# IF YOU GO DOWN TO THE WOODS

Raised on Marvel comics, horror fiction, The Twilight Zone, and other genre entertainment unsuitable for an impressionable young mind, Seth C. Adams knew he wanted to tell stories at a young age. With a Bachelor's in anthropology from the University of California, Riverside, and completing his Master's in North American History at Arizona State University, as an adult he's learned that real life is indeed often stranger–and more frightening–than fiction. He currently splits his time between California and Arizona, and is always working on, or thinking about, his next story.

# IF YOU GO DOWN TO THE WOODS

SETH C. ADAMS

**KILLER
READS**

A division of HarperCollins*Publishers*
www.harpercollins.co.uk

KillerReads
an imprint of HarperCollins*Publishers* Ltd
1 London Bridge Street
London SE1 9GF

www.harpercollins.co.uk

This paperback edition 2018

First published in Great Britain in ebook format by HarperCollins*Publishers* 2018

A catalogue record for this book
is available from the British Library

ISBN: 978-0-00-828025-3

This novel is entirely a work of fiction.
The names, characters and incidents portrayed in it are
the work of the author's imagination. Any resemblance to
actual persons, living or dead, events or localities is
entirely coincidental.

Set in Minion by Palimpsest Book Production Ltd, Falkirk, Stirlingshire
Palimpsest Book Production Limited, Falkirk, Stirlingshire

Printed and bound in the United States of America by LSC Communications

18 19 20 21 22 LSC 10 9 8 7 6 5 4 3 2 1

*This story is about family, friends, and a good dog (which qualifies as both!), and so it is to these I dedicate the novel.*

*To Mom and Dad, for allowing—and encouraging—their weird son to read whatever he wanted.*

*To my own group of Outsiders that enriched my life throughout the school years. We may have never fought off assassins and gangsters, but sometimes just surviving life is a fight all its own, made a bit easier with a good group of pals.*

*To Sheba, Rusty, Outlaw, and Banjo: great dogs, and even better friends.*

# PART ONE

# The Promise

# CHAPTER ONE

## 1.

*This is the night. These are the times.*

I heard these words for the first time from a killer the summer I met the Outsiders' Club. Years passed before I finally understood them and, by then, everyone—my friends, my family, my dog— were long gone: some to the dirt that eventually claims us all, others to the remote reaches of time and memory.

The promise the Outsiders' Club made to each other had a part to play in the way things went down. No doubt about it. But much of it was just life itself, and things beyond our control. Yet I still wonder how it all would have turned out had other choices been made, different roads taken. This is called regret, and it's very important you listen to what it says.

In my case, the long trail of dead that summer demands it.

Sometimes life's fucked up that way. Sometimes the darkness lingers.

Here's what happened.

## 2.

My family moved to Payne, Arizona when I was thirteen. My dad, John Hayworth, got a job as the manager of a Barnes & Noble bookstore, and we moved there from Southern California. Mom, a college-educated woman, decided that being a mother was far more important than searching for meaning in the writing of centuries-dead English novelists, and wholeheartedly supported the move. For those prematurely crying sexism, this was a two-way street kind of respect: Dad supported her, offered to be the stay-at-home parent as she climbed the ranks of prestige in academia. But I think Mom saw more value in passing on her passion for the written word to her children, reading us stories snuggled in our beds or on the sofa, than lecturing youth enrolled in electives, packed like sardines in large lecture halls.

My sister and I had to leave our friends, and though I was sad about some of the people I left behind, I also saw it as something of an adventure. Sarah, on the other hand, sixteen going on retarded, acted like she was saying goodbye to her whole life and every shot at happiness. She had some greasy-haired boyfriend that she was leaving behind, some young stud who thought wearing a leather jacket and slicking his hair back with a few pounds of hair gel made him some sort of James Dean. I thought it made him look like he'd melted butter and greased his head with it.

I told him so once.

He flipped me off.

I laughed at him and gave the old jerk-me-off sign language.

Sarah didn't talk to me for a week after that. That was fine by me. Likewise, I tolerated her like a bothersome rash: it was there, it caused discomfort, but there wasn't much you could do except live through it.

Looking back, I realize she wasn't all that bad. I might even go so far as to say she was a good older sister in some ways. But try telling that to a thirteen-year-old boy, just learning the mysteries of girls and the smaller head in his pants, living in a small house with an older sister who liked barging into his room at any hour to bestow upon him the gifts of noogies, wedgies, and wet willies.

Last, but most definitely not least, I can't forget my dog, Bandit, a German shepherd mix, with some of that mix maybe being wolf. White and gray and silent like some sort of ghost dog from an Indian legend, Bandit was large and stoic and loyal, obedient but obstinate in his own way, and never left my side if I allowed it. He slept in my bed, his loose hairs finding their way up my nose and in my mouth, and my sinuses suffered for it for years. Dad invariably scolded me about keeping that dog in my bed, but there's something about dogs and boys, how they're meant to be, and the years that dog spent with me—warm friend, heartbeats lulling each other to sleep on cold nights—and I don't regret a day.

I remember the long drive through the desert highways to our new home. Hills that seemed to roll to forever in every direction. Sparse trees like stubble on the earth. Mom and Dad took turns driving so the other could rest. Sarah dozed across the seat from me in the back or stared pathetically out the window, a hand under her chin in melodramatic melancholy. Bandit sat or stood on the seat between us, going from window to window, paws on my lap to try to get a good sniff of what was passing us by, and I'd let him, until a stray paw stepped on my nuts, then I'd push him away. I stared out the car windows as well, watched the fiery skies of morning give way to the bruise-blue of afternoon, and remember thinking that though things were changing it might not be all that bad.

I was a simple kid to please. All I needed for contentment and happiness were a good book, some comics, and horror movies, and with Dad a manager at a Barnes & Noble I'd have those things in spades. A whole summer of lazy afternoons, curled in my bed in my room or on a chair on the porch or sprawled on the grass of the lawn, seemed like the superfluous joys of heaven.

The new house didn't let me down in that regard. I'd seen pictures of it my parents had taken on a trip they'd made earlier in the year to see the property, but the still images didn't do the majesty of the place justice.

As Dad turned the station wagon off the highway and onto a country residential sprawl of a road, I found myself leaning forward in anticipation. When we turned the last bend, and I recognized the house from the pictures, I alternately gripped the seat and wiped my palms on my jeans.

It sat on two acres of well-manicured land, carpeted by grass the green of emerald dreams. The whole place was fenced by chain-link, which to some might have made it seem vaguely white-trashy in nature, but to my boy's mind made it seem a secluded fort of a kind. The porch had an overhanging awning and was enclosed by a screen mesh that let you see out but made it hard for others to see in, so all they saw were dark shadows and silhouettes. There was a pool in the back, dry and mossy in places, the cement lining cracked in others, that Dad promised to have repaired and filled soon.

Apple trees dotted the yard, and in the summer the branches were in full bloom and heavy with their juicy burden. The lawn was speckled with the fallen fruit, and as soon as the car braked to a stop with a little cloud of dust, I leapt out, dashed across the grass, scooped up an apple and let it fly. Perhaps thinking I'd filched one of his tennis balls from the trunk without him seeing, Bandit darted out of the car behind me, and charged after the green sphere. Finding it among the litter of others, he spun around in a frenzy, confused and smiling and uncertain by the mass of apples. To his dog's brain, they must have seemed the sweet, multitudinous edible balls of some canine paradise.

"Come on, Joey," Dad called after us, stepping out from behind the wheel and stretching. "There'll be time for that later. We got work to do."

The moving trucks arrived well before us, and the sweat-drenched men had our boxes ready, piled high in totem-like stacks along the porch. Motioning for Bandit to follow, we bounded up the porch steps together. I found the growing stack of boxes with my name written on them in large Sharpie marker letters and began taking them to my new room.

The work went on for hours, and Dad had a cooler set out on the porch, along with plastic chairs, and we all took breaks when we felt like it. Pop open a soda, cram one of Mom's sandwiches in my mouth, and for me it was relaxing. Work, yes, but also fun in a way as I looked out across the desert town in the distance. At times my gaze would drift over to the faraway woods bordering the township, and that dense, mysterious greenery seemed to call to me and Bandit.

Slowly, afternoon crawled into the first evening, purple-black over our new home. My bed set up, having unloaded several boxes of books with many more to go, I sat in bed, the window beside it open. The cool desert breeze drifted in and stirred things with a whisper. A volume of Ray Bradbury stories was open in my lap, propped up by a pillow. Bandit was at my feet, large and furry and kicking his feet occasionally with rabbit filled doggie dreams.

The act of reading usually soothing, I had trouble keeping my mind on the pages before me. My gaze kept drifting to the walls and contours of the room. Realizing I'd spent the last fifteen minutes or so on the same page, I finally gave up and set the book aside.

The room was painted an earthy brown and seemed spacious and snug at the same time. I had my own TV, a gift from last Christmas, and I knew exactly where I wanted it to go. Mom promised she'd call the cable company "tomorrow," and I dreamt of late-night horror marathons. I had boxes of books and comic books yet to be unpacked, and imagined the bookshelves that would line the walls like sentinel soldiers.

There were the other magazines that I had also, buried among my books and filed secretly in between the comics. Magazines of a certain nature all boys must look through at some point, cracking the covers open ever so slightly, ever so slowly, as if lifting the lid to a treasure chest. Treasures they were, too, and I thought of being able to look at these at my leisure in the privacy of my new room.

Then the door to my room swung open and there she was, that rash that wouldn't go away, a look of demented sisterly pleasure on her face.

"You know what I'm here for," she said.

And I said: "Yeah, but I'm all out of Ugly-Be-Gone."

When she charged across the room, I scooped up the book to try and defend myself, and the Queen of Noogies sent me to sleep with bruises and one bastard of a headache.

And the tired realization that some things would never change.

### 3.

I met Fat Bobby first. His real name was Bobby Templeton, but fat he was and knew it, seemed to despondently accept it, and so Fat Bobby he became.

Now I don't know about God or anything like that. I guess I've asked myself the Big Questions like just about anyone else has in their life at some point or another, but I guess my brain is too small for the Big Answers. There isn't much in this life that makes sense to me, but one thing I'm pretty sure of is that there isn't any such thing as coincidence. It seems that how one thing leads to another and that to another, so that there's a whole series of events that gain momentum and become inevitable, is a natural consequence of cause and effect, and there isn't anything coincidental or accidental about it.

I think Fat Bobby was the first in just such a chain of events. I think on how it all ended, the pain and the loss and the misery, and wonder how it all would have been different if I had just passed on by that fat kid in the woods.

But then there wouldn't have come the other things: the friendship, the trust, the laughter.

All things good in this haphazard mess we call life.

* * *

On Dad's first day at the store, I woke up early, thinking I'd cut through the woods and walk into town, maybe check out the local comic book shop, perhaps pay Dad a visit. Lazily excited, I rolled out of bed and stumbled my way to the bathroom across the hall, Bandit following. Starting the water in the shower stall, I waited for it to warm, stripped, and climbed in. Bandit watched with a perplexed expression from the throw rug in the center of the bathroom's tiled floor, as if he wondered why he was excluded from this splashy fun.

After throwing on jeans and a T-shirt, hair still wet from the shower, I raced downstairs. Mom was preparing breakfast, something sizzling tantalizingly in a pan atop the stove. She asked if I wanted some bacon and eggs, and though I was sorely tempted by the smells, I told her my plans and said I'd have Dad get me something from the bookstore cafe. A mild scowl told me what she thought of the nutritional value of a cafe breakfast, but Mom didn't object.

"Just make sure if you're going down to the woods," she said, "don't go alone. Take Bandit with you."

I hardly needed her advice on this, and neither did Bandit, prancing so close behind me that if I stopped abruptly he'd end up nose first in my backside. Out on the porch, Bandit at my heels, Mom called after me and asked when I'd be back. Down the porch and into the yard, I yelled back an "*I don't know!*" and continued down the road.

Our dirt road led to the highway, which in turn led into Payne proper, but as I walked my eyes drifted to the nearby woods. I remembered Dad telling me that a stream ran through the forest and eventually into town. I figured I'd head that way, find the stream, and maybe idle away some time there with Bandit, leisurely making my way to civilization.

The highway led north, while the woods and stream were somewhat westerly. I walked with the sun at my back, the heat coming down like fiery arrows. My hair dried pretty quick, but by the time I reached the edge of the forest I was wet again, this time with a sheen of sweat. Bandit's tongue lolled out like a strip of unrolled carpet, yet he wasn't panting, still moving silently at my side like that Indian ghost dog.

The path to the woods led up a steady incline. When there was still about a quarter mile left to go, I paused with Bandit to rest. From my new vantage point, I looked over the woodlands like a god upon his domain.

To the north I could see the town of Payne, rustic earthy adobe and brick buildings splayed out like an Old West settlement. I could see the roads crisscrossing the municipality from one end to the other, the entirety of the place laid out there below me like a toy model. I half expected to see buggies and wagons and men on horses kicking up dirt clouds, and maybe a blacksmith pounding red-hot metal with a huge hammer. Perhaps a gallows where outlaws and criminals were hanged, looped rope and maybe a corpse swaying in the summer breeze.

I turned back to the woods and, off in the trees a distance, I saw something catch the golden sun like a mirror, twinkling and casting back the light. A hand cupped over my eyes like a visor, I squinted, had to turn away as the sunlight flashed off the object again. I tried to pinpoint its location by some sort of landmark, maybe a tree larger than all the others, or a rock formation that broke the thick landscape around it. There were a couple craggy hills poking about through the surrounding tree coverage, but nothing remarkable.

Nothing I could check on the map in my mind as noteworthy, like a marker on a treasure map.

All the trees looked the same, and though I saw some outcroppings interspersed out among the green landscape, none were very close to that sparkling object. So, I set imaginary crosshairs in the direction of the reflecting light and walked straight as an arrow, hoping for a minimum of obstacles on my route that would make me stray.

"Come on, Bandit," I said, and he trotted at my heels, big dog smile splitting his face as if this was all that he needed: his boy, a sunny day, and a long walk with no particular destination.

At best I judged the source of the bright light to be a couple hundred yards into the woods, and I came to the stream long before I'd trundled that far among the trees and bushes and fallen limbs. The stream was about two car lengths in width, clear water sparkling the sun in a million daggers of light, and at its center I could only just see the bottom. Vague and distorted water-rippled rocks peppered the riverbed. Fish like silvery lasers darted beneath the surface. The sound of the stream moving and rushing along its course was soft music, and a fine spray—wet and cool—carried the current's song in the air.

Bandit had seen the fish as well, or smelled them, and he slipped into the water as silently as he walked, a phantasm entering the flow of the Styx. I settled down on a rock that seemed to be formed just for that purpose. I took off my shoes and socks, thinking I'd dip into the water also, its sharp clarity and cleanness inviting me.

Wiping sweat from my forehead, I wished I'd brought a bottle of water. I thought about leaning over to drink from the stream, but seemed to remember hearing something about fish shit in stream and river water, and it making people sick and giving *them* the shits. Spending the first week of summer squirting diarrhea until my ass was raw didn't seem such a hot idea. So I didn't drink the water, tried swallowing some spit in my parched throat instead.

Reckoning I'd have to settle for just dipping my feet in, maybe splashing about with Bandit a little to cool off, I started to do so. A shout and a loud splash from further downstream brought me to a stop with one foot in the water, the other still on the bank. Leaning in the direction of the sound, head cocked to hear better, I watched the flow of the water to where it ran around a bend in the streambed and out of sight.

Bandit's ears pricked up at the sound also, and he started that way, forgetting the darting fish for the moment. Keeping my voice low, I called for him to wait. We moved along in the water together, boy and dog, one trying to be as stealthy as a ninja, the other naturally so.

A second cry traveled through the air around the bend and, in it this time, I distinctly heard the words *"Please! Stop!"* and more splashing. Despite the high-pitched whine of the voice, and a decidedly embarrassing nasally sound on the verge of being full-blown crying, I could tell it was a boy's voice. A kid probably around my age by the sound of it.

Following the whining-almost-crying and the splashing, I heard laughter, at least two or three distinct voices, and I had a good idea of what was going on. As did Bandit, by the way his ears pressed back against his head and he lowered himself until his chest was touching the water. Ready to lunge, lips peeled back in a grimace, even I found him frightening and had to remind myself this was my dog and it wasn't me that had to be worried.

Around the bend a twisted tree stretched out a gnarly limb as if in greeting. The stream widened here, almost becoming a proper river. The shoreline was rocky and strewn with pebbles and sticks. Three boys, taller and bigger than me, maybe sixteen or seventeen, high school kids definitely, stood among the pebbles and sticks, bending to pick some up from time to time and chucking them into the water. Their target was a fat kid in the water, stripped to his underwear, trying to fend off the incoming missiles with his forearms.

A rock hit him on the breast, a tit larger than most girls', and he staggered. A stick sailed through the air and struck him on the shoulder. Another rock struck him squarely in his massive belly, making the flesh there ripple like a shockwave. This last impact made him stagger again, then topple, and he fell in what seemed like slow motion, hitting the water and sending a splash and wake like a tanker sinking offshore of the Pacific.

"*What's wrong, Bobby Templeton!*" one of the older kids called out, a guy with greased-back hair that made me instantly think of Sarah's boyfriend back in California. The guy wore tight jeans and a white T-shirt that showed his fairly muscled arms. The guy obviously thought he was some sort of biker or something, maybe thinking greased hair and a muscle shirt balanced out the explosion of acne that pocked his face. "*Have a nice trip?*"

The other two guys hooted and hollered at this, as if they'd never heard anything funnier. High fives were exchanged all around. The fat boy tried getting up, his legs and arms like dough, and he slipped again and sent up another large splash. I thought to myself that this might be kind of funny if it wasn't so fucking sad.

"*Bobby Templeton!*" one of the other guys called out, slimmer than the first, wearing jeans and a suede jacket. He was also shaking with laughter, but more in control of himself as he did so, hands casually at hip pockets. He watched the whole thing with a crooked smirk that made me think of serial killers in movies. "*Maybe we ought to call you Chubby Twinkie-by-the-ton!*"

The third guy, ironically, not so thin himself but not nearly as fat as the kid in the stream (Bobby Templeton, I told myself), laughed and threw another rock. This one struck the fat boy on the forehead, and I watched him sort of totter there for a moment or two, a hand going to his forehead, finding blood, and then he toppled over into the water again.

As not numbering among the largest kids ever birthed, I'd been in my fair share of fistfights in school and, like then at the stream in the woods, out of school. I wish I could say I gave more than I got, but I don't honestly know if I'd kept a win and loss scorecard of all my scraps as a kid which side would have the most marks. But Dad had taught me how to throw a punch, much to Mom's chagrin, and also a few sneaky maneuvers with my legs that used my center of gravity and my opponent's momentum against them and in my favor. I'd taken punches before, hard ones, and though I didn't much like them I wasn't scared of getting hit either.

I looked at the older, bigger kids, and knew my chances with all three of them weren't that great: as in no chance in hell. I'd fought bigger guys before, and older guys, so I wasn't really scared about that. It was just a practical matter. I knew I wasn't some superhero, and held no delusions that if I took them all on I wouldn't be leaving there with bruises or worse.

But I had Bandit, and figured that evened things out pretty squarely.

Apparently so did he, because he let out a growl so low and deep and vicious that for a moment I was again afraid of being so near him. He sounded like a wolf then, something primal and ferocious, something wild, and I thought that maybe there wasn't any German shepherd in him at all.

The three high school kids hadn't seen me yet. They'd squatted to choose again among the smorgasbord of missiles about their feet. Targeting the fat kid in the water once more, taking aim.

Then they heard the growl, and froze. Even the guy in the suede jacket with the Charles Manson face. It was as if a monster had just passed by, a thing from nightmares and dark places, and the primitive man in them all took note.

The three of them turned in my direction, saw me, saw my dog. Their gazes seemed more directed at Bandit than me, but eventually the Manson kid turned his eyes my way.

"Hey, kid," he said, nodding in my direction like we were acquaintances. He tried to keep that not-so-concerned smirk on his face, like nothing really bothered him. Like he was somehow separate from the rest of the world. But I noted the bead of sweat on his forehead, watched it start to roll down his face. "Call off your dog."

I'd known his kind before. However this ended up, he wouldn't let it be. I'd interrupted his fun, his amusement, and he didn't like it. It was all there in his smirk and eyes. He'd remember me. He'd marked me.

This pretty much meant I had nothing to lose.

"I have an idea," I said, my voice far sturdier than I felt inside. "How about I take a shit and you eat it?"

What remained of the smiles and good humor of the greasy guy with the head like a planet populated by pimples and the chubby guy was gone in an instant. The lean Manson guy tried to hang on to his smirk, but even that twitched and missed a beat.

"That's pretty brave for a kid with a big ass dog with him," said Mr. Smirk. His thumbs were still in his hip pockets as he tried to remain cool and distant from it all.

"That would almost be funny if it wasn't so fucking retarded," I said. "Talking about being brave, and you there, three against one, and him smaller than you."

I hooked a thumb in the fat kid's direction.

He'd sat up in the stream, blood still trickling from his forehead, watching the whole thing unfolding with an expression short of amazement on his face. He was looking at me and Bandit, and then looking at the three older guys on the shore, back and forth, like he was watching some alien spectacle. I had the urge to check to see if I had tentacles coming out my backside or something.

"He's hardly smaller than us," the chubby guy said, and I almost laughed. It was as if in his tight jeans and black shirt he didn't realize he wasn't exactly Mr. Universe either. Or maybe he did, I thought with something akin to revelation, and that's why he said it.

"The lard-ass pot calling the kettle black," I said, and the fat boy (Bobby) barked a quick laugh before stifling it with a hand to his mouth. The three high school guys gave him a brief hateful look before turning back to me.

"Look," Mr. Smirk said. One hand finally unhooked from his jeans pocket and went palm up in front of him, in a friendly where-is-this-getting-us gesture. "I don't think you realize what you're getting yourself into. Just take your dog and walk away and I'll forget I ever saw you here."

He'd forget me as soon as he forgot how to breathe, and that wasn't anything I was going to hold my breath for. So I decided to roll with it and keep on going.

"Look," I said, giving him the same friendly, conversational palm-up gesture. "I don't think you realize you're a dickweed."

"You fucking asshole," Mr. Pudge said, and took a step forward. Perhaps emboldened by his friend's initiative, Mr. Planet Pimple Head stepped forward too.

Bandit's growl, having continued to rumble through this exchange, rose a notch, from bestial to demonic. Mr. Smirk stopped his friends with either arm outstretched to block them.

"Look," Mr. Smirk started again, "let's make a deal. This is a small town. You're obviously new here. You're not going to have your dog with you every minute of every day. You leave now, instead of killing you, I just kick your ass one time, someday, and then we call it even."

"Look," I said, mocking his nonchalant tone, "I have a deal for you. A counteroffer, if you dumbshits know what that means. My dog rips one of your guys' nutsacks off, and I find the largest rock I can and beat the living shit out of one of you other two. That's two-thirds chance of any of the three of you getting messed up real bad. Either nutsack chewed off," I held one hand up, "or head bashed in," and then the other. Lifting them up and down, my hands weighed something invisible like they were scales.

"Personally," Bobby said, and we all turned to him, equally

surprised that he'd found the guts to talk, "I'd like to keep my nuts."

I smiled at him.

He smiled back.

And there, at that moment, I saw through the pathetic overweight kid who'd been crying moments ago, and knew him for the kid he could be. The friend he could be.

Silence hung in the air like a thick curtain. There were decisions being made in that utter quiet. Gears were moving. For me there was a sense of inevitability, as if these were things that were to always be, like I'd walked into something and somewhere that I belonged. There was no turning back.

"Okay," Mr. Smirk said, tugging on the front of his suede jacket, brushing at lint or specks that weren't there. "You've made your choice." He pointed across the way at me, his forefinger out, his thumb up like a gun hammer. "I've made mine too. I think we'll be seeing each other again someday."

With that he turned away, hands in his pockets, as if nothing at all unusual had gone down. His friends, Mr. Pudge and Mr. Pimple Planet, turned likewise, trying to imitate their leader's nonchalance.

I looked at Bobby Templeton, sitting there fat and pathetic and almost naked in the stream, and he looked back at me and nodded. I smiled and nodded at Bandit.

"*Go for the nuts, boy!*" I yelled, and Bandit, poised in the stream, that growl still in his throat, darted forward. The high school guys looked back, even cool Mr. Smirk, and they saw him coming.

All one hundred pounds of him, teeth long and sharp and white.

Breaking into a run, all coolness forgotten, the three older boys tripped and stumbled over each other and the fallen branches in their path. Crashing through the undergrowth they ran out of sight, leaving me in the stream with a nearly naked fat boy.

# 4.

Bandit came prancing back with an as-happy-as-can-be dog smile splitting his face, though to my mild disappointment without greaseball scrotums and testes dangling from his jaws, just as Bobby Templeton was pulling his shirt and pants back on. Tossed away among some nearby bushes by the high school guys, thorns caught in the fabric poked him in awkward places and he winced and yelped as he dressed. Bandit walked up to him, and though a bit apprehensive, maybe wondering if the dog still had balls on the brain, Bobby knelt to give my dog a good rubdown. Bandit obliged, rolling on his back to offer his furry tummy.

"Cool dog," Bobby said, looking my way.

"Yeah. He's the best."

"I'm Bobby."

The fat kid held out a hand.

"I'm Joey," I said, and pumped his hand up and down like a lever. "Who were those guys?" I gestured with a thumb over my shoulder in the direction the three older boys had run.

"The guy in the jacket is Dillon," Bobby said. "The other two are Stu and Max."

His gaze followed the direction my thumb indicated and, though they were long gone, the worry in the fat kid's eyes was clear.

"Don't worry," I offered. "They won't be coming back anytime soon. Not with Bandit here." I punctuated this with a playful tug on my dog's ear, and he nipped at my hand good-naturedly in return. "Why were they after you anyway?"

Bobby gave a weak little shrug and looked down at the same time.

"That's just what they do," he said, but his slumped, defeated posture seemed to also say this was just what *he* was: the kind of kid others beat on and humiliated. I couldn't exactly argue with that, and so said nothing. "I was just walking into town," he added. "You can cut through the woods and get there faster instead of going down the highway."

I started back around the bend in the river to retrieve my shoes. Sitting on a rock, I pulled them on and laced them up. Bobby hurried to keep up, as if even a few yards of distance between us would put him in danger again.

"Aren't you scared they're going to come after you now?"

"Sure," I said, shrugging, "a little. But I got Bandit and I know how to take care of myself."

"I wish I was that brave," Bobby said, hanging his head so pathetically that I wanted to slap him.

"It's not so much about being brave." Trying to explain, I realized as I was talking I was using pretty much the same words Dad had with me sometime back. "It's about knowing that there's some people, if you give them an inch they'll take a mile. And so you learn to know these people when you see them, and not to take any shit."

"Your dad teach you how to fight?"

Bobby raised his head, looked at me, genuinely interested.

"Some," I nodded. "But someone else can teach you only so much. Then it's when something actually happens, you find out if you've got it or not."

"Aren't you afraid of getting hit?"

Still sitting, I tried to think of how best to answer. Again, finding myself thinking back to the answers Dad gave me when I asked nearly the same questions.

"Sure."

Standing, we started walking again. The sun was still high, its light shining through the trees in patches. I thought to myself how the standoff with the three older kids had seemed so long. It seemed to me as if hours should have passed. Tension will do that to you, Dad had said. Make you think time was standing still or moving too fast for you to handle or both at the same time. I thought this was important to get across to Fat Bobby, but I wasn't quite sure how.

"You never completely get over the threat of being hit, being hurt," I said. "If someone says they aren't scared when it seems like there's something bad going to happen, they're either lying or crazy."

I kicked a rock and sent it sailing into some bushes as I tried to gather my thoughts. A startled squirrel darted out of the brush and up a tree, chattering angrily at me when it found a safe branch. Bandit darted towards the base of the tree, looked up questioningly at the rodent. Soon, seeing his potential toy wasn't coming down, he turned and strode away.

"You get to the point where you just try to give as much as you get," I said, picking up where I'd left off. "It doesn't matter if they're bigger or older. Someone pushes you, you push back. Someone hits you, you hit back."

"And what if you get more than you give?" Bobby said, and his constant uncertainty, his insistence on the negative, the downbeat, the altogether pussy-ness of his whole demeanor, solidified for me. Though I tried to keep my thoughts and words kind, his name for me as Fat Bobby, which also meant Weak Bobby, Sissy Bobby, Yes-I'm-A-Big-Fat-Wuss-Come-Kick-My-Ass Bobby, became fixed in my mind.

"That happens sometimes."

I put my hands in my pockets, clenching them into fists there, then relaxing them. Trying mightily not to get mad at this fat kid who had somehow learned in life that it was okay to get stepped on, to get kicked in the ass. That maybe that's how things were for some people, and there was nothing to be done about it.

"But you go down swinging, and really connecting with at least a few good ones, that person who knocked you down is going to have a fat lip, or a busted nose, and they're going to wonder if it was worth it. That maybe there's easier targets to focus on. Either way, whether you give more than you get, or you get your ass handed to you but you do it throwing punches, you've won."

"That sounds like a hard thing to learn, and a lot of punches to take to learn it," Fat Bobby said.

We'd reached the dirt road that I'd taken from home to the woods, and I stopped. Fat Bobby took a few steps more before he noticed, then he stopped too and looked back at me, his hands in his pockets, his gut bulging beneath his shirt. He stood slouched, shoulders slumped, back bowed, as if a great weight were strapped to him.

"I'd rather have a quick and early hard lesson than to live my life taking shit from assholes," I said, and regretted it even as I said the words. I felt and heard the heat in my voice, and I saw pain and hurt in Fat Bobby's eyes as I looked him up and down as I spoke.

It was obvious what I was looking at, and that I wanted him to know it. *Him.* I was looking at him: his fatness, his complete and utter defeatist attitude, his self-pity bullshit. The hurt my words caused him were immediate, his doughy face falling slack in shame and embarrassment.

"Point taken," he said, looking away from me, looking at his feet, idly kicking at a rock. "Geez," he added, and that was all. Not "geez, why you being such a jerk?" or "geez, don't be an asshole" or anything else that any self-respecting person would have added.

Just "geez," and that one-word response did more than anything else could have. It made *me* feel ashamed. *I* felt embarrassed. I felt like I was one of them. That I belonged with the three high school kids, standing with them and throwing rocks and sticks at the fat boy crying in the stream.

Bandit trotted over to Fat Bobby and pressed close against the kid's leg. My dog looked back at me from that distance, and I saw something like condemnation in his wolfish features. Maybe

I was reading too much into it. Maybe I was projecting my thoughts irrationally onto an animal. But that look from my dog—my friend, my brother—made me feel even shittier.

"I'm sorry," I said, and now it was me with my hands in my pockets, head down, not meeting Bobby's eyes. Kicking idly at a pebble on the ground.

Meekly, I looked up, saw Fat Bobby nod. There was a glimmer in one eye that may have been a tear, or perhaps just the reflected daylight.

"Come on," I said, and started walking again.

I clapped him on the shoulder as I passed by, he fell in beside me, and I knew then that for better or worse we were friends.

* * *

"Your dad sounds pretty cool," Fat Bobby said when we reached the top of the hill. The road overlooked the woods to the west, and to the north the highway led into town.

"Yeah. He isn't bad at all."

"I wish my dad were like him."

"Your dad can't be all that bad," I said, but I remembered the fat kid in his underwear crying in the stream, doing nothing as three other guys assaulted him, and that in itself spoke volumes. That a dad would raise a son like that said more than I needed to know about the man.

I knew my lie for what it was as soon as I said it, and the silence that followed told me Bobby did as well. I turned, cursing myself for not knowing when to shut up.

I looked back over the forest we'd just left.

Remembering the light that had caught my attention in the first place, I scanned the woods for it. Nothing. As before, all the trees seemed one endless growth, no one distinguishable from the rest. Could it have just been the stream water, catching the sunlight in a million little diamond pinpoints?

22

I didn't think so. The reflected light had seemed farther out than where I placed myself to have stopped near the stream.

I wanted to ask Fat Bobby about it, turned to him to do so, and saw a shadow of the earlier sadness and hurt still on his face. A better idea came to me. One that made me feel less shitty as a person and a friend.

"You like comics?" I asked.

Fat Bobby looked at me like I'd spoken some alien language. "I've never really read them."

"My dad runs a bookstore," I said. "Come on, I'll show you some things."

Down the hill, north, we started out, the world stretched out before us in shades of bleached desert-white and earthen browns. Walking along the highway, a dog and two boys, friends, taking the road to where it took us.

# CHAPTER TWO

## 1.

Dad was making his rounds about the store when we pushed through the glass doors. Bandit walked into the store with us, and some old lady with thick makeup like cake batter gave me a dirty look. I looked right back at her and said: "Service dog, ma'am. I'm borderline retarded." She harrumphed and walked away, and I felt proud of myself.

Dad saw us and walked over, gave me a hug. I liked his hugs and never felt embarrassed when he gave me one in public. They were manly hugs, like ballplayers or boxers showing their respect after a long game or twelve rounds of exchanging punches.

He gave Bandit a glance, looked towards me like he was about to say something, and then he noticed Fat Bobby. Dad saw the cut on his forehead almost scabbed over and dry with some help from the summer sun, and turned to me.

"What happened?" he asked.

It was like he had some sort of radar that sounded when something had happened that needed to be told. He called it his Bullshit Detector, and it was backed by a lifetime warranty with an Ass Whooping Clause. For emphasis, he held up his hand and pointed at my butt whenever he said this. My dad never actually hit me when he said this, but the intention was clear: be honest with him or pay the consequences. The consequences were usually his disappointment and displeasure and that was always enough for me. A stern, disapproving look from him and I felt like a worm caught in the sights of a bird.

So I told him what happened and, as I did, he walked us back to his office, motioned us both to sit in the swivel chairs in front of the desk. Pulling out a first aid kit from a file drawer, Dad put some disinfectant on Fat Bobby's cut and two Band Aids in the shape of an X on his forehead.

The office door open, I had a view of the adjacent break room and an employee, a girl about my sister's age, eating her lunch there at a table. She was tall, thin, and her brown hair hung in spirals like little galaxies. Her dress, a flower print affair, clung to her like a second skin, and then there was her skin itself, golden and tanned like she took precise measurements to get it that way. Just so much sun; just the right amount of lotion; a dollop of genetic luck or God's favor; and it equaled something I wanted to run my hands over.

She saw me looking and smiled warmly.

I smiled back, but quickly broke eye contact.

"Pay attention, Joey," Dad said, bringing me back from where I wanted to be, to the real world and the situation at hand, which was far less appealing for my young boy's brain.

"Yes, sir," I said, turning the swivel chair so it faced him.

"I think we ought to call the police," he said. "Throwing rocks isn't fun and games. Those boys could have really hurt you."

He said this last while looking at Fat Bobby, but I knew he included me in that equation also.

"I can take care of myself, Dad," I said, a little louder than necessary for the benefit of the girl in the room behind me. "Plus Bandit was with me," I added and leaned over to pet my dog, saw he wasn't there, spun the swivel chair some more, saw he was out in the break room with the girl.

He had his head in her lap, gazing lovingly up at her as she shook his head from side to side, massaged his ears, and cooed at him.

25

I prayed fervently for God to let me swap bodies with Bandit just for a few minutes. God didn't oblige, and I had some choice words for Him spoken in my head.

Dad saw where my attention had gone again, and he wheeled his chair so he was leaning past me and looking out into the break room.

"Tara?" he called out, and the girl looked up.

"Yes, sir?"

"Isn't lunch just about over?" Dad said, not harshly or mean-like at all, but not overly friendly either. He was irritated at me, and taking it out on her. An image of me dueling my dad for her honor sprang to mind and, in the daydream, I skewered him with my sword, and Tara leapt joyfully into my arms.

"Yes, sir," she said. "I just had to pet this cool dog, though."

She rebelled against my dad by lingering a few moments longer, ruffling Bandit's coat and cooing at him some more with baby talk. Then she was up, throwing her trash into a bin and walking out of sight, but remaining in my heart.

Bandit stared after her for a time before walking despondently into the office where the three of us sat. He settled on the ground beside me with a sigh, as if he were settling for second best. I tried to beam him a mental message.

*Traitor.*

His eyes rolled up at me as if he heard and was bored.

"She's too old for you, son," Dad said, and after a moment to register the words I turned back to face him.

"What? Who?"

"She's fifteen and a half," he said. "It's some sort of work experience thing through her school. She's only here a few days a week."

But I heard none of that, save the first part. *Fifteen and a half.* Round down to the nearest whole number and that left *fifteen.* I was thirteen, with fourteen only a few weeks away. When you thought of it that way, you may as well just say we were the same age.

26

Dad saw my thoughts had trailed off again. Sighing, he brought us back to the subject at hand.

"These boys. Do you know their names?" he asked, facing Bobby again.

Bobby nodded hesitantly, but I interjected before he could say anything.

"I told you, Dad," I said, knowing I was walking on thin ice by objecting to him when he was in a mood like this. Someone had threatened his family, and he wasn't too keen on that. My dad liked books; obviously, he managed a bookstore. But he also had a punching bag in the garage, and he liked chopping wood, and seeing him shirtless like he often was in the summertime to do yard work, you'd think God had run out of flesh and bone and made my dad out of stone.

Once, a drunk man had accosted Mom when we were out for a family dinner. The drunk man had had two not-so-drunk friends with him, egging him on. Dad ended up accosting all three of them, and an ambulance took them away in gurneys for a stay at the hospital, where their busted teeth required of them a diet of Jell-O and apple sauce.

"I can take care of myself," I finished.

"I don't doubt that, son," he said, and though he hadn't raised his voice yet, his face was flat and stern, like a slab of rock with eyes, ears, a nose, and mouth. I knew he would only let me go so far. He wouldn't lose his temper at work either. He'd wait until we were both home, then there'd be that disappointed look, he'd verbalize it, and I'd trail down the hall to my room with my tail between my legs. "But you know how I feel about fighting. There's no reason for it—"

"Unless there's no other option," I finished for him.

"That's right." He ignored my mildly mocking tone. "And here we have an option. And that option is to call the police. Now, Bobby," and here again he turned to face my new fat friend, "can I have those boys' names please?"

Dad, poised over the office tabletop, pen in hand.

Bobby, head bowed, not looking at my dad.

Me, thinking Bobby doesn't know what he's doing. Son or no son, it doesn't matter. My dad wants something from you, you better give it over.

"Bobby," Dad said, his tone prodding and urging, but uncompromising at the same time, "where I come from, when an adult asks a kid something, the kid gives a response."

The quiet between them stretched for a few moments more. The ticking of a clock somewhere could be heard. I thought if I farted it would be like a bomb blast in peacetime.

"Bobby?"

Dad's gaze penetrated like a drill.

I looked at Fat Bobby and saw his double layer chins quiver. I saw that glimmer of a tear in his eye again. *This kid is a real waterworks*, I thought, again with a hint of disgust, and quickly on the heels of that, shame at the thought.

"I ... really don't want you to call the police ... sir," he said without looking up.

"Why on earth not?" Dad asked. He was leaning forward in what he probably thought was a confidential, comforting manner for Bobby. But a large man, muscled and burly, leaning towards you in such a way would seem like a mountain with a face leaning over you, towering over you. The shadow would probably eclipse the sun. "You haven't done anything wrong."

The quivering chins flapped faster. I remembered something on The Discovery Channel about Hubble or other telescopes picking up the wobble of distant stars. Fat Bobby's wobbling chins would have short circuited NASA's instrumentation.

"I ... don't want my dad ... to find out," Bobby said. A single tear began to roll down his cheek.

Dad looked at me, and I shrugged. I saw the same look of mixed concern, mild disgust, and shame at his disgust that I'd felt many times around Bobby in the short time I'd known him, pass over my dad's face.

"Again, I ask the same question," he said. "Why not? You haven't done anything wrong."

Whatever dam had been holding it all back finally gave way under the pressure, and Fat Bobby really started crying. Embarrassed, but also saddened without knowing completely why, I reached out and swung the door to Dad's office closed. In the room with the door shut and the wider world cut off, it was only the three of us, and Bandit too, who again stood and moved to Fat Bobby's side and rested his head on the fat boy's leg.

Dad scooted his chair closer to the crying boy and something amazing happened, something I'd never seen before outside my own home and my own family: he leaned over, pulled Bobby close, and engulfed the large boy in his larger arms. Those arms that had held me before in the aftermath of nightmares or scoldings or the various and countless other things in a boy's life.

"*It's alright, son,*" he said to a boy not his son, and I knew as never before my dad was a great man. He tried to keep his voice a whisper, but it was a soft rumble like a swarm of bees. "*It's alright, everything will be alright.*"

And because my dad said it, I trusted it to be true.

## 2.

Dad gave us ten dollars each and told us to get some comics with it or a drink from the café. With the ten dollars in his hand, you would have thought Fat Bobby was holding the Holy Grail or something, his face was beaming so. His sudden and simple joy made my dad smile, and when Bobby and I made as if to leave the office for the sales floor, Dad stopped me with a hand on my shoulder. I called to Bobby and told him I'd meet him in the comics aisle. He waved, still clutching that ten dollars like it was something magic from a fairy tale.

"You've never chosen your friends easily, Joey," my dad said. "You march to your own beat. Always been a bit of an outsider that way, and I can respect that. If you and Bobby are friends, then he must be a pretty okay kid."

Knowing he wasn't done yet, that he was working his way to what he really wanted to say, I didn't respond. Just nodded my head where it felt appropriate.

"I know you already know this, son," he said, me looking up at him like I was looking up at a skyscraper, "but I want to say it anyway."

I nodded again, waiting.

"It's never okay for a man to hit either women or kids." His hand squeezed my shoulder gently. "A man that does that isn't really a man at all."

Still I didn't say anything, knew I wasn't really supposed to. He was telling me something, something important, and it was for me to listen and take it in. Nothing else.

"I won't call the police this time, Joey. But I want you to stay away from those three guys. They're nothing but trouble. And if you come across them, walk away, head the other direction. Got it?"

I didn't want to, felt like I was already relinquishing my manhood and I wasn't even a man yet, but I nodded and said: "Yes, sir."

I started to walk out of the office, and his hand on my shoulder stopped me again.

"But to be on the safe side ..." he began, then paused.

"Yes, sir?"

"Keep Bandit with you all the time," he finished, and smiled.

I smiled too, and ruffled my dog's coat and slapped him on the flank.

"Yes, sir. You can count on that."

Then I was out the door, through the break room, and into the bookstore, a maze of covers and bindings and that smell of new leather and paper—something akin to what I imagined heaven must be like—I breathed it in, and went looking for my new sad friend in the comics section.

* * *

Comic books and how to read them, and which ones to read, is a thing of intricacy bordering on something like art. You have to read certain storylines to make sense of other storylines, and you have to understand the relationships between characters for those stories to make sense. Furthermore, add in variables like the creative teams, the artists and writers who put together the stories—some of whom shouldn't be doing anything higher brow or complicated than *Archie*; others whose imaginations and love of magic had led them to novels and movies and other creative pursuits—and you have a recipe for disaster unless you have yourself a guide through the whole mess.

I tried being that guide for Bobby, virgin of all things Marvel and DC, allowing him to peruse the rack and shelves of titles. Deftly, I steered him clear of the craptastic stuff that really shouldn't be used as anything other than backup asswipes when the toilet paper recession hit.

When he reached for some sort of Japanese manga garbage, I grabbed it out of Bobby's hands and just barely restrained myself from throwing it across the aisle and stomping on it. I replaced it with a trade collection of a book called *Preacher* by a guy named Garth Ennis.

"Forget that manga shit," I said.

Mrs. Old Lady Makeup was walking by just then and gave me a dirty look. She saw Bandit was still with me and gave another harrumph.

"Sorry, ma'am. I have Tourette's syndrome," I said, and flinched and jerked and twitched my face and said another "shit" just for good measure. She stormed away again, presumably to help the makeup stocks rise for the Wall Street makeup tycoons.

"Read this," I said, turning back to Fat Bobby, pressing the *Preacher* book closer to him, like he might lose it. "It'll change your life."

"Okay," he said uncertainly, eyeing the disturbing cover with confusion. Then his face, confused but still pleased at the prospect of what my dad's ten dollars could get him, fell and slackened again, and I thought to myself, *Oh great, what now?* "Joey, I don't think I can buy this."

"What are you talking about?" I asked, listening but turning back to the shelves at the same time, trying to decide if I wanted *X-Men* or *Spiderman*, or both. "You got ten dollars there, you can get whatever you want," I said, then quickly added: "As long as it's not that crap," and pointed at the manga stuff.

"It's my dad," he said, and though he wasn't blubbering or crying this time around, I could tell that the thoughts that led to that were stirring just below the surface. "I don't think he'd let me read comics. He'd think it was sissy stuff, a waste of time. He'd probably throw them away."

Having been raised on books, novels, and comics alike, the value of comics, both monetary and otherwise, fuel for a kid's imagination, had been ingrained in me since time immemorial. The very idea of someone throwing away comics, discarding them as if they were merely cartoons on paper, horrified and angered me. It was an injustice I couldn't allow.

"We'll keep them at my house," I said. The idea came to me spontaneously, right there, and I didn't know where it came from but it felt right. "I'll get you a separate box. You can come over and read them whenever you want."

That shiny, beaming look erupted again on Fat Bobby's face, that same joyous rapture that had sprung up when Dad had presented him with the $10 bill. It spoke of things too powerful for words, equal parts gratitude, appreciation, and something else altogether. It was as if Bobby were seeing things with new eyes, or maybe just seeing things that he'd never seen before. And it amazed him that things could be this way.

"You'd do that for me?"

He seemed not like a boy my age but a child years younger, looking up at someone they thought a hero. Someone almost worthy of worship. I think I must have felt how my dad felt earlier in the office, consoling this large, fat boy like he was still an infant.

It felt good to be held up this way by someone else.

It made you think, even if in vague and flitting spurts, of the person you could be, if only you had the courage to be a certain way all the time.

"Sure. No big deal."

If possible, his smile grew even wider, like a fissure ripping a massive planet in two. That look of near worship again in his eyes—I felt high and mighty, but in a good way, not an uppity one.

I just hoped he wouldn't build some sort of shrine to me in a closet at home.

That would be sort of queer.

"Thanks, Joey." I shrugged as if it were nothing. He looked again at the comic in his hand. "*Preacher* huh? Are you sure?"

My mouth was open and I was about to say something, when a sound like music interrupted me. The music formed words and a shiver went through me tingling like electricity.

"I'd go with something *Batman* personally," said the voice like music, and I thought, *Oh, this is it. This is what an angel sounds like.* I turned, and there she was, the girl from the break room. "Something by Frank Miller or Jeph Loeb," she said, and my mind quaked with nerdy excitement, my dork sensors reaching overload.

*No way in hell does she read comics*, I thought.

*No way does she know the writers and artists*, I added.

I was in love, and I had no idea what to do next. I shuffled from one foot to the other. I crammed my hands into my pockets and pulled them out again. My face felt hot and I knew I was blushing, probably redder than the sun. I was scared, far more frightened standing there looking at her than I had been back at the stream with the three high school guys. This fear was somehow pleasant, though, and there was no other place I wanted to be.

"Hey, Tara," Fat Bobby said nonchalantly, as if he knew her, and she said hi back as if she knew him, and I thought, *Holy shit, they know each other.* Then I was mad because Fat Bobby hadn't told me this, and this was fucking important information. This was bigger than who shot Kennedy, if there were little gray men in Area 51, bigger than discovering that Atlantis wasn't lost at all but bobbing around right inside your crapper.

I wanted to strangle him.

I wanted to look at her.

I wanted to run and hide.

"Who's your friend, Bobby?" she asked, looking at Bobby, and I thought to myself, trying to beam the message to her like I'd beamed messages to Bandit just a few minutes ago in Dad's office: *Don't look at the fat boy! Look at me! Look at me for the love of God!*

"This is Joey," Fat Bobby said.

Then she *was* looking at me, holding her hand out for me to shake; and I thought, trying to beam the messages at her: *Oh God! I'm gonna melt! Please don't look at me! Don't look at me!*

Taking her hand I felt my face getting hotter, and I wondered if my head exploded and I sprayed chunks of myself all over her and her pretty dress, would she still talk to me? Would she have pity on a headless freak and let me hear her voice again?

"Hi," I said, lamely, and her hand in mine was like worlds colliding, stars going supernova, and all sorts of stuff that I could analogize now, but back then it was a pleasant tingle through my whole body. A lightness in my head and thoughts that I didn't want to ever end.

Smelling something like strawberries, I knew it wasn't me, and it definitely wasn't fat boy next to me, and I realized it was her. It was the shampoo she used on her bouncy, galaxy spiral hair. Or a perfume she dabbed on her neck like I'd seen my mom and sister do. Or it was just the smell of her.

*Tara*, I thought. *The smell of Tara.*

I wanted to lean over and smell that hair. I wanted that smell in my head, in my mind, and I wanted to lock it away in there where I could always get to it.

"Hi," she said back, smiling, and I found myself looking at that smile, those lips, and thinking of touching them. I was looking at her mouth, still holding her hand, pumping it up and down, and I thought that if the Makeup Lady came around a third time I could turn to her and say: *See, I really am retarded*, and it would be true, painfully true.

Turned retarded by way of a girl.

That's got to be a medical condition. I should look it up someday.

I know other guys have felt the same way before. We could start a support group. Sit in a circle, share our stories and have a good cry.

Bandit walked over to her, tail slapping side to side like a feather duster, and she dropped my hand. I held it outstretched there for a moment or two longer, dumb with shock at the loss of the contact. I stared daggers at Bandit, tried to send him some more telepathy.

"*Oh! There's that cute dog! There's that silly dog!*" She knelt and cooed to him again, just as she had back in the break room. Her skirt swished as she knelt, a sound like a whisper, a whisper directed at me. I found myself looking at the curve of her backside, and then quickly looking away when she turned again to face me. "What's his name?"

I told her.

She said some more nonsense to my dog, this time using his

name, and I cried out in my mind for her to say my name. *You know my name! Say my name!*

Then she did, and my heart nearly stopped.

"I like your dog, Joey."

"Thanks," I said, though I didn't really know if that was something to say "thanks" about, and I could have kicked myself.

"Mr. Hayworth, that's your dad?" she asked, and her quick change of subject startled me as easily as everything else about her. I nodded, wanted to say something, but my mouth felt glued shut, and then I thought of what I'd said so far and maybe that was a blessing in disguise. "He's a nice guy. He treats everyone here really well. I mean, I've only met him today and all, but some people you can just tell, you know?"

You got that right, I thought.

To her, I nodded.

Fat Bobby was shuffling about now, left out of the conversation, and I really didn't care. Her words were for me; her eyes were for me. No one else.

"You like comics too?" she said, and I latched onto that single word, "too," and what it implied, what it verified. That *she* liked comics, and that commonality between us was like some invisible bridge running from me to her, and I wanted for all I was worth to run across that bridge to her side of it.

"Yeah." My voice trembled the slightest bit; I tried to consciously still it and, with my following words, it seemed to work. "I've been collecting them for years now. My dad got me into them. I have boxes and boxes of them. Some are really rare, that he gave to me from when he was a kid. I spend all my money on them. Books too, I love books. I love to read."

*Shut the hell up, you idiot,* I told myself, and reapplied some of that glue to my jaws again, swearing I'd try not to speak anymore unless I absolutely had to. And even then to keep my responses to single words. Monosyllabic if possible.

"That's cool," she said.

36

She wore a laminated name tag around her neck, dangling from a cord, and I thought: *That's cool, that name. Tara. Tara. Tara.* I stared at her name tag and repeated her name in my head like a mantra. After a time, I realized it might look like I was staring at her boobs and, thinking that, I actually did, my eyes drifting to the swells there, pushing out against the fabric of her dress like little mountains. I sent out another quick and urgent prayer to God, told Him I forgave Him for not answering my last prayer, swapping mine and Bandit's bodies. This time what I wanted was a lot easier: just miniaturize me and give me some mountain climbing lessons.

By an enormous feat of determination and willpower, I turned my eyes back to her face, hoping she hadn't noticed where my gaze had wavered to and, if she had, hopefully she was too polite to say anything. I hoped for the latter, but readied myself for a fist to the face or a can full of Mace to the eyes for being a perv.

She was still smiling, one side of her mouth turned upward, slightly crooked; something I decided right then and there was the cutest thing I'd ever seen. She kept talking without missing a beat, and for that I silently thanked her.

"Maybe someday I can take a look at your comics," she said.

I shuffled from foot to foot again, hands in my pockets, wanting to stop, knowing I looked like some sort of gimp. My head turned this way and that as I looked everywhere, anywhere but at her, as if following the path of a kamikaze fly buzzing through the air.

"Sure," I said.

*When?* is what I wanted to say.

Where do you live?

What's your number?

You want mine?

All valid options I could have added, but I couldn't. Literally, I couldn't. It was as if those thoughts were stopped by some sort of brick wall, and the words lost in the ether like smoke in a breeze.

"Well," she said, and the way she said it I knew our current encounter was winding down, and I cursed the universe for its cruelty, "I really should get back to work. I'm sure I'll see you around, your dad working here and all."

She made a little dance of a motion, like a pirouette, with a twirl of her skirt, and started to walk away. I wanted to reach out and snag her, pull her back to me like a planet pulling its moon. Down the aisle she glided, moving further away, taking my heart with her, and still I couldn't say anything, not even when she gave a half turn in my direction and gave me a little wave and another one of her crooked little smiles. I tried to wave back, but my hands crammed in the bottomless pits of my pockets snagged there, me pulling frantically to free them.

In that torturous moment I thought she'd walk out of sight and I'd have to wait some unknowable span of time to see her again, but the fat boy saved me. The fat kid who'd been nearly naked in a stream that same day, crying pitifully as he was used for target practice by a bunch of assholes. He, whom I would forever remember as Fat Bobby, whom I would always remember with an uncertain mix of fondness and disgust, called out to the girl who had stolen my young boy's heart, and saved me.

"I guess we'll see you at the fair next week?" he called after her, and Tara stopped, kind of hop-skip-dancing backwards for a moment. With a nod of her head and a one-word reply of "*Yeah!*" muted like a whisper across the distance between us, she turned a corner and was gone.

In the days that followed, morning to evening, light or dark, awake and in my dreams, there was one thing that came back to me again and again. Consisting of two words, those words played over again and again in my head like a song on a playback loop. My heart thudded jackhammer-like against my breastbone, a prisoner pounding against his cage, as I dwelt on the thing in my mind.

The fair.

# 3.

The first trucks began to arrive that Saturday, and Fat Bobby and I watched as the massive diesels pulled into the park at the center of town. I brought Bandit with us, as Dad had told me to and as I would have done anyway, and he lay at my feet while Fat Bobby and I straddled the log-post fence that surrounded the park like it was a huge corral.

Large canvas tents and tarps billowed up and high, supported by their wire- and pole-frame skeletons, like the humps of ancient creatures. Game booths and food stands were constructed also, crews of shirtless and sweat-shiny big men pounding away with hammers and shouting out orders to each other. Glass-cased popcorn machines and the spinning skewers of hot dog vendors; Whomp-a-Mole machines and BB gun shooting ranges; a merry-go-round spinning slowly, hypnotically, on a test run; and the large, imposing monolith of the Ferris wheel, standing tall against the backdrop of the clear summer sky like the monument of some lost civilization—each, in turn, unveiled upon the land like an invocation.

"It sure is something, isn't it?" Fat Bobby asked, downing the last of the soda he'd filched from my house. One corner of a plastic bag stuck out of the breast pocket of his shirt like it was playing peek-a-boo, the sandwich that had been in it, of my mom's making, long gone.

"It sure is," I said with genuine awe, the sounds and sights of the fair coming together like the sounds of a dream long lost slowly coming back.

"This will be the first year I've got to go in a long time," Fat Bobby said. "My mom used to take me. But it's not really the kind of thing my dad likes to do."

Knowing full well this might be a road I didn't want to go down, that such a topic could quickly dispel the glory of the day, I went ahead and asked the question that was on my mind anyway.

"Used to? Where's your mom now?"

The momentary silence before Fat Bobby's answer confirmed for me that we were about to turn down Depression Road, followed by a hard left down Misery Lane.

"She died a couple years ago. Car accident. Dad was driving."

I didn't know what to say to that, and so said nothing. Which may have been the best course of action because, in a few minutes, we were lost in the chorus of the fair's construction again. It was a balm of sorts watching those men work their magic, the tents and rides going up, as if the landscape of a forlorn past were being patched over by something better.

As afternoon stepped aside for evening, the sky going from blue to red to bruise purple, we turned away from the fairgrounds. The clanging and banging of its assembly, its growth, its *becoming*, had a rhythm almost a heartbeat, and there was a sadness to our stride as we moved along: a drag of the legs, a slump of shoulders.

Along the highway, in the deepening night, we walked, and at some point on the long road, we waved to each other and parted; the unspoken desire for the fair between us and the wait for it almost unbearable. Ghost dog by my side, I watched my friend blend into the night and, on the dark road, I continued home.

I was several yards from the turnoff on the highway to our street, when the sound of an engine coming closer rumbled behind me. Stepping further onto the shoulder just for safety, as I had for a half dozen cars before it, I waited for the vehicle to pass on by.

It didn't pass.

Pulling up alongside me, a sleek black Mustang slowed to a crawl, almost like a shadow rolling, a part of the night detached, matching my stride. The electric hum of the windows rolling down was loud in the night. Inside, Mr. Smirk, Mr. Pudge, and Mr. Pimple Planet—Dillon, Max, and Stu—looked out. Clouds of smoke billowed out of the car, drifting up into the night like dragon's breath.

Bandit let out that monstrous growl he'd made back at the stream not so long ago. I knelt to clutch his collar and gave him a bit of a tug, letting him know to stay by me as we walked.

Dillon was at the wheel, but he didn't watch the road. He stared out at me.

The other two were in the backseat, watching me as well.

"Out past your bedtime?" Dillon asked. He had traded his suede jacket for a black leather one and, in the black car in the black night, the effect was disconcerting. He almost seemed like only a head and hands, pale and floating there in the shadow car. "It's dangerous to be out alone this time of night." He looked briefly away from me, out through the windshield at the moon above, like he was confirming the hour. "Bad things can happen at night."

I tried to remember the things I'd told Fat Bobby a few days ago at the stream in the woods. Not to be afraid. Not to take shit. But home, so near, had never seemed so far away.

"Yeah," I said, trying to control the tremor in my voice, "like getting your nuts bit off."

I looked at Dillon in the driver's seat to gauge his reaction, and I felt I'd scored at least a point when I saw a tick of anxiety as he looked down at Bandit. Probably imagining his unmentionables being torn and chewed like a frankfurter and beans. But to his credit, and my growing unease, it was only the slightest of distractions, and then he was looking squarely at me again.

"The brave little man with his dog," he said, and I watched as one of his floating phantom hands left the steering wheel and reached into a pocket of his leather jacket. My first thought, the Southern Californian in me, cried out *Gun! Gun! Run! Hit the ground!* But even as these thoughts fired across my synapses, my muscles tensing to run or hit the ground, Dillon's hand came back out and it wasn't a gun he held.

"I was thinking about your dog, after that stunt you pulled in the woods." I watched him flick his wrist, a quick and simple motion like a magician would do, and a long and silver blade sprung like magic from his fist. "And I think I came up with a viable solution."

That blade, four inches and gleaming with moonlight, held my eyes as effectively as Tara had, though for different reasons. The thought of that knife punching into my dog, ripping into Bandit's guts, tearing the life from him, made my stomach do a little queasy flip. I felt like a small boy, and I wanted my dad.

Hell, I wouldn't have turned away my mom either, had she at that moment come running down the highway to save the day.

I pushed the images away, the momentary horror of what could be, of what I no doubt knew this guy in the leather jacket, driving the deep black Mustang, would do if given the chance. Instead, I tried to snatch the anger that hid behind the fear.

"You ever touch my dog and I'll use that knife to cut off your limp dick," I said. Then, speaking before the thought was even fully formed, as if it were almost a revelation, something inferred from the mists of a crystal ball, I continued. I think it was something like how I'd known the kind of man Fat Bobby's dad had to be, even as I said he couldn't be that bad. "And I'll mail your tiny noodle limp dick to your dad, so he'll know what a fucking pansy ass his son really is."

The tires squealed with the braking of the black car. The Mustang lurched with the sudden friction, and stopped. The pungent smell of burnt rubber wafted up in the darkness.

"I'll fucking kill you," Dillon said, and I looked at him square in the eyes, and his smirk, that lopsided grin like he didn't give a shit about anything, like he was separate from it all, was gone.

His hand held the switchblade with white-knuckle intensity, making his hands even whiter than they already were, contrasted with all the black.

The blade quivered, and the moonlight twinkled upon it.

The driver's door opened, and he stepped out.

I snatched at Bandit's collar again, to let him know he was to follow, and I turned and ran, forgetting all my talk about not taking shit, not being scared.

I ran for the turnoff like I'd never run before, faster than for any track meet or scrimmage ball game I'd ever been a part of. I ran and didn't stop running until I was home, through the door, throwing the lock behind me.

Not wanting to, but needing to know, I peeked through the curtains of the adjacent window. The black Mustang rolled by as if on cue, the windows up so that I could imagine it driven not by a teenage thug, but maybe driving itself, fueled by otherworldly forces. Then it was out of sight down the road, once more part of the night that had birthed it.

Breathing fast and loud and harsh, bent over clutching my legs, I turned away from the window and looked up to see Mom there wringing a dish towel in her hands, looking at me, looking at the door, waiting to see what hordes of hell and damnation had to be on my heels.

# CHAPTER THREE

## 1.

With a whole week before the fair was to open to the public, Fat Bobby and I needed something to do to occupy our minds. We'd spent a couple hours reading comics, and I'd let him go through my boxes and pick and choose what he wanted to read. But I stayed close by as he read them, never leaving him alone for even a second.

I'd instructed him on how to hold and care for the comics properly so as not to crease the covers or bend the binding. Nervously, I pretended to read as well, but watched my friend's elbows and legs shuffling as he sat on my bedroom floor and flipped through the books. He came frighteningly close to trampling the comics at times, like a large circus elephant dancing dangerously close to the gleeful, pointing children, but disaster was always averted.

Finally, filled to the brim with mutants and krytponians, radioactive spiders and dark knights, even Fat Bobby had had enough superheroism for one morning and looked up and asked what we should do next.

I wanted to get out of the house as well, but was afraid to, and so didn't immediately respond.

Sleep the past couple nights had been fitful and restless. I tossed and turned beneath the sheets, disturbing Bandit at the foot of the bed. Outside my window the branches of the apple trees tapped and clicked constantly, as if imploring my attention. Little nubs on the branches looked like switchblades, and every time headlights passed I was sure it was a sleek black Mustang out there cruising through the night.

I hadn't told Mom or Dad about the guys in the car trailing me, or the driver with his gleaming knife. I knew I should; I knew Mr. Smirk—Dillon—was a dangerous kind of guy, not someone who'd be satisfied with just a fistfight. But I thought of the fuss and drama that would follow if I told them. How I'd probably be under house arrest until Dad got a hold of the police and the police got a hold of Dillon, his two friends, and their parents. The thought of missing even a single day of the summer was intolerable.

That was a foolish train of thought. What we as adults call irrational. I knew that even then. But kids aren't the most rational of beings, as I'm sure you know. And boys the least of all.

Gathering up the comics we'd been reading, Bobby and I started slipping them back into their plastic sleeves as we silently considered his question. Light from the dresser lamp shone off the clear plastic sleeves in streaks and whorls of color. Thus bagged, we filed the books into their respective boxes, pushed the boxes back into the closet.

The light off the comics made me think of the light I'd seen from atop the hill on the dirt road overlooking the woods. I told Fat Bobby about it—he seemed vaguely interested—and we got up, went to the kitchen, grabbed a couple sodas and, with Bandit between us, we headed out.

As we walked, Fat Bobby's interest seemed to grow, almost reaching a minimum level to qualify as excitement, and so mine did also, by proxy. He asked questions, and I found myself answering eagerly.

"Was it like a ghost light?" he asked. "I've heard that sometimes people see strange lights floating about in swamps. Was it like that? Ghost lights?"

I shook my head.

"No," I said. "It wasn't like that at all. Besides, there aren't any swamps here. It wasn't no ghost lights."

He looked vaguely disappointed, a scowl scrunching his face and making it look like a pile of unbaked dough grimacing. Then he smiled as some other idea struck him, something better, and the disappointment was a memory.

"Was it UFO lights?" he said, the eagerness in his tone raising his voice an octave and making me remember uncomfortably those high, whiny pleas that had first led me to the crying, nearly naked kid in the stream. "You know, all flashes of blue and green and white as the ship lands and the aliens get out and laser some holes into some cows and stuff."

"No, no." Shaking my head briskly, irritation gaining a foothold, I tried not to let it show. "No, it wasn't no spaceship landing." I wondered if maybe I should put Bobby on some sort of comic book restriction, give his brain a few days to come down from the clouds. "It was like a twinkle or something, you know, when the sun flashes off of something glass or metal."

"Oh," Fat Bobby said, "I think I know what that is."

The disappointment returned to his face, and he started walking ahead of me up the dirt hill. I had to trot to catch up to him. Up at the top, the woods ahead of us a carpet of green, Fat Bobby pointed into the distance.

*Away* from the woods.

My eyes followed the line of his finger and arm and, sure enough, there it was: the light I'd seen—the fallen star—the sun reflecting off some surface in fiery flashes that made me squint. I swiveled my head like a periscope, looking back towards the woods where I'd originally seen the reflective light.

I saw nothing there among the trees as I had the first time.

But turning my head the other way, in the direction Bobby was pointing, and there it was, that bright light like some sort of signal, twinkling, sparkling.

How had it moved? What was it?

I scanned the landscape this way and that, and with each turn of my head I saw something surprising. There wasn't just one flashing light out there among the hills where Fat Bobby had directed me to look. There were several. It was a veritable village of flashing lights, like bits of shattered glass or grains of sand on a beachfront catching the sunrays and throwing them back.

"What is it?" I asked, mystified.

"Come on," Fat Bobby said, "I'll show you."

* * *

The junkyard held mostly dead and dilapidated cars, parked side by side and fender to fender on dirt so barren that I felt sad for the sparse and dry weeds growing out from the cracks, like fingers of penitents from hell reaching through the grating of the earth. We walked the perimeter of the chain-link fence that surrounded the yard, heading towards where Fat Bobby said the entrance was located. As we walked we heard short and harsh sounds like firecrackers exploding, and I again thought *Guns! Guns! Run! Duck!* as the sounds cracked the silence like small thunders.

Bobby saw me flinch, and I looked to him seeing that he hadn't, and he gave me a wry smile that seemed to say *Not always so tough, are we, dumbshit?* and I thought: *good for you, maybe there's hope yet.*

"That's Jim and his dad," he said. "They run the place."

We reached the sliding gate that served as the entrance to the yard, and there a sign read "NO TRESPASSING." As I gazed into the yard I realized that it wasn't as haphazard and slapdash as I'd first thought. There was a large garage in the center of the automotive graveyard, three bay doors rolled up, and inside were various cars and trucks elevated or with hoods propped open. Parts and pieces littered the floor of the garage among shelves and tables full of tools. This wasn't just some scrap or auto yard. This was a mechanic's shop.

"Come on," Fat Bobby said, grabbing the fence. He started to push, and the large entrance gate wheeled open with a screech in its rusty tract.

"Wait!" Looking at the sign and hearing the loud firecracker sounds coming from somewhere in the yard, I hung back. "It says no trespassing!"

"Don't worry." He looked back at me as he slipped inside. "I know them."

Hesitantly, I followed.

As we crossed the yard towards the garage, walking around the cars in various states of disrepair and stages of rust, stepping over flaking tires and old engine blocks like the remnants of machines after Armageddon, I took in the fading chrome and metal, the shattered windshields and sun-cracked bumpers, and thought to myself: *So these are my fallen stars, my great treasure in the woods.* That realization carried with it a light sadness, and a soft sigh, barely perceptible, escaped me as the loss of possibilities played out in my mind. Maybe Bobby's talk of ghost lights and UFO landings had sparked an excitement in me despite my pretenses otherwise. At certain angles, the sunlight glared off of the dead vehicles as intense as it had from far off on the hill, yet this close up the magnificence had left the display and it was just daylight bouncing off scrap metal.

Fat Bobby led me around the garage. The building in the middle of the refuse was like the last fortress on a battlefield, itself pockmarked by age or mortar fire. Then we turned a corner and there, a few feet away, were black people with guns, and with California memories like wartime flashbacks I once more thought *Guns! Guns! Run! Gang war!*

Bobby called out over the gunfire to the duo. Bottles and cans set up on a segment of wooden post some distance away jumped

48

into the air, shattered, or ripped into aluminum shreds as I looked on, and I thought of the anxiety-filled freeway trips through Compton or Long Beach of years past.

The larger of the two, a tall and wiry black man with close-cropped curls of gray peppered hair, turned, saw us, flashed a bright white smile, and holstered his weapon. The second black person, a kid really, no more than a year older than me, if that, saw this, turned to look at us too, and lowered his gun also.

"Hey, my man!" the man said, in jeans and a sleeveless undershirt, grease and oil-stained, looking very much the mechanic. He stepped over to Fat Bobby, held out his hand palm up, and Bobby gave him a mighty slap, a smile brightening his fat face as I hadn't seen it do since my dad had given him the comic book money.

Bobby gestured to the older man, then the boy, and looked at me as he said: "Joey, this is Mr. Connolly—"

"Ernest," Mr. Connolly interjected, and shook my hand with one of his, large and long-fingered and hairy so that I thought of a tarantula as I shook it. I put him at around sixty or so, and yet he carried himself with a mild swagger and confidence of a man thirty years younger.

"—and his son, Jim," Bobby finished, and my hand was released and taken up by the smaller hand of the black kid, wiry like his dad, but his head bald as a baby's. Jim smiled that same flashy ivory smile his dad had, genuine and friendly, and I thought to myself for a fat kid with no friends Bobby sure had a lot of friends.

Tara bloomed in my mind briefly like a puff of smoke, and I smothered the thought and what accompanied it (*the fair the fair a beautiful girl and the fair*) and brought my thoughts back to the here and now.

"Joey saw the light shining off all your cars and wondered what it was," Fat Bobby explained, "so I brought him here. Hope it's not a problem."

49

Mr. Connolly dismissed this with a combination snort and bark of a laugh, and waved the very idea away.

"No problem at all," he said. "You know you can come around here anytime, Bobby." With that Mr. Connolly gave Bobby a massive slap on the back, which he probably meant to be friendly but rocked Fat Bobby on his heels. Turning to his son he gathered up the pistol his kid had been using and started to walk away. "You kids have fun," he said to all of us. And this just to Jim: "Be in for lunch."

Then it was the three of us: Fat Bobby, myself, and the first black kid I wasn't afraid of being shot or stabbed by in a long, long time. And Bandit, of course, off somewhere nearby, sniffing the cars and parts of cars, and the dirt and the thin, dying weeds, scents invisible in the air, there but unseen.

I felt it again, that sense of things moving and me being carried along for the ride. Another link in the chain of events, the moving of the gears, and I felt I was on a trail myself, following it like Bandit to wherever it inevitably led.

## 2.

"It actually wasn't one of the cars here I saw," I told Jim as the three of us strolled casually through the yard, like three buddies on a fishing trip. I'd answered all the initial questions boys always had when meeting each other, like where I was from, where I lived, what I liked to do, things like that. Of course he took to Bandit real quick, which was a point in my favor: a good dog like a sign that said, *Hey, I ain't so bad. I'm pretty damn okay, actually. See, I have a dog!*

"Oh?" he said, twirling a metal pipe he had scooped up off the ground. I noticed his motions weren't clumsy, that the pipe whizzed in circles and semicircles in his hand with deftness and ease, and as sure as Bandit was a sign about me, this was a sign about Jim. It said *I know how to take care of myself* and like a telepathy of some sort I knew Mr. Connolly had bestowed a similar philosophy upon his son as Dad had done with me.

Don't let fear control you.

Don't take shit from anyone.

With just the right twist of his wrist, I knew Jim Connolly could whack something good with that small pipe. Probably without the pipe too, and I knew this was one kid I didn't want to get in any pissing contest with. I was glad we'd hit it off so well.

"Yeah," I said. "It was a lot like the sun shining off these cars here, but it wasn't here. I saw it off in the woods."

"You probably just forgot exactly where you saw it coming from," Fat Bobby said, picking up a stick, trying to twirl and spin it like Jim. The stick went flying out of his sausage-like fingers, sailed dangerously close past my face.

I slugged him on the arm. I checked the punch at the last moment, not hitting him too hard, but Bobby still gave me an injured *What'd you do that for?* look.

"There's at least half a mile between the woods and here," I said. "I'm not fucking blind."

"Geez," Fat Bobby said, rubbing his shoulder where I'd hit him. "Sorry."

"Actually," Jim said, "there's service roads that run all through the woods."

"Service roads?" I asked.

"Yeah, you know, for forest rangers and firefighters and shit like that." He had given me a look when I'd hit Bobby that said: *Don't hit the fat kid.* To his credit he didn't make a big deal about it, and so I made a mental note to myself not to hit Fat Bobby like that anymore, even in play. That Jim would come to Fat Bobby's defense, even with just a look, was kind of cool in my book, and my respect for the kid rose a notch or two. "So it's possible you saw something where you said you saw it."

"I did see something where I said I saw it." The note of challenge in my voice made Jim look up at me, and he flashed his bright smile again. I knew that he was liking me more as well, what with me not backing down from him, even about something as dumb as where some ghost lights or UFO beams had come from.

"Only one problem," he said.

"What's that?" I asked.

We came to the far rear fence of the yard at that moment, and Jim pointed off to where the woods started a hundred yards off or so. A dirt road led off that way into the trees, and there was a barricade across it, large metal crossbeams in the shape of an X. As if for added determent, thick coils of chain looped around the crossbeams, then around two trees on either side of the barricade, and a thick padlock hung at the center where the ends of the chain met up.

"Those roads have been closed for some time," he said.

* * *

I lay in bed that night wondering how the car I had actually seen gleaming with reflected sunlight deep in the forest—not the cars at the Connolly yard that Fat Bobby assumed I'd seen—had ended up where it was.

According to Jim the access road barricades were put in place a long time before, when careless campers or hunters would improperly put out campfires; the embers would be caught in a breeze after the people had left, and acres were burnt to crisp and ashes. Only rangers and the fire department had keys to unlock the chains of the barricades, and hefty fines and jail time kept most people from messing with them.

This left me with only a few options and conclusions.

One, the access road at the Connolly yard that Jim had shown us seemed to be the closest route to the general area in which I had seen my single, distinct, reflective surface, me presuming it's a car. Since that road was barricaded, obviously if anyone had used it, it had been someone with the keys to the chain. This would mean a ranger or the fire department. But Jim hadn't said anything about seeing rangers or fire trucks use that road, and it was a pretty good chance, him and his dad working there, one of them would have seen or heard a vehicle driving that road. Add to that the fact that I hadn't seen any smoke or fire when I had seen the shiny object in the distance, my fallen star, and that pretty much ruled out the rangers or fire department.

This led naturally to conclusion number two. If it hadn't been a ranger or fire truck out there, someone authorized to pass through the barricades, then maybe it was someone with no legitimate right whatsoever. Maybe someone had busted through one of the barricades; an off-season poacher possibly, or kids doing the fleshy tango in an out of the way place, or perhaps a coven of Satanists for all I knew, dancing naked smeared with blood and chanting to the Dark Lord. Sacrificing goats, having orgies, all that crap. But the access road barricade at the Connolly yard, the most direct route to the general area of the light I'd seen, obviously hadn't been run down or forced open.

That didn't mean another access road hadn't been used, and I'd asked Jim how many there were. He said several, exactly how many he didn't know. But they were all barricaded, he said, and the rangers were real regular with their duties, checking on the barricades and patrolling the woods. Fat Bobby verified this by saying that Tara's dad was a ranger, and he always saw the man out and about in his park jeep or truck around town, and when he wasn't around town he was presumably out in the forest, checking on things.

I nodded at this like it made sense, which it did, but inside I was cursing up a storm at Fat Bobby for once again knowing more about this beautiful girl than I did.

So, if only rangers and the fire department could easily get vehicles into the woods, and neither one of them had been there when I saw the bright light on the ground, then that left only one other option I could think of. And it was this one that left me tossing and turning for some time, thinking of adventures and mysteries and all things that made a boy's heart and mind race with life.

What if the car I'd seen shining back the sunlight like a beacon had been there in the woods *before* the barricades had gone up? How long ago would that have been? Years? Decades? And why was this possible car still there after so much time had passed? Was it forgotten? Or did people just not know where to find it? I'd only seen it myself because I'd been on high ground, looking in a particular direction.

That last intrigued me the most for some reason.

If people didn't know where to find it, why not? Had someone put the car out there intentionally? Was there something there that wasn't supposed to be found?

For me, in the long stretch of summer with nothing but time on my hands and a fertile imagination, this wasn't something I could just forget. Plans were already forming in my head and the morning seemed too far away, dangling like a carrot in front of a horse, beckoning, teasing. The night lingered, taunting me, and sleep seemed a misty thing to catch, slipping through my fingers in ethereal tendrils.

### 3.

Fat Bobby lived north down the highway heading into town, about a quarter mile from our place. I hadn't been to his house before, but he'd pointed it out once from a distance when we'd been walking home from town. Whereas my neighborhood seemed something of a checkerboard with immaculate well-tended lawns and freshly painted, manicured houses interspersed with weed-strewn dirt expanses where a lawn had once been, and run-down affairs that could have been boxes and rusted shingles

54

slapped together disguised as houses, Fat Bobby's neighborhood was nothing but the latter. Houses with exteriors of peeling paint like flaky scabs, rusted automobiles parked out front like the husks of dead creatures, and mangy beasts with matted hair chained to posts that I could only guess were some sort of dog, were tossed about his street as if by a tornado.

It was because of these last, the dirt encrusted, sun beaten animals I thought were dogs, that I left Bandit home this time around. That might seem counterintuitive, leaving behind my dog and best protection when I was planning on walking a neighborhood populated by canine monstrosities. But that was exactly why I left him behind. Not wanting Bandit in any sort of dogfight with these sad and horrid beasts, perhaps hosting an early stage of rabies, I trusted myself to outrun these mangy mutts, but not Bandit to avoid getting into a scuffle where he might end up poisoned by the contaminated spit sluicing about their jaws.

Turning off onto Fat Bobby's street, I moved warily along the dilapidated and depressing dirt landscape of his neighborhood. This area held not a hint of the Old West vibe that the town of Payne proper had held for me when I'd seen it from atop the hill. Rather, this neighborhood seemed like a Calcutta or something akin to one of those African villages seen on the Give-Us-Your-Money heartstring-plucking Christian Children's Fund commercials. These weren't homes I was seeing, but hovels, trailers weather-beaten and uncared for so that they seemed not like trailers at all, but like the shells of structures after a nuclear blast. Trees tried growing in a few of the dirt lawns and seemed like the emaciated skeletal structures of ancient beasts, gnarled and twisted by age and decay.

I approached the trailer Fat Bobby had pointed out before, a rectangular thing with duct-taped windows and flaky wisps of what might have once been blue paint fluttering down from its walls, like dying butterflies. Empty lawn chairs sat before it with loose flaps slapping about in a light breeze, like little flags.

I don't know what I expected Bobby's dad to look like; I guess maybe I leaned towards something like Fat Bobby himself, just a larger version. A fat and lazy man with a gut like a beach ball stuffed beneath his shirt, and beer cans littered about his feet like carelessly delivered babies.

But the man in the yard that the trailer sat on, leaning over the hood of a white Toyota pickup, wasn't fat, and the thick cords of muscles glistened by sweat and shiny by sun showed he wasn't lazy. He heard me approaching, stopped fidgeting with whatever part under the hood he'd been fidgeting with, and withdrew from beneath the hood to stretch to full height.

And the height was mountainous.

As I've said before, my dad was a large man. I was used to being dwarfed by the larger of my gender. But whereas Dad was lean and muscled like a fast stallion, Fat Bobby's father was thick and solid like a bull. Mr. Templeton's face was likewise bulbous, as if it was permanently swollen. This wasn't a swelling by anything like a bee sting neither, but a red swelling of meanness, as if there was something on the inside of him that wouldn't go away. Maybe a volcanic pressure, and at any moment he could explode with the force of the heat inside him. He looked at me like he was looking at a fly that had alighted on his food and taken a shit.

He wanted to squash me, no doubt in my mind.

Yet it wasn't personal either. I remember thinking he wanted to squash anyone and everyone. Like the existence of other people was offensive.

Dad was no pushover by any definition of the word, but seeing this man, in torn jeans and a faded flannel shirt like he was some lumberjack-Sasquatch hybrid, I thought of the two of them tangling, Dad and Mr. Templeton, and I didn't think I'd want to place any bets either way.

"What the hell you want?" he asked.

His lips moved beneath a wild beard like a miniature wilder-

56

ness. I wondered if food crumbs and bugs lived in that tangle somewhere, in a little world separate from the one we were in. Maybe there was a whole civilization of lost bits of food and beetles in there somewhere, and when he talked it was like an earthquake and the voice of God from on high to the wee beard folk.

For a moment I thought I'd laugh.

Then I knew if that happened, I'd die, and so I didn't laugh.

"I'm here to see Bobby, sir."

I tried sounding as respectful as I could muster. Afraid of my head being popped like a grape, I think I did pretty good. Fear's a fabulous motivator.

"Are you the kid he's been hanging out with so much?" I thought about answering but he kept on talking, and so I clacked my mouth shut. "He's been shirking his chores, the fat lazy bastard. Gone all day long, comes home late, like this is some sort of motel he can just come and go from whenever he likes."

He paused like maybe he wanted me to say something, but I didn't know what to say so I continued to keep my mouth shut.

"You shirk your chores too? Out here running around like you got nothing to do." Silence still seemed the best option on my end. Then: "Your parents some kind of fucking hippies? Let their kids run around and shit?"

"No, sir," I said, not really knowing which part I was answering to.

"Yeah right," he said, and I didn't know which he was referring to either. Not that it mattered, even with him talking bad about my parents in some offhand manner. I imagined myself briefly trying to stick up for my folks, flipping this guy off or something, and him coming at me, and me trying to use one of the tricky leg maneuvers that Dad had taught me. This guy just laughing as I tried to tangle his legs with mine, or kick at a kneecap like a boulder, and he just twitched a big toe or something and I busted like a little glass figurine.

"May I see Bobby, sir?" I said, deciding politeness was still the best course of action.

"You talk like a fruit, kid." He smiled, and he had teeth yellow-stained by years of nicotine. As I watched he pulled a crumpled pack of Camels from a breast pocket, pulled out its last inhabitant, and lit it up with a lighter shaped like a little pistol. "'*May I?*'" he mocked, murmuring around the cigarette. "'*Sir*,'" he said in a high and whiny voice. "Goddamn queers everywhere nowadays."

At that moment the door to the trailer swung open and hit the wall it was attached to with a metallic rattle. We both turned at the sound, and there was Fat Bobby standing in the doorframe. It took a second or two for me to notice what was different about my friend. The dark ring around his right eye seemed to call my gaze to it, like the target circle of a dartboard.

I looked back at Mr. Templeton.

He looked at his son, then looked down at me. It was clear he knew what I'd seen but he didn't seem much concerned. As in not at all.

"You know what happens in another body's family isn't none of your concern, don't you, fairy boy?" he asked, and immediately, obediently, I nodded. "You don't doubt that if you caused me any sort of trouble I wouldn't think twice about bouncing you around some, do you?"

I shook my head. No, I didn't doubt it one bit.

"Good," he said, then he looked from me back to Bobby, still standing silent and slouched in the doorway of the trailer. "Get out of my sight."

Turning back to the Toyota he leaned once again under the hood.

Bobby stepped off the porch lightly, making almost no sound, which, with his girth, was a tremendous feat of skill. Slowly, he walked towards me, moving as if he were trying to avoid disturbing a beehive. When he was close, he waved for me to follow and together we walked softly away from the miserable trailer, out of the neighborhood like a Third World ghost town, and onto the highway. After several minutes of silence like a period of mourning, I finally opened my mouth and told him what I wanted to do.

Fat Bobby smiled as I spoke, and with that smile the effect of the black eye seemed to dwindle. Though we cheered up considerably talking about what we were going to do, time and again I turned to look at my friend and that shiner and, in my mind, I saw the fist that caused it coming down like a hammer.

* * *

On the way to the Connolly yard, we stopped at the hill on the dirt road overlooking the woods. I immediately saw the object casting back the sunlight that I'd seen before, far out into the forest among the thick carpet of trees. Fat Bobby saw it too, and I actually heard him breathe out something like an '*ahhhhh*' of amazement.

"That isn't ghost lights or a UFO," he said.

"No, it isn't," I said and looked at my watch. It was approaching noon, and I tried to think back to that day I'd first met Fat Bobby, and what time I'd been standing on this very hill. It could have been around noon. Which meant that the object down there, be it abandoned car or something else, for some reason only reflected the sun at a certain time of the day and from a certain angle.

This was intriguing, and I was eager to get on with our plans.

"Come on," I said and started to walk again. Bobby lingered for a moment, as if the light down there held him by a tether and was reluctant to let go. I knew the feeling. It's that thing between boys and the mysterious, the unknown. Like an umbilical cord that gives and returns life.

* * *

Before hitting the Connolly yard we stopped by my house to pick up Bandit. The aroma of fresh cookies wrapped about us like tantalizing fingers as soon as we walked inside. We stayed awhile, watching my mom in the kitchen pulling out trays lined with brown baked delights and scooping them onto the counter to cool. We wanted them hot and begged for them, and Mom gave us each a handful. A glass of cool lemonade that fogged the glasses just a bit accompanied this feast, and we ate slowly, enjoying every bite and swallow as if they might never come again.

Mom noticed Fat Bobby's shiner, but she didn't say anything. She gave me a look and I gave her one back, and somewhere in that secret exchange she understood the message: *Not now. I'll tell you later.* She nodded as if she'd actually heard this, told us to enjoy our cookies, and then was off somewhere else in the house.

As we were putting our glasses in the sink, Sarah came down the stairs in a summer dress, and her hair and face were all done up like for some sort of pageant. *Date*, I said to myself, and had to smile. Apparently, her true love in California was forgotten. Out of sight and out of mind.

She saw us in the kitchen, saw my blooming smile, and pointed at me threateningly.

"Don't say a word," she said, and that was like an invitation.

"I think you need more makeup," I said. "We can still see your face."

There was something in her other hand, the one not pointing like a dagger at me, and she wound up her arm and threw it and, too late, I saw it was her sandals and one of them hit me in the chest. The heel was broad and thick and it hurt when it struck. I laughed, though, seeing my sister's face had turned red with the jab.

"You don't want him to know you're a mutant on the first date."

And here came the other sandal, fast, and I stepped aside at the last moment and it sailed by my head, striking the refrigerator with a thump. My sister stomped determinedly towards me, and that was when Mom stepped back into the kitchen from the living room and planted herself between us.

"What on earth is going on in here?"

"Oh, Joey!" my sister bawled. "Why do you have to be such a retard?!"

She was away and back up the stairs as quick as she'd appeared, not even bothering to gather up her ballistic missile sandals. Upstairs a door slammed, the impact reverberating throughout the house. I imagined her in her room or in the bathroom, staring at herself, wiping her face clean and trying again with the makeup and lipstick and whatever other chemicals and goop girls used.

That made me smile.

That smile made my mom frown.

It wasn't one of her vaguely comical-puzzled frowns, either, that asked *How did this happen?* Rather, it was one of her dangerous and angry frowns that said: *What the hell is your problem?* and sometimes ended with her whapping me upside the head. In moments, under that reproachful gaze, my smile dwindled and then faded altogether.

"Why are you and your sister so mean to each other?"

I shrugged. Looked down and away from her disappointment.

"You know someday it'll just be you and her," Mom said. "Your dad and I won't be around forever."

"Yes, ma'am," I murmured.

"Someday you'll need each other."

"Yes, ma'am," I muttered, really thinking: *Yeah, right, like I need a rash on my sack.*

"She's growing up, Joey. Jokes like that aren't so funny anymore. She needs to feel good about herself."

"Yes, ma'am," I said, head still hung low.

"You might not understand now, but someday you'll meet a

girl and want to say nice things to her. Then maybe you'll think back to now and the things you said to your sister."

I thought of Tara. I thought of the things I wanted to say to her. I thought of her in her dress at the bookstore. The shape of her. How the lights caught in the swirls of her hair. Her smile and her skin like velvet.

Suddenly, the things I'd said to my sister indeed didn't seem so funny. But I wouldn't—couldn't—admit as much to my mom. So I settled with another "Yes, ma'am", and then my mother was moving upstairs, trailing after my sister, and me and Fat Bobby were free and so we headed outside. Bandit trotted along beside us.

"Why are you so mean to your sister?" Fat Bobby asked after we were across my yard and back on the dirt road.

"Because she's a dork," I said, as if that explained it all.

"She's kind of pretty."

I looked at him like he said the sky was falling, and I saw his face was red. I remembered how I'd felt around Tara, and I thought to myself, horrified and wanting to laugh at the same time, *Fat Bobby is sweet on Sarah!*

But rather than laugh at him I just kept walking, adding these words in response:

"If by pretty you mean pretty stupid, then you got a point."

### 4.

Back at the Connolly yard we slid through the large sliding gate again and picked our way through the rusted heaps of automobiles and parts and piles of parts. From a distance we saw Mr. Connolly and Jim lying on rolling boards slid under an old Chevy in the garage. A clang and scuffle of metal on metal from beneath the car preceded the emergence of father and son when they heard our approach. Oil and grease-stained, the duo waved at us instead of shaking hands. We pulled Jim aside and started to tell him the conclusions I'd come to and what we wanted to do. Pretty soon he was nodding along to our words and one of his flashy white smiles spread across his face.

Although we stood grouped together in a corner of the garage and kept our voices low, Mr. Connolly lingered nearby wiping his hands on a towel. I knew he'd overheard some of what we were saying. He didn't make any objections, but instead smiled one of his own bright smiles, as if he wished he were a boy again and could come along with us.

"If you boys are going down to the woods, stick together. Have fun and be safe," was the closest he came to any admonishment, and then: "I have some calls to make and other office work. Be home for dinner, Jim."

With that Jim's dad opened a side door and disappeared into the room beyond. Jim walked to a small refrigerator humming along one wall, opened it, and fished out three bottles of water. Handing one each to me and Fat Bobby, he led the way out back, across the rear of the yard, and opened the small gate at the end of the walkway. Side by side, with Bandit doing his ghost impersonation padding along silently about us, we walked to the barricaded access road, stepped around the barrier and into the dense forest beyond.

* * *

Shadows and light passed upon us and the earth as the sun stabbed through the branches overhead in intermittent fashion. Green-heavy limbs and thick brown trunks rose all around us, so that walking the access road through these I felt as if I'd entered some fantasy world; a deep woods in which some wily wizard or wrinkled witch holed up in an old shack cast spells and charms. Looking in either direction off the road, visibility lasted only feet or a few yards at best, and then it became like a wall, the trees and the branches and the bushes obscuring things.

Deep in the woods the quiet around us was startling, so that we talked to each other just to break the silence. I thought that this far in the forest there would be sounds: birds twittering and things moving in the trees and bushes. Maybe the rustle of leaves and branches as a breeze sidled through like someone in a crowd. But this was as if only a painting of a forest, just colors and shapes, with no real life to it.

"Why is it so quiet?" I asked, my voice loud in the otherwise vast silence.

"Most of the animals around here are migratory," Jim said. "They're always moving and sometimes all of them are moving at once, so they're gone for awhile and you get this."

He made a vague gesture to indicate the silent world around us.

"Kind of creepy," Fat Bobby said, looking about nervously with little jerks of his head, as if he were trying to watch all directions at once.

"Not really," Jim said. "I think it's kind of peaceful."

Initially, I felt inclined to agree with Fat Bobby, thinking the silence and stillness of the forest was sort of spooky. I could imagine things out there in the trees or hiding in the bushes, watching us, biding their time. Creatures with fangs and claws, and holes where they dragged their prey kicking and screaming into subterranean dens. But as we continued to walk along the access road, the quiet began to lose some of its macabre atmosphere.

I was reminded of the calm and stillness I most enjoyed reading in. When my parents and sister were elsewhere and I was out on the porch, or in my room, with a comic or a paperback spread in my hands, and there seemed a hush over the whole of the earth. A stillness just for me, as if the universe were holding its breath just so I could enjoy my book.

So that when the soft running of the stream began like a whisper, and then a little louder as the road curved towards it, I was almost disappointed at the end of the silence. The appearance of the stream meant we were heading in the direction of where I'd initially met Bobby, and it was past that spot where I would have continued in my beeline for the mystery object, be it UFO or fallen star, if I hadn't been interrupted.

I pointed this out, and we crossed the stream. The tinkling of the water seemed an invitation for us to join it and speak freely.

"So, you going to hit the fair?" Fat Bobby asked Jim as we splashed across.

"You bet," Jim said.

"Why don't you go with us?" I said.

"Sure thing," he answered with a curt nod of his head, as if he'd been waiting for the offer.

On the other side the world awoke as if we'd crossed some threshold, some barrier between dimensions. The twitter of birds, two at least, calling and answering each other, was like the last song on earth, eerie and almost unnatural, following so soon after the preceding quietude. We stopped our talk in unison to listen to it, unconsciously rolling our steps to reduce the noise of our passing. Farther out in the woodlands other critters chittered and yapped, joining in on the chorus.

Soon the stream gurgled more distantly behind us, fading, and then was gone. A break in the trees to the west revealed one of the rocky outcroppings I'd seen that first day on the hill, trying to locate a landmark against which to find the fallen star. The outcropping rose like an ancient monument, and its stones like natural steps led to the top. I imagined natives with torches walking to the peak, and up there an altar and a bound virgin, willing sacrifice to the sun god.

I told Jim and Bobby how I'd seen just such a craggy hill near the light source.

"Maybe we'll see something from up there," Jim said, and so we broke the path of our straight line, heading on over to the foot of the monument hill.

The climb was easy and took only a few minutes, as if the stones and rocks scaling the hill had indeed been put there as steps to aid just such as us. Flat stones sat upon a grassy area at the top, with one large stone standing upright that if you looked at from the right angle looked like one of those Easter Island heads. Unfinished maybe, as if the sculptor had decided halfway through that there were better things he could do with his time. We sat with our backs against it and sipped our water, looking out over the top of the woods, daylight pouring down on us hot and bright.

"It sure is high up here," Fat Bobby said.

"Yeah," Jim replied, "kind of cool."

"Like we're on a tower, looking down on our kingdom," I said.

"You use words like a writer," Jim said, and his tone made this something like a compliment. "You ever think about being one someday?"

"I don't know," I said, when in fact that was all I ever thought about my future being. Whether it was books or comics, or something else I hadn't thought of yet, it was stories that I wanted to tell. "What about you?"

"What about me?" Jim said, playing with the cap on his water bottle.

"What do you want to do, you know, when you grow up?"

"I don't know," he said, his brown skin beading with sweat under the high sun. "My dad wants me to do some kind of police work. Says I've got the brains for it. That I can see things and figure out how they work or how something happened."

"What does your mom think?" I asked, earnestly, but also with a kid's curiosity as I had yet to meet his mom. A mental CAUTION! detector blinked in my mind's eye, recalling Bobby's tragic answer to a similar question not so long ago. Sometimes things were better left not knowing about, and I hoped this wasn't one of those times.

"I don't see her that much," Jim said. His tone was matter-of-fact, so devoid of either anger or sadness that I knew he had to feel one or the other. Perhaps both. "She met my dad young. She was still in college when she got pregnant. Had real big plans to become a lawyer. So Dad offered to take sole custody after I was born, so she could stay in school."

I pondered this, turning it over. It seemed to me that Jim's ability to control his emotions was just the kind of temperament an officer of the law would need, and so I said as much.

"I bet you'd make a good cop."

Jim smiled, nodded slightly in an unspoken gratitude, our blooming manhood inhibiting anything further. I then turned to Fat Bobby.

"What about you, Bobby?" He looked over at me all surprised-like, his mouth open just a bit, as if he'd never expected to hear someone ask him this question. "What do you want to do?"

He shifted uncomfortably for a second or two, then grew still and looked out over the woods like he was trying to find something. He looked about to speak a couple times, his mouth working like words wanted to come out, and then he'd close his lips and grind his teeth. Jim and I looked at each other, and he offered me a shrug. When Fat Bobby finally answered, it was brief and to the point and spoken matter-of-factly as if it hadn't taken him such a time to say it.

"I want to be gone from here," he said, and I think we all knew that *here* meant his home, his dad, and the things like that shiner dark around his eye. I remember praying something at that moment, not like a formal prayer or anything, but just silently offering up some words to God and hoping He wasn't too busy to hear them when they drifted His way.

Please God, let him find his way out of here, let him find what he's looking for.

And, in the end, when all's said and done, isn't that pretty much what every prayer is about?

Some minutes later Jim bolted up and pointed and said: "*Look!*", and I stood up and Fat Bobby did too. Following the line of his finger, we saw out to the west not more than half a mile away among a thick copse of trees, a flash of something, maybe glass, maybe metal. We started down from the rocky hill, our lookout tower, and found our way back to the access road. I wanted to cut directly through the forest in the direction of the light, but Jim suggested we follow the road a little more, and so we did. Not a hundred yards away we found that the road branched, and in one direction it continued east and in the other it looped back, heading northwest.

There was an old faded rectangular sign fallen on the ground covered by rust and weeds. I bent and tore away the weeds, but the rust I could do nothing about, and the sign remained mysterious and unreadable. For all we knew it read "DEATH AHEAD FOR STUPID BOYS," but it didn't matter. We took the northwest branch, which looped us back in the general direction of the light.

This branch of the road was weed strewn and deeply pitted and rutted, as if it had been in a state of disuse and in need of repair decades ago. Never tended to when it was still in use, now abandoned it seemed an artefact, a remnant of some ancient settlement recently excavated. Maybe awaiting a second death, when in the course of eons the earth would swallow it again under the dust of ages.

Bandit found his way easily enough and bounded along ahead of us, muzzle to the ground, sniffing and snorting as he followed trails that we could never see. We didn't bound speedily and confidently about like him. We picked our way carefully along the half-hidden road, planning and measuring each step, lest a foot slip into a hole or rut and one of us snapped an ankle like a twig.

I don't know exactly where I expected to find the proposed abandoned car, if a car it actually was, but smack dab in the middle of the road like it was waiting for us wasn't among the possibilities I imagined. I thought of finding a cave and the car somehow in the cave (how we saw reflected light from within a cave, this scenario my imagination didn't answer; it just seemed cool, a car in a cave!). Or the car rolled down a ditch and blackened by the flames of its explosion in the distant past. Or maybe up in a tree as the forest had grown around it, lifting it up in its branches so that it ended up like a tree house of sorts.

But right there in the middle of the road … no, that's not what I expected at all.

Yet that's what we found, an old Buick family affair, color long flaked away so that it was gray with the metal beneath, gray and drab, like the husk of a giant metal beetle. The forest had indeed begun to grow around it, and roots and weeds were tangled about what remained of the tires and crawled up along the grill and bumpers. The headlights were busted, shards of plastic and glass like tiny daggers littering the forest floor. We walked around the thing reverently, in silence, and tried to peer in the windows, but they were covered by years of bird shit and dirt caught in the wind and slapped onto the glass like a second skin.

Jim tried one door, Bobby another, and I a third, and all three were locked or rusted shut. Jim tried the fourth door, only to find it likewise immovable. Bandit circled the car, sniffing, poking his head underneath it, searching, his tail pumping like a crank. Eventually, we settled on the front bumper and drank from our bottled water, only Bandit still running about the car, trying to get at what was in it.

"Well," Jim said after awhile, "we found it."

"Yeah," I said, staring out at the woods, not knowing what I was feeling, whether it was disappointment or just not having all the answers at once.

"I wonder what's in it?" Fat Bobby said, and that was what we were all thinking about. Those locked doors were like a challenge. They were defying us with their stubbornness not to open and reveal to us what was inside. "Why don't we just bust the windows?" Bobby said, and he bent over to pick up a fist-sized rock from the ground.

We looked at each other and then with a shake of our heads dismissed that idea. It would be like vandalizing a museum or a church: it just wasn't right. We wanted to get into the car, but we wanted to do it the right way. In a way that respected the car, and how it had sat here for years waiting for just this moment, waiting for *us.*

"We'll get it open," Jim said, and he said it like it was so, like there was no alternative, no other possibility. "Don't forget, my dad owns a car yard."

I thought to myself, *Yeah, that's right. If anyone can find a way to open the thing, it's this guy right next me.* My momentary funk dissipated, and I was able to just sit there like I was at a park bench, enjoying the setting.

"We'll come back," Jim repeated, as if settling the matter. "We'll open it."

So it was settled, and so I knew it would be.

But the fair was tomorrow, and we made our plans for that as we made our slow way back towards the highway. And in the wake of the events of the day that followed the car was for a time, if not forgotten, then relegated to some back row of our young brains, in the shadows, biding its time.

# CHAPTER FOUR

## 1.

The day of the fair arrived and, to my distress, the whole family was going. I should have expected such a possibility, but thoughts of the high Ferris wheel and rollercoasters and haunted houses and finding Tara somewhere there, radiant in the lights of the place, pushed out all other considerations. I hadn't even entertained the notion that my parents and sister would want to go also. So when Dad made his announcement and started herding us to the door, I moved with exaggerated sloth-like shuffling strides impossible to ignore.

"What's wrong?" he asked when we were all in the foyer, each jockeying for one last look in the standing mirror.

"I wanted to go with my friends," I said, unable to keep a certain tone from my voice that I knew wouldn't go over well with my dad.

"Well, you're going with us."

This last brooked no argument, stated with a not so subtle, unspoken warning that I would go with them or not at all. In protest, I made sure my feet plodded through the door and onto the porch with a little extra emphasis.

Bustled into the car, dressed warmly for the night in coats and sweaters, we rolled away onto the highway. I scowled in the backseat, staring daggers at my family. Sarah didn't seem perturbed by this at all, and with some new guy she'd met I thought she would have put up a bigger fight than I had with Dad. But she seemed smug and happy as can be, and I thought I knew why. She was probably meeting the guy at the fair, and was thinking that she'd slink away from the rest of us when we were actually there, batting her lashes and mooning over Dad to win him over.

Figuring I could probably do the same thing, except for the batting the lashes part, I tried to keep my spirits up. Truth be told, it wasn't all that hard to do. As the highway made its final slow descent into town, the great lights of the fairground rose outlined against the early evening sky. With its rollercoaster loops and arches stretching high, it seemed like an alien city, some strange metropolis landed upon our world.

The noise of the fair drifted to us before we even arrived. Traffic slowed to a crawl as we approached, and the laughter and screams of those lifted above carried on the night wind, through the streets, and into the windows of the cars turning into the parking lot.

The long snake-train of vehicles moved forward inch by anxious inch, until we pulled up alongside a booth, and an attendant leaned out of a window. Dad took some bills out of his wallet and handed them over to the attendant, saying: "Two adults and two children." The attendant disappeared and then popped back into view like a jack-in-the-box, handing over four tickets to my dad and then waving us through.

We found a parking space far enough away so that when we climbed out I could look up and there were the humps of the rollercoaster, like the arched spine of a fierce dragon. Over there a ways the Ferris wheel stood like a portal and the lights of the cabs all around it twinkled in a vast "O". The screams of the people high upon it wafted down, shrieks of joyful fear like a primal, cultic chanting. I wanted to be up there with them, and it was all I could do to refrain from tugging at my parents' sleeves like the child I was but no longer wanted to be.

Dad passed out the tickets and we pocketed them, heading across the parking lot and to the arches that admitted us.

Just as we walked in a young man approached, in nice pressed pants and a collared shirt and a denim jacket. He said hi to Sarah, and then turned and shook my parents' hands and "sir"-ed and "ma'am"-ed them and I knew then without a doubt that Sarah had planned this.

She indeed batted her lashes at Dad and did this pouty thing with her lips and pulled on his arm and said: "Please, Daddy, oh please." Mom leaned over towards Dad and whispered in his ear. With an exasperated sigh he waved Sarah away. She leaned over and pecked him on the cheek and then she was prancing away like a doe with this nice looking guy not at all like the grease ball from California, and that surprised me. But not so much as the fact that Dad had let her go in the first place when he made such a fuss about it being a family night. I was angry at Sarah for getting away so easily, but angrier with myself that I hadn't planned ahead like her.

So I gave it a try and asked Dad if I could go looking for my friends. For a second I even considered trying the batting the lashes thing and pulling cutely on his arm. But at the last moment I decided to hang onto a bit of self-respect and just stick to the begging.

"No," he said.

I thought about making a scene, but then Mom leaned towards him again. She had one hand on his chest and one finger was kind of stroking him gently, prodding him.

"Come on, John," she said, and she did this persuasive lilting, soothing thing with her voice a thousand times better than my sister's blatant mooning. *Sarah, take some lessons from the master,* I thought, holding back a smile. "Let them have fun."

"This was supposed to be a family night, Linda," Dad said.

Mom snuggled even closer to him.

"We can have fun too," she said, and I thought, *Oh, barf!*

73

But I thought of finding Tara out there somewhere, among the crowd and the booths and games, and her pressing close to me like Mom was to Dad. The Puke Factor immediately went down a few levels. Dad smiled at Mom. You could see he was trying not to but losing the battle. Finally, he handed me a twenty from his pocket, ruffled my hair, which I hated, and waved me off. I ran before he could change his mind.

Under the lights and the shadows of the towering wheel and coaster, the people of Payne, shoulder to shoulder, moved almost as one mass, one creature. An ocean of people, and I ran and was drowned in the magic of it.

## 2.

I looked for my friends for a bit, trying mightily to avoid the game booths and rides until I found them. Until I saw this booth with water guns where you had to shoot into the mouths of these clowns that looked to me like portraits of John Wayne Gacy, not cheerful funny clowns at all. The water in the mouths filled up these balloons, and if the balloon on your target popped, you won a prize. It was the prize wall that caught my attention. Lined up rank and file on little shelves were these big plush superhero toys of Spiderman, Batman, Superman, and others, and I thought: *Wow, that's pretty dorky,* but really what that meant was I thought they were cool and wanted one.

Fishing the twenty from my pocket I walked over to the game booth. Only two of the six seats were taken, so I sat and gave the attendant my twenty, and it was a dollar a game so I got nineteen back. On my first try I found that the water stream from the gun arced high and I missed the maniacal clown's mouth for a couple seconds and sprayed his eyes, forehead, and chin while trying to adjust my aim. I thought to myself if this was John Wayne Gacy he would have raped me and chopped me up for the mess I was making of his face.

When the water gun was empty I passed another dollar across the counter to the attendant. He flipped a switch, and when the gun was full again, he said: "*Ready!*" I pulled the trigger and the water started to fly. This time I aimed low, adjusting for the arc, and though I was closer to the clown's blood-red open mouth, I still splashed around a bit and the balloon only got half full.

"Shit," I muttered and passed over another dollar. As my water gun was filling up again I saw this body sitting down on the stool next to me. I turned and there was this face like the moon, and a smile that made my heart skip a beat.

"Hey cowboy," Tara said, as she passed a dollar over to the attendant and he began to fill the gun in front of her. She wore jeans and a jacket, and she straddled the stool like a cowgirl. "Bet I can beat you."

Her voice was like a spring breeze through grass and tumbling leaves, and I thought I could smell her breath on the air. It was dew after the rain, flowers, and a clear blue sky.

I smiled, took hold of my gun.

"What are the stakes?" I asked, taking careful aim at Gacy's mouth.

"Whatever the winner wants," she said.

Smiling, she gave me this squinty look.

"That's kind of broad and vague. I don't have much to give."

Somehow I found the courage to meet her gaze.

She laughed, a brief sound like raindrops on a rooftop or feet tapping a dance.

"Then you better hope you win," she said. The attendant told her the gun was ready. She looked at me. I looked back at her, smiling so broadly it ached, telling myself I must look like an idiot, and not caring. "On the count of three."

I turned to stare down the killer clown.

*You're going to choke on it*, I told that painted face staring back at me.

"One," she said.

*You're going down, clown boy*, I taunted telepathically at Mr. Gacy.

"Two."

I tried thinking of what I'd ask for if I won. I wondered if she really meant what she said: *Whatever the winner wants*. I thought of a lot of things I wanted at that moment, and they made this shivery feeling go up and down my body.

From the corner of my eye I saw the arc of water shoot out of her gun, and I was still waiting for the *Three!* It took me a moment to figure out what was happening. I looked over at her and laughed, and then back at my target and pulled the trigger.

My aim was true this time around, but she had a head start and her aim was nearly as good. I watched as our balloons filled with water, mine always a bit smaller than hers, and then her balloon was stretching, growing, expanding until parts of it seemed almost translucent. When it burst she dropped the gun and lifted her arms to the sky and shouted: "*I won! I won!*"

I laughed and so did she, and she pointed across to the prize wall and chose the Spiderman plush toy.

"Two out of three," I said when she was seated again. Spiderman resting on her lap seemed to look up at me with a smug satisfaction. "You cheated."

Her crooked smile aimed my way and she laughed and reached over and gave me a little shove on the shoulder. My skin tingled there even after her hand was gone, like a phantom presence.

"Can't stand losing to a girl?"

This seemed a taunt in more ways than one.

"No," I said. "Losing to a girl's just fine by me. It's losing to a cheater I can't stand."

She gave another one of her tinkling laughs, and I wished I could record that sound and play it back whenever I wanted.

"Okay," she said, her head kind of rising a bit and doing this cute bob like one of those springy bobble heads on the dashboards of cars, "Mr. Macho has to beat a little girl. Two out of three."

She passed over another dollar to the attendant.

"No cheating this time," I said, passing over another dollar also.

"No cheating," she agreed.

We waited for the guns to fill and the attendant to give us the ready. I looked over at Tara and she was looking at me, and those eyes were like crystal balls and in them I saw what I wanted my future to be.

"On three," I said, and she nodded. "This time I count."

She laughed, and my heart raced.

"One," I said, taking aim then looking back at her. She was all concentration, looking down the sight of her water gun at the clown in front of her. The tip of her tongue poked out of a corner of her mouth, and it was the cutest thing I'd ever seen. I needed to make a list of the cutest things I'd ever seen when it came to her.

"Two."

I turned back to my own devil clown. Put the painted bastard in the crosshairs.

I waited for the count of three, letting the silence hang between us. I counted the seconds away in my head, *one, two, three …* still not saying the last aloud. I waited, ticking the moments by in my mind … *four, five, six, seven …* and finally, in my periphery, I saw Tara lower her gun and turn to me.

"Something wrong?" she asked, and then I pulled the trigger, my grin impossibly stretching wider.

"*You booger!*" she shouted, turned back to face front, took aim, and fired.

This time my balloon filled faster, though she gave it a good run. My balloon burst, splashing the ground beneath it. We both laughed, and she gave me another of those shoves on the shoulder.

"You cheater!" she said.

Laughing, she wiped at her eyes, tears of laughter rolling down.

"I learn from the best."

I ran a forearm over my own eyes.

I pointed at the Batman plush toy on the prize wall, and the attendant brought it to me. I propped the Dark Knight in my lap, like Spiderman was in Tara's.

We took a few moments to regain our composure. We each slid another dollar across the counter to the attendant, dancing back and forth between us and his other customers. We waited for the guns to fill.

"Now the tiebreaker," she said. "Winner takes all."

"And this time," I said, "really, no cheating."

"No cheating." She crossed her chest with a finger. I watched where her finger trailed, making the X between the swell of her breasts, and my mouth went dry. I turned my gaze back to her face. "Cross my heart."

She faced front again.

I did the same, taking aim, looking down the scope of the gun at the evil clown in front of me.

"We'll both count this time," she said. "To make it fair."

"Okay," I said, not looking away from my target.

The attendant gave us the ready.

"One," Tara said, and I heard her shuffle in her seat, probably to take better aim.

"Two," I said, finger tightening on the trigger.

I waited for the *three* count, tensing in my seat. I heard her shuffling again and thought to myself: *Good, she's nervous.* My mind drifted and I thought again of what I could ask of her if I won. The possibilities were almost too much for my brain.

"*Three,*" came the final count, and it was right next to my ear, a puff of breath like an ocean breeze. Startled, I dropped the gun and turned. Tara was moving back into her seat, lifting her gun, aiming, and pulling the trigger, smiling and laughing like the night was hers. The evening air carried that laughter like it belonged to it.

Her balloon was filling fast.

My gun sat on the counter in front of me.

The tingle of her breath against my ear lingered, that feeling of a phantom touch like when she'd shoved me on the shoulder, now intensified a thousandfold. I picked up the water gun and pulled the trigger, trying to aim and splashing nothing but the wall, missing the psycho clown completely.

Tara's balloon burst and she jumped from her seat and did a little dance. She came up behind me and put her hands on my shoulders and shook me, leaning over and laughing in my ear.

"*I won! I won! I won!*" she said. She pointed at the Superman toy, and when the attendant got it down for her, she put it under one arm and Spiderman under the other.

I smiled, but inside I felt cheated. I'd lost, and now all those things I had thought about wouldn't ever happen. Still, she was here beside me, and that wasn't bad at all.

"Come on," she said and took me by the arm and pulled me along beside her. "I saw Jim and Bobby near the Haunted House earlier. I told them to wait for us."

"Wait," I said, as she tugged me along. "What about what the winner gets?" I asked, surprised that I'd had the guts to say it, even as I wondered how she knew Jim, how all these people—Fat Bobby, Jim, Tara—knew each other, and feeling a bit like an outsider.

"I'll collect later," she said mysteriously. She gave another cute bob of her head, and then she was pulling me again, away from the water gun booth and into the lights and the people. I saw none of it, only her hand on my arm, and I hoped the night would never end.

### 3.

Jim and Fat Bobby were in front of the Haunted House just as Tara had said they'd be. Eager and anxious, they jogged towards us and herded us back towards the line. Jim saw the Batman doll under my arm and gave me this wry grin like he wanted to call me a sissy, wanted me to *know* he wanted to call me a sissy, but was doing me a favor, and wanted me to *know* he was doing me a favor. It was all pretty complicated, and I threw him a look that I hoped let him know I got the message and appreciated it. About twenty or so people were ahead of us, and I took the time to look at the Haunted House.

The place seemed constructed of clapboard and leftover wood too termite infested and splintered to be used for proper construction. The walls were adorned by murals of wailing ghosts and bloody-mouthed vampires and zombies with ropes of brains dangling from their maws. I thought to myself that a retard with crayons and markers could paint better than those murals, even if said retard also had Parkinson's and periodically went into spastic fits and banged his head against hard surfaces. The line of patrons waiting to get in went down the center of a rubber foam stone graveyard, each tombstone with a stupid name like 'Boo Gravely' and 'B.L. Zebub' etched on it.

I would have complained and asked that we go do something else, but everyone else seemed eager to get in, and so I kept my mouth shut. Besides, Tara was beside me and so I figured the night was still a winner.

Finally at the front of the line, each of us handed over a dollar, accepted our ticket, and went up the steps and through the door. The door shut behind us and my opinion of the place soon changed.

The first room was dark and in the sudden dark it was sort of frightening. A woman's voice ahead of us gave a shrill little gasp, and someone with her laughed nervously, like he was saying: *I'm not scared at all little lady, but my, it sure is cute that you are.* In the dimness, red and blue lights started to flash, and a fog machine somewhere pumped in whirls of the stuff from vents in the floor and walls, so that soon you looked down and your feet and ankles were gone in the mist. As we stood about, sections of the walls began to flip open and behind them were women done up like Anne Rice vampires, in long and flowing immaculate gowns of reds and purples and black. They writhed their bodies in a slow and deliberate way, and offered passersby lascivious looks. They hissed at us and bared fake fangs. Trickles of fake blood ran down the corners of their dark red lips, running down the slopes of their chins and necks. A sign above them in glowing neon green lettering read "THE DEVIL'S BRIDES."

"*Oh, brother,*" Tara muttered from behind me and prodded me forward with a hand to my back.

"*Why does Satan get all the bitches?*" someone called out behind us. Even distorted, bouncing off the walls with a tinny echo, the voice for some reason sounded familiar.

Hoarse laughter answered it from somewhere ahead of us, past Jim and Bobby.

The next room was lit by yellow lights and candles set into the walls and covered by protective glass. Tables, counters and shelves crowded the room, and it was obvious it was supposed to be some sort of library or laboratory or a combination of the two. Glass cases covered the surfaces of the furniture, and inside many of the cases were glass jars filled with what was supposed to be formaldehyde but looked suspiciously like Mountain Dew. Floating in the viscous fluid were fetuses vaguely human, grotesque and disturbing because of that similarity. All of them were deformed in some manner, staring out at us with glazed, plastic eyes.

Here was one with an oversized head. There one with two heads sprouting out from each other like potato spuds. Another here with no head at all. One counter had floating and bobbing fetuses with too many hands; over this way one with three legs; right over here just a torso, bobbing like a buoy in a yellow ocean. Others had limbs fused together; too many fingers on each hand; noses and ears and eyes misplaced. Some had flesh like lizards, scaly and thick; others with spiny tails growing at the ends of their backs. In other cases were skeletal remains, and here were skulls misshapen with bony protrusions like jagged boulders; skulls with too many eyeholes; skulls with jagged shark-like teeth. A sign hung in this room as well, glowing bright in the dimness, and it read "THE DEVIL'S CHILDREN."

"At least Lucifer doesn't shoot blanks!"

The familiar voice from behind us.

The laughter ahead of us answering it.

Moving forward again and we came into a hall of mirrors. Lit only so that you saw the mirrors just before you ran headfirst into them, the mirror room was a maze of shadow and reflected shadow. Here too a fog machine poured in a mist from vents in the floor, so that it seemed like you were floating in the darkness, the darkness reflected and the mist below. The mirrors distorted things in disturbing proportions. First there was a big fat Joey in front of me, and then after a turn a skinny Joey almost ten feet tall, his head nearly touching the ceiling. I saw a squat and dwarfish Joey, and a Joey with a squished in face like he was sucking on the world's sourest lemon. Lost in my many reflections, it was a moment before I noticed Jim and Bobby had disappeared out of sight ahead of us. I turned to make sure Tara was still with me, and seeing her vague form there I continued forward.

A squeal issued from behind me a moment later. Tara ran into me from behind and I was pushed forward, bringing my hands up against the mirror looming before me. It didn't shatter as I feared it would, imagining the tiny shards raining down on me and carving me up.

I turned and faced Tara. Her face was pale and seemed to float before me.

"What's wrong?" I asked, grabbing hold of her hands without thinking about it.

"Someone … grabbed me," she said.

She cast an anxious glance behind her. I looked that way too. Saw nothing but the darkness.

"What do you mean?"

"Someone ... pinched me," she said. "You know ... on the butt."

I looked behind her again, balling a fist, but then she was pushing me forward once more. Alone there in the mirrors and dark and mist I lost my moment of bravery as quick as it had come, and let myself be propelled forward. We turned corners quickly but cautiously, our other selves imitating us in their distorted bodies, mocking us, and then there ahead of us, I saw Jim and Bobby, and ahead of them an exit sign glowing red, and an arrow pointing the way.

"*Come on,*" I said as we moved up alongside them, wondering why they hadn't moved towards the door. Then I saw the others, two silhouettes on either side of the door, one thin and one fat, both taller than any of us.

Footsteps came up from behind me, moving fast.

A metallic *snik* and something cool and sharp pressed against my throat. I froze, refusing even to swallow, afraid that one movement, that small ripple of flesh, would split my skin against the blade and a hot crimson wave cascading forth would be the last thing I felt.

"*Where's the dog, fag boy?*" Dillon's familiar voice issued from behind me. I could hear the smirk in his words, even though I couldn't see his face. A puff of breath, stale and heavy, whispered in my ear. "*I see you and fatty have yourselves a slut and a pet nigger now.*"

Giggles from the shadow people guarding the exit door.

"Quite a gang of fucking losers you have going," he said, and I said nothing. "You know I'm going to fucking kill you, don't you?"

*Here it was, then,* I thought to myself. He'd promised me that night on the highway, in his black car like a slick rolling shadow. He'd said he would, and now he was going to.

"*But first let me demonstrate on your dolly,*" he said, and I felt

83

the plush Batman torn free from under my arm. I'd forgotten all about it with the knife at my throat, and now with it gone I felt the wetness of sweat under my arm. I sent out a silent apology to the Caped Crusader for bathing him in that most unfavorable of ways.

The blade moved away from my throat, yet still I didn't move. My limbs felt weighted by cement, my feet rooted to the ground. I wondered where all the other people were in the Haunted House. What had happened to all the people behind and in front of us? Then I thought of Dillon trailing us, maybe slinking along like an oily eel, and his buds, Stu and Max, in front of us. Could they have maneuvered in such a way as to make sure no new people came in, and waited for the rest to leave?

I thought maybe they could do just that. They were just the sort of kids—not really kids anymore being in high school, definitely not the size of kids—that even most adults wouldn't challenge. Just in the short time I'd known him, I could easily imagine Dillon lingering at the entrance to the Haunted House, directing patrons to come back later, his wicked smirk all the average person needed to take a hint and walk away.

There was a harsh ripping and tearing, and I vaguely saw in the darkness Batman's white cotton guts spilling out. More laughter from the shadow guards.

Still I didn't move.

But Tara did.

A passing of air and I felt more than saw her twirl. In my periphery I saw her kick out low and fast, the glint of a burnished sandal. A *smack* echoed loud in the small corridor and I thought of my sister throwing her sandals at me just a few days ago, and one of them sailing past me and hitting the refrigerator with a solid *thump*.

This was louder.

Sensation returned to my body, blood rushing to the extremities, and though it was gone I felt the haunting touch of the blade at my throat. That cool touch wasn't something I'd ever forget.

Turning in the weak light and the murk, I saw Dillon's dark form hopping up and down, holding a leg at the shin. I thought of the things my dad had taught me, the punches and the kicks. How if you had to fight, if there was no option but to fight, then fight hard and fast, bring your opponent down quick.

I moved forward, building momentum in the small space between us. As I darted forward I reached out with my hands, felt the leather of his jacket, snagged it and pulled him forward. My head shot forth like a piston, my forehead met his nose, and there was a sharp *crack* like a twig broken underfoot. A spray of warm blood sprinkled my head. Something gleamed in the darkness there, like ripples of water in the moonlight, and I saw it was the knife—he'd dropped the knife—and it hit the floor with a clatter. I pulled him closer and brought a knee up and into the softness of his belly, and felt the air go out of him in a *whoosh* like a vacuum sealed container being opened. I let go of his jacket and Dillon crumpled to the ground in a dark heap.

Just two or three seconds for this all to happen, and yet it felt like an eternity.

Remembering the shadow guards, I turned to meet them even as they were just moving themselves, hearing their leader and realizing that something was wrong. The not-quite-as-fat-as-Bobby, yet still pudgy Stu moved first, and I saw Jim's dark form, a shadow in deeper shadow, dart forward, bent low, charging like a bull. He collided with the bigger kid, drove him back and hard against a wall. The room shook with the impact like a quake had passed.

Seeing his friend go down, tall, lanky, and complexion-challenged Max moved next.

I pushed Fat Bobby with all my strength and his greater weight overtook that of the taller guy, like a child's wagon disappearing under a freight train, and now, moving, stepping over and on the

85

figure under him, Bobby ran to the door, opened it. Colliding with each other, bumping and shoving, Tara and Jim joining us at the threshold, the four of us spilled out the door and into the night beyond.

We ran until the Haunted House, its foam rubber graveyard now too realistic for my taste, was far behind us, lost amidst the people and the lights and the sounds.

## 4.

"Was that Dillon Glover?" Tara said. Fat Bobby and Jim both nodded. "What the hell does he have against you?" This last was directed at me.

I explained to her about the day at the stream and coming upon Bobby. How the three guys had been throwing rocks and sticks at him, though I left out the part about Fat Bobby being almost naked. I glanced at him and saw the look of gratitude on his face and gave him an almost imperceptible nod.

"Wow," she said. "We should tell our parents."

Reluctantly I agreed, and I saw Jim nod too, though Fat Bobby remained silent. We walked the midway and kept close to other people and stayed in the lights. Remembering the sound of his nose crunching, I didn't think Dillon would be feeling up to coming after us anytime soon, but it didn't hurt to play it safe.

Jim's father was the first we came upon, him sitting at a table taking hunks out of a large hotdog and great gulps out of a big soda, so big it almost looked like a pail. He saw us approaching and rose to greet us and ushered us to the table. He asked if we would like anything to eat. Then he saw the looks on our faces, and his dark face took on this scrunchy scowl that made me think of a black hole in space, eager to swallow planets and devour them. Jim explained to his dad what had happened, and Mr. Connolly's scowl deepened.

"Those fucks," he said, and followed with: "He really pulled a knife on you?" I nodded, and he repeated his initial words. "Well, let's go find everyone's parents, and then I think we'll be calling the police."

Fat Bobby spoke up, and we all looked at him.

"My dad's not here."

"Well, then," Mr. Connolly said, "you stick with me and I'll give you a ride home. Come on, let's get moving."

We walked around for awhile and came to my parents next, coming out of the exit area from the Ferris wheel. They were still holding hands and my mom was pressed close to my dad. Dad saw us, apparently read something in Mr. Connolly's demeanor, maybe like the looks me and Jim gave each other and seemed to understand without words, and he came jogging up to meet us halfway.

Dad and Mr. Connolly shook hands, and their eyes met and something passed between them. Mr. Connolly repeated what Jim had told him, and at the end of it my dad had given more than his fair share of "fucks" and "bastards" and "shits," more in those few minutes than I'd ever heard from his mouth before. Quite a little gathering now, we all walked the midway until a few minutes later we found Tara's father, whom I didn't know from anyone else in the throngs milling about, but she pointed out for our benefit.

The man was tall, taller than Jim's dad, and slightly gawky, but not strangely so. His height and angular features made him seem like a bird of prey, and when he heard the story Dad and Mr. Connolly told him, he seemed only more so. His face settled into this passively hungry-like expression, his fingers curled like talons wanting to grip and tear something.

The adults moved a distance away, Jim hung by his dad, Fat Bobby with them, so for a moment it was just me and Tara under the awning of one of the areas set aside for tables and the diners using them. Our parents were exchanging numbers, pens and scratch paper pulled out, scribbling and babbling, talking about the police and what would happen and all three men talking about kicking asses and busting heads. No one paid us any mind under the awning. The moon up above like a pearl seemed to shine its light directly upon Tara and I.

Tara was holding my hand, I looked at her, and there was that crooked little smile that set my heart to beating like a drum. She said something, but my heart and my blood pumping drowned it out.

"What?" I asked.

She smiled and gave one of her little shoves.

"I'm ready to collect," she said, and I heard the words but they didn't make sense for a moment. It was like I was hearing her through water. All I could think was: *I'm here in the moonlight with a beautiful girl.*

She leaned forward and her lips met mine. I think I tasted the stars.

# CHAPTER FIVE

## 1.

A deputy came to our house that evening and took an initial statement from me, jotting down the things I said with a little nub of a pencil on a little yellow pad of paper. The deputy said the sheriff would be by in the morning to hear everything himself.

Mom hovered over me hen-like, behavior she normally didn't indulge in. It was as if she thought maybe I had broken and just hadn't shown it yet, as a teacup with hairline fractures will crumble with one ill-timed jostle. She made me hot chocolate, sat on the sofa with me, and occasionally pecked me on the cheek or forehead and ruffled my hair. Even Dad walked by a couple times and grasped my shoulder with a firm hand or clapped me on the back and said he was proud of me. I grimaced at these gestures, but didn't complain too much. I enjoyed sneaking glances at Sarah sitting on the stairs, watching all of this with a frown and a scowl, like she'd won second place in a contest.

I offered her little smiles.

She offered me the bird.

When it was time for bed, however, I went upstairs, climbed under the sheets and closed my eyes, only for the door to open a moment later. My sister stood in her pajamas, outlined in the threshold. She flipped on my desk light and walked in without waiting for an invite.

"Sarah, please, not tonight," I said, almost pleaded, covering my head with my hands to defend against the coming noogie.

"Oh, stop whining."

She crossed the room and sat on the edge of my bed. She was silent for a spell but I knew she wanted to say something. From the firm set of her lips and the frown of concentration, it seemed like something important, too. This was strange because all she ever had to say to me were taunts when she was rubbing my head with her knuckles or pulling my underwear so far up my crack I thought it'd come out my mouth.

I said nothing and waited.

"Did you really get a knife pulled on you today?" she asked.

I nodded, letting my hands fall off my head but keeping them at the ready.

"And your friends were there too? That girl I saw with you at the fair?"

Sarah had walked up with her new boyfriend just as the gathering of parents and the exchange of phone numbers on the midway had begun to dissipate. I nodded again.

"You whooped that guy good, like you said?"

I didn't know if it was right to feel good about beating someone up. Dad said no, you did what you had to do to take care of yourself and your family, but when you started feeling good about violence it meant you were in trouble. Not legal kind of trouble or even trouble with friends or family. It was an inside kind of trouble, he said, in your heart and soul, that warned maybe you were losing a little of what made you different than those people that tried to hurt you. I thought of this, tried to hold on to it, but when I nodded again in response to Sarah's question, I felt a little surge of pride and had to smile.

Just a little one.

"That's good," my sister said. "I'm glad you're okay."

"Thanks."

"How come you don't fight back with me?" she asked, and I knew what she meant: the noogies and wedgies and Indian burns.

"Because you're my sister."

By the light in the hall outside my room, I saw my sister smile. She leaned down and gave me a hug. I didn't know what to do, and I kind of froze for a second. Then, awkwardly, I put my arms around her and gave her a little squeeze.

"I love you, Joey,"

She kind of trembled for a moment or two, like she might cry.

I'd never seen Sarah cry before. The closest was when I drove her near to tears of frustration with my jabs, like I had in the kitchen when she launched her sandals at me. I didn't know what to do again, so I just held her tighter, and she squeezed me back and then stood up and walked out of my room, closing the door behind her. I was left confused, baffled, still not quite sure what had happened, so I turned over, buried my head in the pillow and tried to sleep.

But the events of the day replayed again and again in my head: the sounds and sights of the fair, the confrontation in the Haunted House (the feel of the cool blade against my throat and the crunch of Dillon's nose), and the kiss under the moonlight. Alternately terrifying and alluring, such thoughts kept me tossing and turning, and sleep was a long time coming.

## 2.

If I thought the morning would bring some reprieve from the chaos and exhilaration of the evening at the fair, like the rising of the sun would wash it all away with its golden light, my hopes were dashed right quick. Not five minutes out of the shower, striding downstairs in fresh blue jeans and a flannel shirt, my mom's sausage and pancakes calling me with their smells and the sizzling of the frying pan bringing water to my mouth, the doorbell rang. Not yet having left for work, Dad went to answer it.

Looking over my shoulder from the breakfast table, I saw a fat man in a tan and brown uniform filling the doorway.

Overshadowing my father with his girth, I saw the bronze badge pinned to the breast of the uniform, and remembered about the sheriff. Dad stepped aside, letting the man in.

The sheriff doffed his hat respectfully and wiped his boots on the mat. He had jowls like a turkey wattle, but as he followed my dad into the kitchen and to the table, I had to re-evaluate the sheriff as I was afforded a closer look at him.

Yes, he was fat, but it was the kind of fat with muscle hidden beneath it, so that he seemed formed by barrel kegs stacked atop each other. His hatless head was bald and caught the light from the chandelier over the table, like an oiled bowling ball. He shook hands with everyone, his gaze seeming to hang on Mom and Sarah a bit long, and I wondered if Dad noticed this.

The sheriff's hand gripped mine a tad too hard when he offered it to me, and I knew that with a little more pressure he could snap my bones like matchsticks. He had a smile on his face that said: *Hey, aren't I a friendly guy?* and the smile was fake, plastered on like the frozen expression carved upon a mannequin.

Bandit gave a low growl from under the table at my feet. I shushed him with a gentle hand around his muzzle.

I looked over at Dad, saw his face was set and the tension there was obvious. I thought to myself: *What did I miss here?* With only Dad and the sheriff standing, the rest of us sitting at the table (Bandit under it), the sheriff spoke like he was on a stage addressing an audience.

"Folks," he said, gesturing with his hat like a teacher with a meter stick at the blackboard, "I'm Sheriff Glover. I understand there was some sort of mishap at the fair yesterday?"

He looked at me when he said that last part, his eyes concealing something like contempt, as if he was studying a bug he wanted to step on. That smile was still pasted on his face, like he was trying to hide something beneath it, which was his true self.

"Between you, young man, your friends, and some other boys?" he asked.

I nodded.

Dad spoke even as my head was beginning its bob up and down.

"Mishap is one way to put it," he said, and the flat tone hiding the anger beneath let me know that, yes, Dad had seen the sheriff's glances at Mom and Sarah. He'd probably seen the jackal beneath the smile, as well. If I'd had the sense of something not quite right with the sheriff, then it was a safe bet my dad had also. "Someone pulled a knife on my son."

"I was getting to that," the sheriff said, now facing my father.

"And one of those 'other boys' was *your* son, Sheriff," Dad continued, and I saw the sheriff's bowling ball head go a shade of red as quick as a lava lamp. "Dillon Glover, right? Mr. Connolly filled me in on that little fact."

"Now, there's no reason to get hostile," Sheriff Glover said. One hand went to his holster and the gun there, like all he needed was a little prodding and he'd pull the piece out and start with the pistol whipping, or worse. "I was about to touch on my boy's misdeeds before you interrupted me."

"Misdeeds?" Mom scooted her chair out and stepped up beside my dad. "Your son cornered Joey in that rundown shack of a Haunted House and threatened to kill him."

Her tone was fiery yet controlled. A flame eager to be stoked to a blaze. Sheriff Glover gave my mother an icy stare.

"Where I come from," he said, "women still know their place."

Sarah's silverware clattered loudly on her plate.

"Where you come from is Planet Asshole," she said.

I looked at my sister with shock and awe, and sudden respect. I barked a quick laugh before I could stop it.

The sheriff spun his head towards my sister. His face had gone from lava red to sun fire scarlet. I thought his cranium might blow as the volcano inside him erupted.

"Upstairs," Dad said, pointing at Sarah.

She looked at him as if stung, but did as she was told, stomping away towards the stairs. The sheriff watched her go, eyes wide and angry, and then he turned them on me. A smile still split my face like a great fissure. I broadened it a little and showed my teeth for the sheriff's benefit.

"You too," Dad said, now pointing at me.

I followed Sarah without argument.

I climbed the stairs and saw my sister at the top step, sitting down. She shushed me with a finger to her lips and motioned for me to sit with her. I did, moving slow, so as to not cause any creaks or moans of the floor or walls or banister. We sat and listened, and the shadows of our parents, and the larger, rounder shadow of the sheriff, played on the wall below like a shadow puppet show.

"Mr. Hayworth," the sheriff said, his voice trembling with embarrassment and anger, "you should really teach your family manners. They ought to respect authority."

"You're one to talk," Dad said. "What have you taught your son, Sheriff? To pull weapons on people? Or just how to take a beating?"

I stifled another laugh, and Sarah and I turned to each other and mimed a high five, beaming at one another.

"Now you watch your mouth, mister," Sheriff Glover said, and his shadow self raised an arm and pointed a finger at my shadow dad's face. "I came here to try and make peace." The shadow sheriff wagged a shadow finger like a wand. "It's obvious our boys had a little misunderstanding. That's what happens with kids."

"Your kid's almost eighteen, according to what Mr. Connolly tells me," Dad said. "Not too much longer and he won't be a minor, and then he won't have to worry about my son at all. Next time, he ever comes around my family, I'll wipe the floor with his ass and send you the cleaning bill."

Mom's shadow stretched an arm around Dad's, as if restraining him. I thought that was a good idea. For the sheriff's sake, not Dad's.

94

"You threatening my son, Mr. Hayworth?" the sheriff said. His shadow moved a step closer to my dad's.

"Yep," Dad said. "And now I'm threatening you, Pillsbury."

The laughter building inside of me almost made me stomp my feet in giddiness, and Sarah restrained me by pulling me close to her. Her red face revealed she was having the same struggle.

"Mr. Connolly told us how your son runs amok around this town," Mom chimed in. "Don't think our kids will stand by like some of the others around here."

"That's the third time I've heard that nigger's name in five minutes," the sheriff said. "I don't want to hear it again. Niggers and cunts ... they both ought to know their place."

This time it was Dad's shadow that stepped forward on the wall movie screen below us. Shadow Dad and Shadow Sheriff were now almost toe to toe.

"Did I hear you right, just now?" Dad said, his tone low and menacing. That tone reminded me of Bandit's growl. "I think it's time you left."

He took another step forward, and the sheriff took a step back. Dad kept moving forward, and the sheriff continued falling back. The shadow show switched to real life as the two men appeared below in the foyer. Like a dog driving cattle, Dad herded the big, round man to the front door.

Mom was there to usher him through the threshold, giving a little curtsy as the sheriff stepped out onto the porch. Sarah and I moved up the top step and behind the banister to stay in view of the action.

"Thanks for the visit, kind sir," Mom said and started to close the door.

The door stopped short of shutting, a large boot in its way. The sheriff looked through the opening and shared a glance between my mom and dad. Then he cast a sly, furtive glance up and over and past Mom and Dad standing there at the door, and his eyes found mine, peeking through the uprights of the banister.

He smiled at me, winked, and then looked back at Mom and Dad. He put his wide-brimmed hat back on and tipped it to them.

"I'll see you folks around," he said.

He removed his boot from the doorway and walked away.

### 3.

For the next couple days I wasn't allowed to leave the house. I wasn't too happy about this turn of events, and I let my parents know it by stomping around and slamming doors and giving them evil eyes that would do a gypsy proud. I even performed a little mental curse against my dad involving explosive diarrhea, hopefully in a public place. There was no shrine or sacrifices involved, though, so I doubt the dark gods were impressed.

Dad said it was just for a few days to let things cool over. He didn't think Sheriff Glover was foolish enough to act on a grudge, at least not openly. Even if he was a major asshole, as Sarah had rightly judged, he was just one man in the department. And there were county and state police to worry about should the good sheriff bring any undue attention his way, Dad elaborated. Local law enforcement were notorious for wanting to maintain autonomy in their little corners of the world.

This was all well and good, but a few days may as well have been a hundred years. This was summer, school a distant and unfathomable notion, with long days of doing whatever I wanted, and there was the fair still going and I hadn't done the rollercoaster or Ferris wheel yet. There was a certain girl whose lips still lingered on mine with a vague electric feeling every time I thought about it, which was just about every other second.

And those odd seconds? Those were taken up by the memory of the blade against my throat, its cool touch and sharp edge. I wouldn't admit this to my parents, though. They'd probably insist

I see a therapist, where I'd be pressed into admitting how many uncles had touched me (none) and how often I put on women's panties (never). I'd then be told it was alright for a guy to cry, whereupon my masculinity would be forever lost as quickly as if a surgeon had clipped off my sack.

I tried to occupy myself by reading, trying to lose myself in comics and Bradbury stories. The events of the past few days had been more exciting and yes, frightening, than any fiction, however, and the stories only fleetingly held my interest. Even the terrifying aspects of the experience at the fair only added to the exhilaration of it all.

Fear made the blood pump and rush, letting you know you were *alive*. Likewise, the smell and kiss of a young girl screamed *alive*. I wanted to be *out there* with my friends, and I thought about the car in the woods and what was in it and how, as long as I was in here, I'd never know.

I ran about the yard with Bandit, tackling him and wrestling him down, and though it was fun for awhile as all things with my dog were fun for awhile, it wasn't as fun as being *out there* with him and my other friends.

Fat Bobby came over a couple times, and he sported a freshly busted lip, only just scabbing over. He read my comics, and added a few he'd somehow bought on his own to his collection in the box in my closet. He even tried some short stories by Bradbury and Matheson and King, but it seemed he liked the pictures and always went back to the comics and graphic novels. We played catch in the front yard, and he even tried chasing Bandit around a couple times, but Fat Bobby got winded easily and that didn't last long.

Then, one day, the third of my house arrest or quarantine or whatever my parents thought of it as, we were on the porch, Fat Bobby and I, and that old familiar sad, depressed look came over his face. The sour expression scrunched up his features, like he'd bitten into a Ho Ho full of shit.

"What's up?" I asked, leaning back on Bandit's curled form behind me like a backrest.

"I was thinking about the Haunted House."

"Yeah. Pretty crazy stuff, wasn't it? But we got through it."

"No," Fat Bobby said. He kind of stomped his foot like he was on the verge of a tantrum. "You and Jim … and even Tara … got us through it. I didn't do anything."

"You ran down pimple face," I said.

"You pushed me into him," Bobby said, giving me a look that said: *Don't throw me any bones.*

"The point is he went down," I said, knowing it sounded lame even as I said it.

"The point is he went down because of you, not me."

The point he was making was obvious, and the hard fact was that I couldn't really argue against it. He *had* done nothing, and if it wasn't for Tara's quick thinking when the knife had been pulled away from me, and me and Jim reacting … well, let's just say that the night could have ended very differently.

So I didn't throw Bobby anymore bones, but just let the quiet linger between us for a bit. I knew he wasn't finished. I had an inkling of where this was going, but I felt it was important for him to say it, not me.

"I was wondering …" he said, staring out off the porch at the yard and the butterflies fluttering about over the grass like they were spelling out a secret message just for him. "Your dad showed you how to fight, didn't he?"

I nodded, said: "Yes."

"Do you think he'd show me?"

I put an arm around him, clapped him on the back. I told him I'd ask, and we sat there for awhile on the porch, under the sun, with the blue sky like a blanket over it all.

* * *

Day four of my "just a couple days" incarceration and I was starting to lose patience with my parents. I knew arguing with my dad wouldn't do any good, so when he got home from work in the early afternoon, I asked him about showing Bobby some moves. Dad considered this for a moment, his eyes occasionally drifting to Bobby's fat lip, and then he nodded. Bobby smiled, and we followed my dad out to the garage.

With my parents' cars always kept in the driveway, the garage was free for other purposes. From one end to the other, corner to corner, the four walls showcased hammers and spades and drills and saws hung on hooks. The whole center of the garage was taken up by exercise equipment. At the forefront of the garage was a cleared area of the floor covered by blue tumble mats. Beyond that there was one of those Bowflex machines, a stationary bicycle, a treadmill, and free weights resting on a mat. In the middle of all this, like the centerpiece of a shrine, was a man-sized punching bag, supported by a weighted base at the bottom, and tied to rafters at the ceiling for extra support. Dad worked this bag at least an hour a day, and there were duct-taped areas where his punches and kicks had eventually torn holes in the bag's hide. I worked the bag with him sometimes, when I wasn't lost in between the covers of comics or other books.

He led Fat Bobby with a hand on the kid's shoulder over to the mat that surrounded the big bag. My dad took off his work shirt and underneath he was wearing a T-shirt, and his biceps and forearms looked like granite wrapped in flesh.

"Okay," he told Bobby without preamble. "Show me what you got. Hit the bag."

Fat Bobby looked at me, then at the bag, and he kind of cocked his head at it like he didn't know what it was or what it was for. Then he let out this sigh and wound his arm about and swung it at the bag, and it was like watching a fat bear just out of hibernation throwing a lazy paw at a tree. His fist bounced off the bag with a pathetic sound like a sweaty butt cheek peeling off a leather seat. Fat Bobby's face reddened with shame.

Mine did too.

Dad didn't miss a beat though.

He moved behind Bobby and squared the kid's shoulders, showed him how to balance and carry his weight. He turned Fat Bobby's torso this way and that, back and forth in little semi-turns like a spindle. He told Bobby how to throw the punch with all his weight, to lean into it for momentum. Dad went through the motions with him a couple more times and then stepped away and gave Bobby the go-ahead.

Bobby kept his feet anchored like my dad had shown him, cocked his arm back, and threw a jab while turning his upper body with the punch. This time the bag shook with the impact, and Dad slapped my friend on the back.

Fat Bobby's face colored again, this time with pride.

They went at it for awhile. Dad showed him how to stick and move, to keep your opponent off balance; how to move in with a blow for maximum impact; how to feign low and come back high. Pretty soon Fat Bobby looked like a greased ham, sweaty and glistening. Dad called for a break and fetched water from the nearby fridge, gave a bottle to Bobby, and leaned back against a wall.

"You want to watch me and Joey go a round?" Dad said to Bobby. Bobby nodded eagerly, and Dad looked over at me, kind of smiling. "You up for a round with the old man?"

"Sure," I said, and I stepped over to the wall where some gloves and headgear were hanging. I took them down, threw the larger pair to my dad, pulled the padded headgear over my head, and put on the smaller pair of gloves. "One condition."

My dad was already dancing around the area at the forefront of the garage, where the free mat space was. He threw a couple jabs, a few kicks that cut through the air like bullets, and he smiled at me.

"Name it," he said.

"I land one hit," I said, smiling back at him, "even just *one*, and I get to go out with my friends."

He was already shaking his head before the words were out of my mouth.

"It's too soon, son—" he began, and I cut him off.

"Scared I'll knock you a good one?" I threw a few jabs of my own, then followed with some of my own kicks, which whizzed through the air pretty good if I did say so myself.

He was still shaking his head, even beginning to unlace the gloves he'd just put on. Unperturbed, I went for a cheap shot.

"Don't want to pull a muscle?" I said, and that stopped him. He gave me a stare across the garage like a gunfighter giving someone the once over in a dusty saloon.

Dad had pulled a muscle in his lower back the year before while working the bag. It wasn't something he liked brought up. It reminded him he was getting older.

"What counts as a hit?" he asked me, lacing the gloves back up, pulling them on tight and snug with his teeth.

"Head, face, and body," I said, making my way to the mat and kicking off my shoes. Dad did the same, his bare feet padding on the mat as he shuffled about.

Fat Bobby watched all this from the sidelines, eyes wide and mouth agape.

"You know you're not fighting some punk kid this time, don't you?"

Dad smiled down at me, dancing around, circling me.

"Yeah," I said. "This time I'm fighting a cripple who should be in an old folks home."

His smile widened and he began to move closer, his circles tightening.

"I'll try not to spank you too hard," he said and threw an intentionally slow jab, testing me.

"I'll try not to knock out your dentures," I said and moved

quickly in with a flurry of jabs, some low kicks, and an uppercut.

My dad dodged these or batted them away like annoying insects buzzing about him. He gave me a little shove that sent me off balance and tumbling to the mat. I rolled into the fall and came back rabbit quick on my feet.

I danced around him, watching his legs and arms, trying to find the weakness in his defense, watching, waiting. I was still watching, waiting, when his right leg darted out and caught me high on the shoulder. Though he checked the kick at the last moment, it sent me sprawling on the mat again.

I rolled again to my feet, this time not so gracefully.

Dad smiled at me, slapped his gloved fists together.

"Let me know when you've had enough, little man."

"Let me know when you've crapped your Depends diapers, old man," I said and darted in for another flurry. He batted them all away again, and gave me a couple rabbit punches to the back and top of my head just for fun.

I snarled and went for some kicks to his thighs and belly. He pushed these away. Stepped close and ruffled my hair in that way I hated and then shoved me away again. I kept my balance this time, but just barely.

He laughed at me and did an impression of me stumbling about that looked like a drunken wino tripping along a street corner. Fat Bobby burped out a small laugh, too, and I turned to him and stared him down and he shut up fast.

"Fine," Dad said, and relaxed his stance, started for the laces of his gloves with his teeth. His chuckles died down as he freed his hands and, hanging up the gloves, he turned back to me. "Fine, go out with your friends. But you all stay together, and Bandit still goes with you."

Still wanting to fight, but visibly letting my face settle and relax, I worked at my gloves and went past my dad to hang them up. I turned around and made as if to head back to the house.

Dad was already headed that direction. I jogged to catch up to him.

"One thing, Dad," I said.

"What's that, son?" he said and started to turn to face me.

"I still want my one hit," I said and cold cocked him on the chin.

I didn't hit with all my strength, of course. I wasn't stupid. I put just enough behind the jab to startle him. But it was like hitting a brick, and probably hurt my hand more than it did his face.

Surprise rolled down his face like a curtain, and then a smile. Like the champion and winner that I was, I ran away fast, laughing and taunting my dad all the way.

Not until later, when I needed him, did I realize I'd left Bandit behind.

## 4.

Fat Bobby told me how he and Jim had told Tara about the abandoned car in the woods and that they'd been spending a lot of time down there together since the night at the fair. He said there was probably a good chance Jim and Tara were there now, and that got me all nervous and angry inside, thinking of Tara out there alone with another guy.

"What do you guys do there?" I asked as we walked the now familiar dirt road to the hill, where we would then start down and make a beeline for where we now knew the access road and the car to be.

"Just talk really," Fat Bobby said and shrugged, as if it were no big deal.

But it was a big deal for me: two guys out there alone with my girl. That's how I thought of her: *my* girl.

"Sometimes we climb up Lookout Mountain—"

"What?"

"That's what we call that rocky hill we climbed. Where we saw the car closer up that first time, me, you and Jim?"

He said this with the smallest hint of exasperation, like he was talking to someone hopelessly out of the loop. Which I guess I was in this regard, and it pissed me off.

"Oh," I said.

We entered the trees and they closed in around us with branches outstretched as if in embrace. There at the edge of the woods, under the branches but not lost in them yet, I heard an engine. Bobby and I turned around to see a cloud of dust rising as a car rolled down the dirt hill. Slowing, it parked maybe a dozen yards away from us. I saw the siren bubbles on top, dead at the moment, and the seal on the hood and doors. I knew I should have run, pulling Bobby with me, but I stayed where I was, under the trees, as if that were protection enough.

The driver's door swung open, the engine still idling, and Sheriff Glover stepped out. The dirt clouds behind him and drifting away gave the impression of a magician appearing in a puff of smoke.

"Well, howdy boys," he said, one hand at his belt where his gut hung over in a huge bulge like a monstrous pregnancy. He tipped his hat to us. "You know these woods are dangerous. Not to mention off limits if you're minors. Need parental supervision."

He made a show of looking around, and then he scratched his chin as if puzzling over a problem.

"Now," he said, and a cruel grin came over his face, "I don't see your parents around, do you?"

Neither of us answered, but I took a step back and pulled Bobby with me.

"Now don't go nowhere," the sheriff said, moving across the distance between us. "It wouldn't be very responsible of me to let you kids go running off by yourselves."

"Leave us alone," I said, turning. Thankfully Fat Bobby turned with me, and we quickened our pace. But he was fat and didn't move so fast, so that it was either run off by myself or stay with my friend.

I stayed with my friend, and then the sheriff was on us, hauling us to a stop with one meaty hand on each of us.

"You need to learn some manners, boy," he said and shoved me, and I went down hard on my butt. A shock of pain went up my tailbone, throbbing. He still held Fat Bobby by a fistful of shirt, but he was looking down at me. "Your daddy's got a bit of a mouth, and so does your sister and mama." He grinned and showed teeth that were large and tobacco stained. "But mouths on women I don't mind so much, if put to good use."

I had an idea of what he meant and my face went red. With embarrassment or shame, I don't know. Probably both.

I got up and ran at him, and he lifted a big boot and I stupidly ran headfirst into it. I went down again, now with a throbbing in my head to match the one on my ass. He shook Bobby, hard, as if punishing him for my crimes.

"You uppity little bastard," he said, shaking Fat Bobby, but looking at me. My friend started crying, really blubbering, and this time I couldn't blame him. I was pretty scared too. This wasn't some teenager with a knife. This was a lawman, he was big, and he had a big gun at his belt. "I told your folks I'd be around."

His free hand—the one not shaking Bobby like a carpet needing aired out—went to his belt, and I thought he was going for the gun. I thought of looking down that muzzle, black and long like a tunnel, a tunnel to places I could never come back from, and I was close to crying too. It was like having the knife blade at my throat again.

But he didn't go for the gun.

He went for his nightstick, pulling it out of its loop like a sword from a scabbard.

"I think you need a little correcting," he said, and now Bobby was tugging at the large hand that held him, scratching at it, pulling back on the fingers. The sheriff turned towards Bobby and brought the nightstick around, slicing through the air like a baseball bat. It *thunked* Fat Bobby on the temple, and my friend's eyes rolled up and he went slack. Sheriff Glover let him go and Bobby fell to the ground like a heavy sack.

"Now your turn," he said, facing me again, taking a step in my direction.

I stared at Fat Bobby, crumpled on the ground like a broken doll, like I imagined Batman with his stuffing guts pouring out looked like on the floor of the Haunted House. I saw the blood trickling from his head and I remembered the blood trickling from his head that day at the stream when the final rock had hit him. I was scared, scared that I was looking at my friend dead on the ground.

The sheriff took another step towards me, and I crab walked backwards on my hands and legs, then pushed myself up and to my feet. The nightstick rose again in the sheriff's grip and started down in another arc. I turned and ran, and something hard clipped me along the collar. I stumbled, found my balance, kept running.

*Fuck!* I screamed at myself. *Where's Bandit?* And then I remembered I'd left him home after sucker punching my dad and running off, and I screamed at myself again. *Fucking moron!*

The forest seemed to spring out of the ground around me, trying to box me in. Pines and firs like large blades of grass made me feel like an ant, an ant in a large world, and everything in my way. Everything an obstacle as I ran from the man close behind me, the sheriff, a police officer, someone I was supposed to trust, gone mad. He was swinging a nightstick like a stick at a piñata, and I was the target. The prizes that would burst out of me if one of his swings connected wouldn't be candy, however, but busted bones and blood and maybe bits of teeth. ·

Stomping across the stream, splashing, my footfalls landed awkwardly on the silt and soil beneath the water. I slipped. My knees banged against stones. My palms shredded skin on pebbly silt. I rose and kept running.

Close behind and getting closer: larger and louder splashes.

Skidding to a halt at the access road, I saw the rusted sign fallen in the weeds. I turned, remembered the divots and ruts in the old road, danced about them, leaping and jumping. But the sheriff didn't know about the ruts or was too enraged to mind them, and I heard a tremendous *thump* and a cry of surprise more than pain.

Risking a glance back, I saw he'd fallen. I was gaining ground on him, but he was already standing again. No ankles twisted or femurs poked out of his thighs, unfortunately, and the nightstick was still in his hand. His big arms and legs pumped, his momentum building like a bull looking to gore. Spittle like rabid foam flew from his mouth as he yelled after me, his face flushed red.

My lungs burned, my chest hurt, but I pushed my body harder, faster. A slight turn in the pitted road and there it was, the car, and there perched on the hood, tossing rocks about, my friends, Jim and Tara. Hearing my footfalls they looked up in surprise, saw me, saw the monstrosity behind me, and in unison they leapt off the hood. Dust rising in little plumes as their feet met the ground, they each stooped, scooping something off the road like laborers picking a field. I was confused for a moment, wondering why the fuck my friends were picking daisies when there was a crazed sheriff behind me keen on murder. Understanding blossomed a moment later however: *ammunition!*

I slid like a runner diving for home, and the dirt ground scraped my skin like a potato peeler. I came rolling to my feet, and in either hand I held rocks. Big rocks. I stood to take up position by my friends, their arms already cocked and ready.

Sheriff Glover skidded to a stop some yards away from us, the nightstick in his hand held aloft like a conductor's baton. I think he wanted to play the *Smashed Kids Concerto, in C minor.* But he saw what was in our hands, and froze in indecision.

Breathing hard, he tried to catch his breath. His chest rose and fell like a great bellows. His gaze fell on the Buick for a couple beats, and he gave this slight lift of his eyebrows, like he'd stumbled on something he'd forgotten about.

Then we were the center of his attention again.

"Big trouble ..." he wheezed, "... if you throw those ... at a peace officer."

"What about for chasing a kid with a nightstick?" Jim said.

"I don't ... need no smart mouthed ... nigger boy talking back to me," the sheriff said. He let the nightstick fall to his side, then deftly slid it back into its loop. His hand went to the gun and pulled it free. He pointed it at us, and yes, the tunnel of the muzzle was as black an eye as I'd imagined. "I'm not playing games with you little shits. Put the goddamn rocks down."

I thought about it. I think we all did.

In the end we stood our ground, holding our rocks like they were talismans.

"You going to shoot us?" Tara said. Her voice trembled, but only just so, and her courage made my young heart yearn for her even more.

Sheriff Glover smiled at this like he was saying: *Hey, now you're getting the idea.*

"Sheriff sees gang up to no good," he began. "Follows them into the woods where they ain't supposed to be. Sees them vandalizing stuff maybe. There's this car that maybe was stolen awhile back. So he confronts them, and the kids throw rocks at him, so he has no recourse but to open fire."

His smile widened. His lips looked like two big pink earthworms, writhing and wriggling in the creases of his face.

"Think you can get all of us?" I said. "If one of us gets back and tells a different story, you think you'll get out of this scot-free? Shooting three kids dead? Don't you think that'll be all over the news?"

His smile faltered, the wriggling earthworms going still.

There was a shuffling sound from behind him. A rustle in the trees as something cut through the air like a bullet. The sheriff stumbled forward. The gun went off, kicking up dirt and grit not two feet in front of me. He turned, a hand to the back of his head and coming back blood-specked.

Fat Bobby stepped out from the trees, stones in either hand—his head likewise bloody.

"No one's hitting me anymore, shithead!"

His scream was something fierce, like a primitive warrior letting loose the hunting cry. Fat Bobby spun his arm and another rock went flying.

Sheriff Glover raised his gun hand.

Jim, Tara, and I moved as one, arms spinning, rocks sailing.

Pelted like an Old Testament sinner, the sheriff screamed and his gun fell to the ground. We picked up more, the three of us from behind him, Fat Bobby from his front, and we threw them, most of the stones finding their mark.

The sheriff fell to his knees. One hand, bloodied at the knuckles, tried to find his fallen service pistol. Jim darted forward and kicked it away into the bushes. Fat Bobby met Jim halfway and, skirting the sheriff, walked back with him to our side, near the old car.

Each of us reloaded, stones in either hand.

The sheriff, hands outstretched before him like a man praying, scooted on his knees so he was facing us. He seemed to be crying blood, trickles of it running down his face. He was trembling with rage or pain or both, and his eyes, ringed by blood, looked inhuman.

"Go away," Fat Bobby said.

"Leave us alone," Tara said.

"And don't call me nigger," Jim said.

I thought that about covered it all, so I said nothing. Just stood there in those tense seconds that seemed to drag on forever.

"You ... goddamn brats," he whispered. "Fucking ... losers ... you think this is ... over?"

"It better be," I said, finally finding my voice. "Or do you want how you hit a kid in the head with your stick, how you pulled a gun on others, in the paper? And don't forget my dad. Hurt any of us and he'll shove your gun so far up your ass you'll be shitting lead."

"Now get out of here," Jim added. "And don't let your son and his friends bother us no more. This here area belongs to us."

The sheriff looked from each of us, back and forth, and there was death in his eyes. I knew he'd kill us if given the chance. He looked towards where Jim had kicked the gun. We all raised our arms, ready to let loose another volley.

Lastly, he considered the Buick again.

He stood, turned, and walked away from us, giving one last menacing look before disappearing into the green like a phantasm.

### 5.

We stayed there for awhile, letting the calm of the forest work its magic. When we felt we'd recovered somewhat, gathered our thoughts and bearings, we likewise gathered around the hood of the old rusted Buick, like generals around a battle map.

"A lot of people don't like us," Jim said, and there was nervous laughter.

"Yeah," I said. "I keep getting called a loser. Hurts my feelings."

"Maybe we should start a club or something," Fat Bobby said, kind of smiling.

No one laughed at that, and we kind of looked around at one another. Me and Jim longer than the others. He raised an eyebrow at me, and I shrugged at him. *What the hell?* we were saying to each other. More than that, though. Not just *What the hell?* but maybe *Why not?*

"The Losers' Club," Tara said and we all looked at her. "Like the Justice League, only not as cool."

I smiled at her, and she at me, and there went my heart again.

"That has a nice ring to it," I said. "But it's already taken."

I thought of what my dad had said not so long ago, back at the store when I'd brought Bobby in after the confrontation with Dillon and his pals at the stream. *You've never chosen your friends easily, Joey. Always been a bit of an outsider that way.* These three, in their own ways, were as much outsiders as I was. And I'm not so sure I chose them as friends, as we chose each other. Or something else entirely brought us together. Something beyond our control. Something written into the very machinery of the world. There was the sense again, as I stood there with my friends near the old Buick, of things not so much building momentum, but falling into place.

"How about the Outsiders' Club?" I said, feeling the words as they rolled off my tongue. They sounded somehow right. As if I wasn't making a suggestion, but merely declaring something we all knew to be true.

Tara and Bobby looked at each other, then back at me, nodding in turn. Jim kind of shrugged, but I could see a gleam in his eyes.

"We'd need special names," I said.

"Oh, geez," Jim said and passed a hand over his face. I remembered the look he'd given me at the fair when he'd seen the plush Batman under my arm. "How about yours is Joey the Dork?"

I smiled, said: "Why not."

"I'm Fat Bobby," Fat Bobby said, as if he'd read my mind. He said it with a sort of pride that made me smile.

"You got quite an arm," I said, looking at Tara. "You nailed the sheriff right between the eyes."

"Yeah," Fat Bobby said. "You don't throw like a girl at all. You should be in the major leagues."

"Tomboy Tara," I said, and she slugged me on the shoulder.

"Saying I look like a boy?" she said, that crooked smile like a quarter moon playing at her lips. I blushed, feeling the heat in my face, and I think that was answer enough for her.

111

Last of all we looked at Jim, and he kind of gave us this challenging look, daring us to say something.

"And I guess I'm Nigger Jim?" he said, and he looked at each of us in turn. None of us said anything, and he gave a little chuckle. "Nigger Jim, huh? Bunch of racist honkeys." But he was smiling now, we were all smiling, and he stuck his hand out over the hood of the car and said: "To the Outsiders' Club."

Fat Bobby put his big hand out on top of Jim's brown one.

"The Outsiders' Club," he said.

"The Outsiders' Club," Tara said, her hand going out and grasping theirs.

There was a buzz in the air, I thought, and something pleasant tingled down my spine. I put my hand out on top of Tara's, on top of them all.

"The Outsiders' Club," I said. "We always watch out for each other, no matter what."

"No matter what," they all said as one.

And that's how it was for the rest of our days together, until the end.

# PART TWO

# The Car and the Collector

# CHAPTER SIX

## 1.

I saw the man in the fedora and long black coat for the first time outside our house at night.

Initially asleep, Bandit's growling woke me up slowly. At first I thought it was part of the dream I was having. High up with Tara at the top of the Ferris wheel, she was leaning forward for another kiss. That's when I heard the growling, and in the dream the growling was juxtaposed with the groaning of the Ferris wheel. It was falling apart around us, bolts and screws and beams falling away, until it was just our bucket seat in the night sky. Then that was falling, too, like an elevator cab cut loose of its cable.

The ground rose up quickly to meet us.

As we plummeted, I screamed and Tara laughed, saying: "Come on, kiss me!" I turned to her and it wasn't Tara, it was Dillon and his dad, Sheriff Glover, and they were both stuffed inside the dress Tara had been wearing. Packed in there together like Siamese twins, Dillon had his knife, and his dad had his gun. Both were leaning towards me saying: "Kiss me! Kiss me!" over and over. The glint of the knife in the moonlight was like an eye; the dark tunnel of the barrel of the gun, a mouth.

The Ferris wheel bucket seat slammed into the ground.

I woke up with a start, pushed the blankets aside, and saw Bandit at the window, growling. I called him softly to me but he wouldn't come. I stood and walked quietly to the window, avoiding the areas of the carpeted floor that I knew squeaked, not wanting to wake my parents.

At the window I pushed the curtains aside and there he was, down there on the road in front of our house. The wide-brimmed fedora hat cast shadow over his face like a veil. His long trench coat billowed out behind him like a cape as he walked. His hands were in the pockets and shuffling about in there, as if he was idly rattling change.

He looked like someone without a care in the world, just out for a stroll.

Maybe if I opened the window I'd hear him whistling.

The man in the fedora and coat walked briskly but casually by our house, turning his shadowed face and looking up once as he passed. I knew he saw me framed in the window and I wanted to back away, draw the curtains shut, but I didn't. Then he was down the street and gone in the night.

Tired, the webs of sleep still strewn across my mind, I told myself he was just a guy out for a walk. I climbed back in bed, motioned for Bandit to follow. But I pulled the covers up high, nearly to my chin, which I hadn't done since I was a small child, watching with dread the shadowed corners of my room.

## 2.

I got to go to the fair again the day before it left town, though my parents insisted I do it during the daytime, and the whole Outsiders' Club went with me. Because it was daytime, the Haunted House was closed, which none of us really minded, but so were some of the other attractions that depended on night for their appeal. Among these was the Observatory, a darkened walk-through attraction that took you through a pitch-black building with the walls and ceiling lit by stars and planetary effects. Big-headed aliens that glowed green and tinfoil spaceships were placed in strategic positions in unsuspecting corners, so you'd turn and there, right in front of you, was one of the butt-probing, cow-mutilating Roswell creatures. Also closed was the Laser Maze, in which kids ran around with light guns and dorky-looking, clunky vests and got to shoot each other.

I'd been looking forward to both of those, along with other attractions, and was disappointed that I wouldn't get to do them and that this was probably my last visit to the fair. But I got to go on the coaster, and the ups and downs and quick turns made me feel sick, though I was smiling when it was over. We hit the Ferris wheel, too, and like in my dream it paused at the top so that I was alone in the sky with Tara. But Jim and Fat Bobby were in the bucket seat immediately in front of us, and they constantly turned and waved at us or called to us, so we didn't kiss.

But I held her hand, and it was warm and smooth. Just that simple touch, up there in the sky, all the world seemingly below us, was good enough for me.

We did the water guns again, shooting at the John Wayne Gacy faces and popping the balloons. I chose a Captain America plush from the prize wall, which I thought appropriately patriotic with the Fourth of July just around the corner. Before we left, Tara turned her gun on me and soaked my face and the front of my shirt. Jim thought this was funny and turned his on me too, so I called him by his Outsiders' Club code name and shot him back. Then Fat Bobby was soaking all three of us, and when he got to Tara he aimed at her chest instead of her face. Pretty soon breasts tipped with hard nipples were poking out against her blouse like missiles.

I thought, *Whoa, good job Fat Bobby*, and Tara saw me looking, gave me a mighty slug in the ribs, turned and gave Jim and Bobby one also. We three quickly put our guns down, but by that time the game booth attendant was shouting at us about the mess we were making and we ran off laughing.

We left the fair soon after, but it was only early afternoon, so instead of calling my mom as had been the plan when we were ready to leave, we started walking. None of us had eaten at the fair, not even Fat Bobby, so we stopped at a sandwich place and we all chipped in and bought lunch. We ate on the patio, at a little table with an umbrella over it. The walk and the sun had dried Tara's blouse pretty quick, and I was disappointed at this, having been enjoying discreet peeks since we'd left the fair.

Then she spoke and my mind was immediately occupied by other things:

"So, when are we going to open the car?"

And with that one sentence we knew where we were going next.

* * *

At the Connolly yard Jim's dad greeted us, clapping each of us on the back. He stooped to give Bandit a rubdown, whom I insisted we stop at my house to pick up, not wanting a repeat of the last excursion to the woods when a certain sheriff had pulled a gun on us. Mr. Connolly looked to be in the same or similar grease-stained shirt and pants that he'd been in the day I met him.

When I had the chance I leaned close to Fat Bobby and said: "*Seems like he's always here. Jim too.*"

Bobby nodded and said: "They live here."

I blinked, mildly surprised, and so was about to ask where they slept and used the bathroom, when Fat Bobby pointed at a couple doors near the rear of the garage in one corner. One said "RESTROOM" and so that part of my unspoken question was answered easily enough. Next to this door was another that said "EMPLOYEES ONLY" and Bobby nodded at that one.

"That's where the living room and bedroom are."

To some people I guess this would be a sign of poverty, people living in the same place they worked out of, but to me it was kind of cool and I didn't think much about it after that.

Jim told his dad what we wanted to do, and Mr. Connolly walked away and rummaged through a couple drawers in a shelf on one wall. He came back with something that looked like a corkscrew and a length of flat metal notched at one end. Handing these items over to his son, Mr. Connolly saw my questioning look and the puzzled expressions from Tara and Bobby as well.

"Lock pick," he said, Jim holding up the corkscrew device to punctuate his dad's words. "Slim Jim," he added, and Jim held up the notched length of metal, giving a reproachful look at me, Bobby, and Tara to head off any would-be jokes. "Be surprised how often doors get jammed or the lock just doesn't work or someone's locked their keys inside the car. These suckers will pop just about anything open."

"Thanks, Mr. Connolly," I said, again surprised at the things he was letting us do, like he knew that abandoned car had been out there just waiting for kids to find it. Like that was how things were supposed to be.

He smiled at us and then gave us a cautionary wag of one long, dark finger.

"Now, if you kids find anything dangerous or … well … just plain weird, I guess, and you think you need to tell an adult … you come to me first. And we'll see what's what."

We all nodded our understanding and appreciation for his help. Then we were out the rear of the garage, over, under or around the barricade like scurrying monkeys, and onto the access road and into the forest.

### 3.

Jim tried the driver's door first, inserting the notched end of the Slim Jim beneath the lip of the rubber trim lining the window. Scraping sounds of metal on metal issued from inside the lining of the Buick's door. Kneeling, hunching, leaning, Jim tried applying the Slim Jim at different angles, yet the lock didn't pop and the driver's door didn't budge.

"Why don't we just break the windows?" Fat Bobby said.

"*No!*" Jim and I said in unison, turning on him with vicious glares. Again, it was that unspoken feeling, like we were at work on something sacred here, something that deserved respect and maybe a little reverence. Busting the windows of this beat-up old car would be like desecrating a church and the mere suggestion offended our sensibilities.

Jim tried once more on the driver's side door, pushing and sliding the length of metal around. His grip on the Slim Jim slipped, his hand struck the car, and he cried out and stuck his thumb in his mouth.

He stepped away from the window, leaving the Slim Jim inserted there like a surgeon's implement left sticking out of a body on a gurney.

"You give it a try," he said, nodding to me and getting out of the way. "Dad never showed me how to do this. Looks easier than it is, I guess."

I walked up to the door, aware of Tara and Bobby leaning on the hood, watching. Bending for a better angle, I grabbed the haft of the Slim Jim with both hands, wiggled it, pushed it, slid it back and forth.

There was a pop and a rattle, and then that familiar little *click* of a car door unlocking. I looked up, and everyone was staring at me expectantly. Jim moved up close again beside me. Tara and Bobby pushed off of the hood and stepped closer.

I reached out, grasped the door handle, lifted up, and with another *click* the door swung open. There was a silence for a spell, as we tried to register what it was we were seeing.

Do you remember an old Disney cartoon called *Duck Tales*? In the cartoon there's an old, miserly character appropriately named Scrooge McDuck. McDuck had a huge bank vault hidden beneath his massive mansion, and an enormous lock and door that protected what was in the vault. What was in the vault?

Money. Jewels. Treasure.

Tons of it. Bills and gold coins and gold bars and statues of gold, seemingly yards deep, piled wall to wall. In almost every episode, Scrooge McDuck would dive off a perch above the vault room and its treasure, and he'd splash into the precious stones and gems and gold bars and bills like he was diving into a swimming pool or the ocean. He'd kick his feet and swing his arms, and it *was* an ocean, an ocean of riches.

In the front seat of the old Buick, and spilling into the backseat, were sacks of money. No gold or jewels or gems, but lots of green, green money. Rubber-banded stacks of hundreds spilled out of the open sacks like an afterbirth. On the seats, on the floors, a few on the dashboard. Everywhere, money, and I wondered if I could dive into it like Scrooge McDuck, jump into it all like it was a pile of autumn leaves.

My thirteen-year-old imagination took mere seconds to begin considering the possibilities of so much money. What I could do with it; what I could buy. Books and comics, by the hundreds, the thousands. Within days my room could be wall-to-wall books. Hell, I'd need a second bedroom, maybe a third. Shit, I could buy a whole house just for the purpose of holding all my shelves of books.

Somehow, Tara, Jim, and Bobby squeezed in that little open door with me. Seeing what I saw, I was nudged this way and that as they each strained and craned to see what was in there.

"Move over, Joey the Dork," Jim said, jostling me, and then, "Holy shit," when he saw how the stacks and piles spilled over into the backseat of the Buick.

He picked up a banded stack of hundreds from the nearest open bag, riffled through it like you'd see gangsters do in movies. He was making little sounds under his breath, soft little huffs and puffs, and I wondered what was happening. Was he going into some sort of seizure or fit? Then I realized he was counting the stack. When he came to the end of the stack, he started again and riffled through it once more before looking up at us.

"That's ten thousand dollars," he said, his voice hushed and tremulous, like he was afraid, even out here, someone would hear him.

"Just that one stack?" Tara said, her tone also betraying her excitement.

"Just this one stack," Jim confirmed.

"There must be hundreds of stacks in there," Fat Bobby said, his head and face real close to mine, so that when he spoke he sprayed me like a sprinkler. I pushed him away and backed out of the car door.

"Which could mean …" I said, trying to do the math in my head, carrying zeroes and cussing when those fucking zeroes got all crowded and got me confused, so that I had to start over. "Millions of dollars …" I finally whispered, giving up on an exact figure and settling for an estimate.

"Millions …" Jim repeated, pushing his butt side to side to brush the seat free of its stacks and bags, sending them in a small avalanche down to the footrest area so he could sit.

"Hey," I said, and for a moment no one looked at me, everyone's eyes still on the interior of the car and the mountains of green paper. "Let's check out the trunk."

Three heads swung my way in near unison, and three smiles grew wider.

Jim stood, reluctantly dropping the banded stack of hundreds on the passenger seat. Together, the four of us walked around to the rear of the Buick. We lined up there, and as if knighting me, Jim passed over the corkscrew-like lock pick. He described briefly how to work it, how to feel for the actuator that controlled the rod that pops the lock, and I felt very important, entrusted with some vital task.

I inserted the lock pick into the trunk's keyhole, turned it.

Leaning close, I heard the tap and rattle of the actuator. I turned the pick some more.

The lock popped easily. The trunk sprung open an inch or two.

Grasping it under the latch, I swung the trunk lid up.

The head seemed to be looking back at us from the confines of the trunk: the sockets empty, strings of hair still attached like frayed threads to the skull, the teeth in a rictus-grin as if ready to bite.

Screaming, we jumped back in near unison, the sudden sounds in the still forest sending birds from the trees aflutter. Branches and leaves rustled at their departure like a crowd whispering among themselves. The echoes of our screams came back to us, and in the otherwise quietude it could have been the skull talking, returned from the land of the dead, finding its voice, and eager to share its secrets.

\* \* \*

A few moments passed before I gathered my wits and stepped back towards the rear of the car. To me, the open trunk lid looked like a mouth, and I had little desire to see again the morsel inside. But no one else was moving, and it seemed someone had to do something.

Bandit had run up to us when we'd shouted, abandoning whatever other scents had previously occupied him. Now he followed me as I moved towards the car trunk, his body low, his legs tense, his tail straight out, reading my fear.

I held the corkscrew-like lock pick out in front of me, like it was a *Star Trek* phase pistol and I'd use it to vaporize the skull if it suddenly chose to spring up at me, its teeth clacking as it sought my throat. At the bumper, I realized my gaze was moving rapidly in all other directions, taking in the sky, the trees, the ground, keeping the trunk and its contents in the periphery. Now, there, I had to look, and I lowered my eyes and saw again the nearly fleshless skull looking up at me. Its strings of hair looked like little insectile feelers prodding the air.

I felt my heart thudding, my stomach churning with my recent lunch. Fighting the urge to retreat again, I stayed where I was, tried to be clinical about the whole thing. Like Mom when me and Sarah had been younger, and we'd cut ourselves or smash a toe or finger, and she'd doctor us. Whispering, consoling us, she'd tell us it was no big deal, the pain would pass. I tried that with myself, consoled myself, told myself it was dead. *It* was a person, but now that person was dead. It really shouldn't be any worse than looking at road kill on the side of the road, or a bird dropped dead in the front yard.

But it *was* different.

This was a person, not road kill. What I was seeing was what *I* was underneath, what I was made of beneath the flesh. It was what my friends were made of, my family, and it was what we'd all be someday, every last one of us.

*That* made it different.

As I examined the trunk and what was in the trunk, I realized it wasn't just a skull nestled among the spare tire and the tire jack. It was just that the skull was more prominent, tilted upward leaning against the long deflated spare tire.

The rest of the body was there as well, poking out from faded and holey clothes little more than scraps of cloth. The arms were atop the chest, bound at the wrists. I leaned closer, pinching my nose against a smell I expected but, tentatively, discovered wasn't there. I guessed all the parts that stunk had long ago flaked away. A black powder and mush coating the lining of the trunk put meaning to a word I'd only read about in horror novels and comics: decomposition. I choked back a rising surge of vomit, and leaned forward a few dreadful inches nearer.

Closer, I saw that what bound the wrists was fishing wire, its thin filaments catching the sunlight like a silky spider's web. I scanned down the length of the body, the bones, and saw that the feet were bound as well at the ankles.

Bandit hopped up on his hind legs, forepaws over the edge of the trunk, and leaned in for a sniff. He whined and jumped down.

I knew how he felt and started to back away myself.

Then I looked at the head again, that skull with the pits for eyes looking back at me, and I saw something I hadn't noticed at first. Leaning in once more, this time I noticed there *was* a smell, faint but stale and pungent. An old smell that I was glad was long faded to this vague remnant. My attention was on the top of the skull, and I leaned in even closer. Some of those wiry strands of hair were dangerously close to my mouth and nostrils. I wondered if I was breathing in corpse dust, if right at that moment little microscopic pieces of the dead thing were finding their way inside me, *invading* me.

On the top of the head was a hole. Cracks radiated from the hole, as if the head had been struck by something.

Stuffed in the trunk.

Money in the car.

A picture was forming in my head, of possibilities, of likelihoods, and I didn't like it, didn't like the picture and the pieces coming together, what it all meant. I turned on spaghetti-legs to my friends, and I saw that all of them had drawn closer as I'd been inspecting the skeleton. I hadn't heard them, and their nearness, when I'd last been aware of them farther away, was unsettling. I stepped back and struck my head on the open trunk lid.

"*Shit*," I muttered and rubbed my head.

"Is that a hole in its head?" Jim said.

I nodded.

"What does it mean?" Tara asked, now moving past me to look back into the trunk, nearly as close as I'd been. Tomboy indeed.

Fat Bobby raised his hand as if he were in a classroom, and

125

we all turned to him, knowing maybe what he was going to say, not wanting to say it ourselves.

"Murder?"

That one word seemed loud out there on that old road with just us and that car, alone, and the rest of the world a world away.

## 4.

"Nothing there, huh?" Mr. Connolly asked when Jim and I arrived back at the car yard.

We'd decided that Tara and Fat Bobby would go on home instead of coming back with us. Between the four of us we'd decided that they were the weakest liars. For Fat Bobby it was a unanimous decision. I guess we all felt that because of his all-around nervous and awkward presence, he wouldn't be able to tell a lie convincingly. He protested, almost whining. But we didn't give, and eventually he agreed to go home and let me and Jim talk to Mr. Connolly. Tara outright told us she sucked at lying, had problems even telling her mom dinner was good if she thought it really blew the big one. So she went home as well.

We agreed to get together again the following day, at noon, on Lookout Mountain, to talk about what we were going to do next.

"No, sir," Jim said in response to his dad's question. I gave something of a noncommittal shake of my head, like I was showing how disappointed I was that that was the case.

We stood in the doorway to one of the side rooms in the garage that served as Mr. Connolly's office. He had a phone clasped to his ear between his shoulder and cheek, one hand over the mouthpiece. It was the first time I'd seen this room, and I took a moment to look around, mildly surprised at what I saw.

A high-end-looking computer sat on the big oak desk in the center of the room, with a printer and fax and big speakers and a widescreen monitor. Bookshelves filled with automotive volumes lined the walls end to end. Filing cabinets tall and wide sat in two corners. It was all really sophisticated and professional-like. Not what I'd expected from seeing the orderly mess of the car yard itself and the garage.

"Nothing at all?" Mr. Connolly said, as if genuinely interested. When we shook our heads again he said: "Bummer", and went back to his phone call.

"That was easy," I said to Jim when we closed the door to his dad's office.

"Yeah," Jim said, but his tone didn't seem as upbeat as mine.

* * *

I lay in bed early that evening, Bandit draped across my feet warming them for me, arms behind my head, worried, restless, and excited. Part of me was thinking about all that money, an amount, a number, that was almost beyond my comprehension. I thought about all the comics and books and other stuff I could buy with it.

The other part of me was thinking of that long dead person, nothing but bones now, and that hole in its head. I was young, and the idea of all that money to spend was exciting and fun to think about. But I was old enough that I knew about death, had seen some violence, and knew that what had happened to that person stuffed in the trunk was real, and could happen to me.

I was thinking how I should probably tell my parents, and they'd call the police. How maybe despite our agreement to meet tomorrow and talk about it, one of my friends had possibly already told *their* parents, and then the money would be gone. Probably forever. I was smart enough to know we had probably been looking at drug money, or a big bank heist, or maybe something altogether different and infinitely worse. Cars full of money didn't just happen by accident.

Neither did dead people in trunks.

I didn't know what to do, and the minutes crawled by like I was in some sort of temporal anomaly.

The bedroom door opened and something white sailed through the air to land on my face. I took it off and held it up. A pair of my jockey shorts.

"Your stupid underwear was in my laundry again," Sarah said from the doorway, a laundry basket cradled under one arm. "So many skid marks, maybe we should put you back in diapers. If you're not going to wash your stuff, at least keep it out of mine."

She reached into the basket again and came out with a pair of my socks also. She threw those too. They landed on Bandit's head and hung there like rabbit ears. He opened his eyes, yawned, seemed bored, and went back to sleep.

"Stop trying my clothes on then, perv," I said. "Cross-dressing went out of style with *Silence of the Lambs*."

She flipped me off.

I flipped her off back, raised her a double.

"You're so mature," she said with this haughty tone, as if she'd already forgotten she'd thrown dirty underwear and socks at me and my dog.

"You're so ugly," I said, and shielded my face with a forearm, as if hiding from Medusa.

She gave me this scowl and a sigh like I was such a headache and bore to deal with. She started to turn around to leave, but then I thought of something and called her back. Sarah gave this long-suffering sigh again and at first I didn't think she'd stay, but she turned around and put her free fist to her hip, like she was a queen entertaining a court jester more idiotic than entertaining.

"What?" she said. The look in her eyes told me noogies and a proper wedgie were in my future if I said the wrong thing.

"You still thinking of taking those journalism electives next year?"

She stood there silent for a moment, eyes squinty, suspicious, like she was waiting for the punch line. When I didn't follow with anything smart, she said: "Yeah. Why?"

"You think you got what it takes to investigate something?" I tried to throw in a little note of challenge, like maybe I didn't think she was.

"What do you mean?" she said, and though she still held that high and mighty queen look, she set her laundry basket down and took a step into the room.

"Close the door first," I said, and she did. "And you got to swear not to tell anyone else what I tell you."

"Oh, give me a break—"

I sat up and cut her off.

"I'm serious. This might be something big."

You could tell she was still doubtful, but her interest was piqued. Probably imagining herself as a future Lois Lane going for a Pulitzer. Seeing that I wasn't going to say anything else until she swore, she raised her hand and, in a melodramatic voice, like a bad actor, said: "I swear upon my heart and soul and the love of baby Jesus."

I thought her acting voice sucked, thought about saying so, that she should stick to journalism, plus the added benefit that the audience wouldn't go blind from looking at her hideous mug, but thought better of it and gestured for her to sit down at my desk. She did, scooting the chair a little closer to my bed and, in the moonlight coming through my window, I told her about the car and the money and the body. Again there was that sense of things moving, gears turning, of events rolling forward and gaining momentum.

When I was done, I could see she doubted me some, but maybe not enough that she thought I was completely off my gourd, maybe just exaggerating a bit. She tapped the armrest of the chair with one hand, twirled a strand of hair with the other.

"Show me," she finally said. "Then I'll see what I think we should do."

"Fine," I said and told her how tomorrow I was meeting Tara, Jim, and Bobby at noon.

"No. Show me tonight."

# CHAPTER SEVEN

## 1.

Down the hall, my parents' bedroom door closed at ten o'clock, the creaks and squeaks as they settled for the night carried softly through the walls of the house. Sarah had told me to be ready at midnight, and I lay beneath my covers already in my shirt, jacket, and jeans, watching the minutes on the nightstand clock pass.

Struggling to keep my eyes open, the lids fluttered shut like lazy butterfly wings. A couple times they snapped open, my mind screaming that I'd missed the appointed time and my sister had left without me, only to see but a few minutes had passed. Then came the gentlest of knocks on my door, and it swept inward slowly. With the fedora-wearing man still in the back of my mind, I thought of a crypt door opening, and I half expected a fanged monster to come leaping in at me.

No fangs, but a monster in her own right, my sister walked in and over to my bed. She leaned over and shook me. I slapped her hands away. She reached down and grasped my face, shook it. I slapped her away again.

"*I'm up, I'm up,*" I whispered. As I struggled out of the sheets she continued to poke and prod at me, just for the hell of it, so that I got up in a funny spastic dance.

Bandit was up, too, his eyes alight in the shadows of my room.

"*Let's get going,*" Sarah said and gave me one last hard pinch on the upper arm, punctuating it with, "*This better be worth it.*"

"It is," I said.

We crept out of the room like burglars, me shutting the door reluctantly on Bandit, afraid of the clacking of his nails on the hall floor waking my parents.

\* \* \*

The dirt path made a pale stripe through the dark abyss of the night, and it seemed we walked a trail suspended in nothingness to either side and just the road at our feet. We had flashlights we'd filched from the foyer closet and the bright beams like lasers slicing the night proceeded ahead of us. Up the hill we trudged, pausing at the top where I'd first seen the light of the abandoned car, then down the other side. The woods stretched out before us and the trees reached hungrily for stragglers.

"Hope there aren't any wolves or bears or anything," Sarah said as we drew nearer.

"As a Sasquatch, you shouldn't be too worried."

She turned and shoved me.

At the edge of the woods we halted for a moment like we'd reached a barrier, some borderland whose crossing marked a certain passage. With a shared look and synchronized deep breath, we pushed through the trees and into the woods.

The bright, pale coin of the moon hanging above in the purple sky showed itself only intermittently between the roof of the branches above, like a child playing peek-a-boo. There were hoots and chirps and other sounds, and occasionally a bush or branch would rustle. We swung our flashlight beams in the direction we thought the noises came from. Sometimes a limb shook a bit as if something had just occupied it, or the quick flash of reflective eyes winked from the deep shadow. Subconsciously, we moved closer to each other: who was protecting who I can't say.

We came to the stream and in the night it looked like a river of oil. Slick and black, the whispers of it running over stone was a constant white noise, like some fanatical survivalist had left a television with bad reception on somewhere deep in the forest. Leaves and twigs sailed the surface like tiny vessels.

Sarah looked up and down the stream, searching for large stones for footholds to cross the water without getting wet.

"Got to wade through it," I said.

"Damn," she said. "Probably cold this time of night."

"It's not the cold you have to worry about. It's the piranha."

"Har har," she said, giving me a look colder than the night. "Very funny."

"Don't worry though. Since it's only your feet in the water, I'm sure you'll be safe. The smell should be a natural repellent."

She punched me on the shoulder and, though I smiled, what I really wanted to do was rub my arm. My sister didn't punch like a girl.

"If you could bottle the odor and sell it to deep sea divers, you'd be a billionaire," I said, and she hit me again on the same spot. The throbbing there ached to the bone, and I shut up.

We took off our shoes and started across the water. The stream was indeed cold, and trying just my toes first didn't do me much good, rather made me want to turn back, so I just took a deep breath and dunked them in and started walking. My sister was close behind, and I heard her gasp at the first feel of the water over her feet. I made melodramatic stomps through the water that sent up splashes, and her gasps went a few octaves higher.

"*You ass!*" she hissed.

I felt a shove at my back between the shoulders and I went stumbling forward, fell to my knees. The water splashed up to my face and each trickle of it hitting the bare skin of my hands and arms and neck and face was like a dagger poking. My knees and shins landed painfully on stones in the water, and between those aches and the cold I grimaced and clenched my teeth.

"Okay, okay," I said. "We're even. Help me up, please."

I held out my hand, and my sister splashed up beside me and grabbed it.

"Serves you right, dork," she said and started to pull me up.

I pulled back, fast and hard, and she fell into the water beside me. As she fell, I was already up and striding towards the shore. Both of us had had the presence of mind to keep our flashlights held high and out of the water, and as Sarah got to her feet she targeted my face with her beam so that I had to hold a forearm up to shield against the light.

"You're so dead."

Her jeans were soaked and her shirt and jacket up to the ribs.

"Have to catch me," I said and started to jog, fast but not too fast so that we'd lose each other. I found the ruts of the access road soon enough, and my sister's light chasing me I saw well enough to pick up my speed. That was the way it went for a bit: my sister cursing me, telling me she'd kill me, me laughing and running by moon and flashlight. Until we came to it, the old Buick, paint-flaked and rusted. A giant dead thing of metal there in the middle of the rutted road.

But something was different, and I stopped in my tracks.

Sarah skidded to a halt beside me, started to grab my forearm with both hands, began to twist the skin in opposing directions for one hell of an Indian burn. When she saw I wasn't reacting, that something else had my attention, she stopped.

"What's wrong?" she asked.

I pointed at the old car.

Its doors were all open, like the wings of a gigantic insect. We—me, Tara, Jim, and Fat Bobby—had closed the door we'd popped before we left. The trunk as well.

Slowly, I moved closer. Walking wide around the car, I shone my flashlight into it. The money was gone. All of it. Something else nagged at my mind then, something more terrible than missing money.

I took long sideways strides around to the rear of the vehicle. The trunk was open too. I stepped closer, peered over the lip of the trunk to see inside.

The body was gone.

"*Look out!*" Sarah yelled, still standing where she'd skidded to a stop behind me, several yards away.

The rustle of leaves was all I heard. A whisper of movement from the corner of my eye caught my attention. Something black moving. Something billowing like a curtain in an open window. I started to turn, caught a glimpse of a figure moving like liquid. Atop the figure, atop its head, a wide-brimmed fedora, like those hats detectives wore in old black-and-white movies.

Then I couldn't turn any further because there was an arm around my throat. Another arm wrapped around me like a tentacle, pinning my own against my sides. I tried to struggle but it was like fighting iron. Flaps of cloth slapped my sides and legs, and I peered down, saw corners of the long coat flapping into view like little flags snapping in a high wind.

I remembered the figure from a few nights prior, walking the road in front of our house, looking up to my window like he expected me there. Strolling away like a passerby in the park.

"Let him go!"

Sarah, rushing forward.

A cool, sharp, and familiar pressure at my throat. My sister stopped, which I thought was wise. I didn't much want a second mouth carved into my throat, to watch that new orifice spew blood like scarlet vomit.

"Where is it?"

A conversational tone, as if nothing was amiss.

"*What?*" I croaked, feeling the kiss of the blade at my throat.

"This is the night," the voice said, and the words baffled me. "Great things can happen at night." He spoke calmly but with a passion, as if he were reciting poetry. "This is the night. These are the times."

Obviously, to this man these words meant something. To me it sounded like the ravings of a whack job. I thought of telling him so for just a fraction of a second, then realized a whack job who recited whack job poetry probably wouldn't be too hesitant about relieving me of my head. I kind of liked my head right where it was. I looked at it every morning in the bathroom mirror. It wasn't anything special, but it was mine and I kind of had an attachment to it.

"*I … don't understand …*" I said, relying on honesty, or at least a semblance of it. I understood his first words—*Where is it?*—assuming that he was probably referring to the money. My declaration of ignorance was in response to his whack job-beatnik-spoken-word crap. The stuff about the night and the times.

"There was a sum of money," he said, almost whispering into my ear like we were friends sharing a secret. His breath was sweet and minty, like he'd been sucking on candy preparing for a long awaited kiss. "It was in this automobile. Now it isn't."

"What do you want?" Sarah said, taking a daring step forward.

I felt the man's head shift behind me as he fixed his gaze on her. Sarah stopped her approach immediately, as if she'd heard the command in a game of Red Rover.

"You may call me the Collector," the man said. His sweet and minty breath and his snapping flag coat touched me delicately in different places. "I collect things that are owed, and at times I collect things for myself."

The iron tentacle-like arm around my body suddenly loosened and fell away, but I didn't move. That intimate touch of the blade was still there at my throat, and that held me rooted more than his arms ever could.

The ruffle of cloth on cloth as I felt and heard him go into one of his coat pockets was loud to my panic-heightened ears.

He pulled the hand out a moment later and held something out for Sarah to see. I couldn't see it, his arm too low and me not daring to lower my chin even a fraction of an inch, lest I stir the knife to action.

"Here is something I collected recently."

He made a swift flicking gesture like he was tossing a coin. Something indeed was tossed, but it wasn't a coin.

I followed it through the air as it rose into view in a wide arc, and Sarah's light rose to trace its path. Pale and crooked like a large, dry noodle, one end red and raw, the finger sailed through the space between us and my sister, then dropped out of my view. It hit the ground with a faint sound like pebbles being idly and gently jostled by a foot.

Sarah screamed.

Then she had the presence of mind to realize what this might mean for me if she pissed off this nutjob, the Collector. She cut off her shriek with a hand clapped to her mouth like a clamp.

"It matters not whether you live or die," he said, whispering to me, but I had no doubt including my sister as well. "All I require is what was in the car, and you may continue to live."

"I … don't know … where it is," I squeaked.

The slightest pressure was added to the knife, and I felt it press into my throat. I felt its edge first kiss, and then bite. I felt a trickle of coolness down the slope of my neck. Blood-drool from the site of my proposed new mouth.

I pissed my pants.

I'm not proud of it, but I'm not ashamed of it now or then. Have one big bastard of a knife pressed to your throat and see how brave you are. Besides, I think that was what saved my life, wetting my pants like a big fucking baby.

It was an honest response. It made me as genuine as any words could have.

"I believe you," said the Collector. The knife left my throat and I heard the almost inaudible sounds of his footfalls receding.

The rustle of leaves dancing as he withdrew from me and back into the shadows that birthed him. "You have two days to find where it has gone, and then I'll be back to collect. Here. Midnight. Either the money, or you. Your choice."

As he faded into the night, his voice drifted back to us once more like dark music carried on a breeze:

"I've disposed of one body already. If necessary, more can be added to that grave."

Alone then, my sister and I, me in the warmth of my piss-soaked jeans, my sister breathing hard and fast, puffing a chill mist, and a lone finger in the space between us. That pale digit a reminder of what could have been, what still might be.

## 2.

"Where is it?" I demanded, grabbing Fat Bobby by the front of his plaid shirt and shaking him.

Sarah had come with me to the meeting of the Outsiders' Club atop Lookout Mountain. Though the light of day cast everything in summer hues of greens and browns and blues, the events of the previous night were just as fresh and urgent as they had been when they occurred, and all the world seemed darker to me, muted. Sleep hadn't come at all the night prior, and I was tired and frightened and angry.

I shook Fat Bobby a few more times and then Sarah, Tara, and Jim pulled me away from him. Jim especially was rough with me, yanking me and propelling me away with a nice good shove, so that I clenched my fists and targeted him next. Bandit barked in confusion, not sure what was going on, who the bad guy was and who he should bite.

"Where's the money, Jim?" I said through clenched teeth. "This guy wasn't joking around."

By shouts and curses I'd already told them what had happened the night before, about the Collector, and how he collected things owed and sometimes for himself. About the severed finger sailing through the air, its stub of bone poking out catching the moonlight and sparkling for a moment like a grim jewel.

"If you'd calm down for a fucking second," Jim said, seeing my fists and making a couple of his own, just in case I guess, "that's what we were going to tell you."

"Then tell me."

"You're standing on it," Jim said.

I looked at my feet, and the rounded and stoned peak of the mountain we were standing on. I saw nothing out of place: no freshly dug and refilled hole; no stones rolled out of and back into place to hide things under.

"What're you talking about?" I said, getting angrier by the second. My throat was buzzing with that phantom sensation of the blade pushed up against it.

"Next to it might be more accurate," Jim said and walked past Bobby, holding his shirt together where my yanking and pulling had ripped a couple buttons loose, to the tall upright stone that looked like an Easter Island statue.

I followed him.

Stretching on tiptoes, Jim reached for the top of the upright stone and boosted himself up to a sitting position atop it. I did the same. He leaned over, and so did I. There it was, in a recess made by the upright stone and others behind it, perhaps a yard deep and less than a foot wide: the canvas sacks, the green banded stacks of bills glimpsed through the open mouths.

Sarah strode over and boosted herself up also, leaned over, saw all the money, said: "*Holy shit.*" I scooted and leapt back down to the others. Jim did the same, dusting his hands on his jeans after he landed. Leaning over for a few moments longer looking at all that money, Sarah came down last, like she was reluctant to leave it.

I knew the feeling.

"Why'd you move it?" I asked.

"We were afraid someone might find it," Fat Bobby muttered.

He had that hurt expression on his face, that pitiful slacking of his cheeks and mouth that made me want to slap him and made me feel rotten at the same time.

"Who the hell would find it?" I asked, knowing the stupidity of my question even as I voiced it, and not giving a shit. I'd had a goddamn knife to my throat the night before, and I'd pissed my pants in front of my sister, so I wasn't in such a good mood.

"Well, Joey, obviously someone was looking for it," Tara said in a soft, lilting tone, trying to defuse the situation at hand.

"And don't forget Sheriff Glover saw us on the road with the car," Jim added, his fists finally relaxing, fingers hooking into his pockets. "We couldn't leave the money there after he'd seen the car."

I couldn't help but feel betrayed that Tara was the one who spoke the obvious truth. It *had* been foolish to leave the money in the car. Especially after the confrontation with Sheriff Glover.

That didn't mean I had to like being kept out of the loop. *I* was the one who'd found the car and led us all to it. I'd brought us all together, and I should have been included in all things. Then I looked at Tara's face, her eyes, her mouth, those brown curls, and I softened considerably. I took a deep breath and calmed myself.

"Did you recognize him?" Jim asked. "Either of you," he added, looking at Sarah too. He still had a mild look of irritation when he looked at her, and each time he did he'd quickly look at me with a sort of accusatory stare. I knew what he was silently asking me: *Why'd you bring her?* As in: *Why is she part of this now?* And though I was irritated and angry, I guess I understood. I imagined how I'd feel if I'd arrived to find any of them had brought new people into the fold, so to speak.

"No," Sarah said.

I shook my head.

140

"Nothing?" Jim said. "You didn't get a look at his face? You didn't recognize his voice?"

"No," I repeated.

"And we have two days until he comes back?" Tara said. She and Jim exchanged looks, and I knew that they were thinking along the same lines. I felt left out, wanting to know what it was they were thinking.

Sarah and I nodded again.

"A *finger*?" Fat Bobby said and we all turned at the interruption. He had blanched, as he had when I'd first mentioned the finger. He kind of half turned, his cheeks puffing a bit, as if he might throw up.

Tara and Jim turned back to me, ignoring him.

"I say we do what the Outsiders' Club does best," Tara said.

Jim smiled, apparently knowing where she was going with this declaration. I had a vague idea, quickly forming, but didn't want to say anything yet. I didn't much like the idea that was forming in my head. I remembered what had almost happened last time.

"Let him come," Jim said, sharing another look with Tara, and she was smiling now too. "We'll be ready."

Certain of what they intended now, or something close to it, I spoke:

"Throwing rocks isn't going to stop this guy."

"What are you talking about?" Sarah asked.

Reluctantly, but seeing no way around it, I told my sister about the confrontation with Sheriff Glover. How he'd hit me and Bobby, pulled his gun on us, and we'd all countered with rocks, beating him bloody. I thought Sarah would insist we tell Dad and Mom then, tell them everything, and the worried expression that passed over her face made me think she was considering just that. I needn't have worried, however, as the look of concern was quickly replaced by a smile, and she high-fived me.

"Joey's right," Sarah said, and she got that irritated look from Jim again, and I got mine, and I knew he wasn't happy about an

141

outsider giving her opinion on things. "We're not going to stop this guy with a bunch of rocks."

"Then we use more than rocks," Tara said.

What that implied I didn't know or wasn't ready to admit to myself, but it scared the hell out of me. It seemed we were being pushed in a direction, like maybe down the very hill we were standing on. Propelled forward and rolling down and gaining momentum we'd soon be going so fast that we wouldn't be able to stop ourselves. Not until we crashed, that was, and that sense of losing control worried me. But I didn't know how to share those thoughts with my friends. Didn't know how to put them into words that would carry the weight of the feeling.

"Wait," Jim said. He was still looking at Sarah. "Who said anything about 'we'?"

He pointed at her to punctuate his words.

"I'm involved now," my sister said, her hands on her hips and this look on her face like she was ready to walk over and rip his nuts off if he argued the point. I wouldn't put it past her either. The line between noogies and testicular removal seemed a small and fine one to me.

Jim wasn't so easily cowed.

He'd never had a sister. Didn't understand his folly.

"The hell you are. This is our money."

"It won't be anyone's money if the police hear about it," she said, and she gave Jim this triumphant smile, like she was saying: *Top that, jerk.*

"You'd do that?" he said. Jim's face had gone paler than I ever imagined a black person's could. It looked like the transformation of Michael Jackson packed into a couple seconds.

"I just might."

They looked at each other and the clash of wills was almost tangible, like a military skirmish was playing out right before us. I could almost hear the sounds of battle, and the screams of the dying.

I was fairly sure my sister was bluffing. The fact that she'd gone with me the night before to the woods and the access road, and her acknowledgement that it would take more than stones to stop the Collector, revealed that she was as invested in this as the rest of us. The car was *our* find. The woods and the road that had hidden it, our place, our *realm*. These things belonged to us, in ways not fully explainable in words. I'm not so sure I understand it even now. But it was our duty to protect these things—the car, the body that had been in it, and yes, the money—for as long as we could.

Yet I'd be lying if I said I wasn't worried then and there, watching the battle of wills between my sister and friend. Everything seemed perched on a razor thin edge in those passing moments. If pushed the wrong way, it could all end in a moment.

Jim finally let out this deep sigh and then looked at me.

"Fine. She's in."

As if it was by his decree and not his submission that this was concluded.

Tara moved forward and gave my sister a hug, and for some reason this was embarrassing. The tension about us seemed a tangible force lifting and floating away. I sighed in relief, and my body eased.

"Nice to have another girl in the club," Tara said, and Sarah smiled.

"You need a code name," Fat Bobby said, and we all turned to him, like we'd forgotten he was there. I saw a steaming pile of something chunky on the ground beside him, and realized he indeed had vomited.

"Code name?" Sarah said.

"Yeah," I said, and I began to go down the roster, gesturing at everyone. "Tomboy Tara, Nigger Jim, and Fat Bobby."

"And what about you?" she asked.

"You can call me Master," I said.

"Yeah, right. How about Joey Pisspants?"

My face turned red. I shoved her, she shoved me back. No one asked for elaboration on my proposed new nickname, and I was grateful.

"How about Ugly?" I suggested, shoving her again.

"How about I kick your ass in front of your girlfriend?" she said, and slapped me upside the head. Bandit jumped up between us, wanting in on the game. His paws left a smear on Sarah's blouse, and she pushed Bandit away.

"Dammit, Joey," she said, brushing angrily at the smear with her hands. "That dog's retarded."

"At least his nickname isn't Ugly," I said.

It went on like that for a few moments more, until she hit me a pretty good one on the shoulder, and I tried not to show how much it hurt. But I thought about her threat and didn't much want to get a wedgie or noogie in front of Tara, and so ignored the further insults coming to mind and stood a safe distance from my sister, rubbing my tender arm. Jim and Tara took the opening to start talking about what we'd do, and "more than rocks" was the understatement of the year. What we were talking about doing was something, even at that age, I knew could never be undone and would be with me until the end of my days.

### 3.

We'd finished our little club conference atop Lookout Mountain with Jim, Tara, and Bobby going back to the Connolly yard to see to some preparations. Sarah, Bandit and I headed home in the off-chance that we were being watched. We didn't want the Collector to get suspicious or anything if he was the one doing the watching.

Jim had pointed out the fact that the Collector could have been watching us up on Lookout Mountain during our whole talk, and that maybe he saw us boost onto the upright stone and peer into the recess there. That when we left he'd come out of hiding, find the money, and that would be that.

When Jim said this, we all stopped what we were doing, even Bandit, as if he sensed the direness and inherent threat of Jim's words, and stood and looked around at the trees around and below us. I watched for the slightest shake of a branch; listened for the slightest snap or pop of crushing footfalls; saw and heard nothing but the forest. No one else did either.

There was nothing else we could do but proceed as we had planned. Either the Collector was watching us and now knew where the money was, or he'd concluded last night that it had been hidden somewhere far away and discreet, and was confident in his promise of violence to see the money brought to him.

The Outsiders' Club silently parted ways at the edge of the woods, without a goodbye or even a wave, as if the task we were about demanded solemnity rather than joviality. I was actually appreciative of my sister's presence, along with my dog's.

The weight I felt pushing on me seemed too heavy to bear alone.

* * *

Now, you'd think a missing body, a buttload of money, and a creepy guy in a fedora and coat calling himself the Collector threatening to kill you and your sister, would be enough for God or Fate or whatever ran the universe to put on one kid's plate at any given time. But you'd be wrong, because apparently God's got a mean streak or Fate was a neglected stepchild and is working out issues or something.

When Sarah and I arrived home we were greeted by the following scene: our dad in the yard face to face with the lumberjack-Sasquatch, Mr. Templeton. The way Bobby's father stood, legs firmly set and arms crossed at his chest, and the close proximity with which our father planted himself before the bull-like man, made it clear that this wasn't an impromptu PTA meeting.

The tension in the air was like a substance you could reach out and touch. We were in the driveway, Dad and Mr. Templeton a short distance away in the green summer grass of our yard, and though I knew Dad had seen us approach, he never once let his eyes drift away from the larger man in front of him.

I'd forgotten how truly huge Bobby's dad was. He was a mountain sprouted legs.

I remembered that day at the trailer trash neighborhood, the street like a ghost town or a Third World village. Seeing the man turn to me. The feeling of being the focus of his bored and sleepy anger, like it was something that was always there, this rage, but dulled or lazy by its constancy.

I remembered how I'd thought the bearish man could break me like a twig.

I held that same conclusion as I watched him and Dad square off.

This wasn't me he was facing this time, though, and my dad was no twig.

"Where's my boy?" Mr. Templeton said.

He had the same or similar flannel shirt and jeans he'd had on the day I'd first seen him. His lumberjack outfit. He asked this question as if he'd asked it a time or two already, and there was something like a disinterested irritation in his tone, if that made any sense. Like he expected my dad to answer, but really didn't give a shit either.

"I already told you," Dad said. "I don't know."

Dad's shirt was halfway tucked in, half hanging out like a drooping lip, as if he'd been in the middle of dressing when he'd become aware of his visitor outside. Mom was on the porch, a vague silhouette behind the screen and leaning on the handrail, wringing a dish towel or drying her hands or something else. All I knew was that towel was getting manhandled and hadn't done

146

a damn thing to anyone. Which meant Mom felt what I did. That thick tension like a fog or a curtain that you could brush at in front of your face.

Something was going to happen.

And it wasn't going to be pretty.

"And I already told you I think you're full of shit," Bobby's dad said, again, not losing his cool but just stating a fact. Bored and tired. "He's been spending a lot of time with that brat of yours," and he hooked one large thumb over his shoulder directly at me. That frightened me, him knowing I was there without even having turned to see me. Then he *did* turn to look at me, and I froze like an animal in the headlights of an oncoming car. "Where's my boy, little faggot. He's been shirking chores, that fat fuck, and I want to know where he is."

He even took a step towards me.

And that's what started it.

Dad grabbed Mr. Templeton—inches taller and many tens of pounds heavier—and spun the bigger man back around to face him.

"You don't go near my son," Dad said, and he was as cool as Mr. Templeton, only not disinterested or bored at all. He was very interested, and beneath his calm exterior, very mad. "You don't even talk to him."

Looking down at Dad, then looking to the side to see the hand clasping his shoulder, Mr. Templeton smiled a beast's smile. I saw those yellowed teeth again, stained and worn like ancient tombstones. Then his eyes rolled back to Dad, and the smile grew.

"Take your hand off me," he said to Dad, grinning in such a way that you knew he wanted exactly the opposite. He didn't want Dad to take his hand off of him at all. He wanted Dad to leave it there, so he could take it off himself.

"Get off my property," Dad said, leaving his hand right where it was.

"Tell me where my son is."

"Fuck you."

The fist came like a piston, so fast that I hardly saw it, nearly as fast as I'd ever seen Dad move, and Dad moved like an eel. I never thought such a large man could move so fast, and I wanted to shout out to warn Dad. But the motion was faster than my ability to form the words and I was stuck like Mom and Sarah, unable to do anything but watch.

Which was fine, because Dad wasn't there when the fist arrived.

He'd somehow moved *behind* Bobby's dad, came up and under the arm, hooked the larger man in some variation of a half nelson, lifted, swung with his hips, and Mr. Templeton went through the air, over my dad's back, and slammed the ground like a falling tree. A grunt issued from the bigger man as his back struck the ground and the air tried to *whoosh* out of him, but the next moment he was back on his feet and facing Dad as if he'd done nothing but tripped and stumbled.

"You're dead, little man," Mr. Templeton said and took a strong stance, his legs spread and his knees bent. He lifted his large, meat-slab fists like a boxer, bounced a few times on the balls of his feet, and started throwing punches.

If possible, and if my eyes could be trusted since I hadn't seen much the first time, Fat Bobby's dad moved even faster this time around. The punches actually buzzed through the air like large insects flapping wings.

Dad batted the first couple away with ease.

Mr. Templeton moved in closer, quickly.

Dad batted a few others away, tried a swift kick at the bigger man's legs. He may as well have tried kicking a redwood. The sound of Dad's leg hitting the other man's was like meat hitting brick. If there was any effect on Mr. Templeton, he hid it well. In fact he smiled.

Dad must have been as surprised as we were. I knew he'd kicked with his all and had expected the larger man to go down again. When he didn't, Dad paused, and that was when the next

148

punch caught him square in the head. He stumbled backwards. Mr. Templeton rushed in close, bent low, and threw some body shots. The pounding on Dad's sides and stomach sounded like hammer blows.

He took them, and he still stood, but his face scrunched up in pain.

This close in, Dad brought up a few quick knees, striking the other man in the thighs and ribs and abdomen. More grunts and gasps from Mr. Templeton, but he kept swinging, at the body, the head, switching back and forth with a steady rhythm.

Dad had his arms down, and took most of the punches on the forearms, protecting his ribs. It was like two machines pounding each other, both fueled and fired, and it was impossible to tell which was getting the worst of it.

Mom was at the steps of the porch, the screen door open, wanting to come running down and do something. She knew better than to get in the middle of such flailing, though, and could only watch.

Sarah and I knew to stay away as well.

But there was one other, and his low and menacing growl let me know he was ready, just waiting for the word. I hesitated a moment, not knowing what my dad would want me to do. Dad wasn't getting the worst of the exchange, but he wasn't giving any more either. I honestly didn't know what would happen if it continued.

Who would be standing.

And who would fall.

Somehow, unlike my dad, I didn't think Mr. Templeton would be satisfied with a fall. He wouldn't stop until my dad was a sack of pulp and broken bones.

That's what decided it.

I gave the word.

"Bandit! Go!"

And like a bullet, he did.

In one bound my dog flew over the short brick wall dividing the driveway and yard. His feet landed on the grass with cushioned thumps. Two strides to cover the distance, and then he leapt into the air and I thought: *Wow, he flies!* and I wouldn't have been surprised to see my dog sprout wings and flutter about the yard. His jump carried him into the center of Mr. Templeton's back, right between the shoulder blades. Dad had the presence of mind to see Bandit's approach, while still keeping his eyes on the other man, and when the dog struck he stepped aside and Bandit's weight and impact sent dog and man tumbling to the ground.

A flurry of teeth.

Strands of spit flying.

The speckled red points of blood raining down on the marble garden stones and walkway.

Bandit snapped and his jaws clacked, and cloth and skin alike tore under his assault. Mr. Templeton, at first surprised by this attack, then sobered by his own blood, quickly recovered and started pounding at Bandit's head and body with his fists, while trying to keep his forearms between my dog's teeth and his own face. I watched fist after fist slam into Bandit's head, his face, his body, and finally I couldn't take it anymore. I ran and jumped the low dividing wall much as Bandit had done. I landed in the yard and kept running.

"Dad! He's going to kill him!"

I screamed in pain and misery, with a fear deeper than what I'd felt when it had been my dad that had been taking the beating. Such is the irrationality, and beauty, of the love between dogs and boys.

Mom, somehow down the stairs of the porch without me seeing her, intercepted me, bear-hugged me, carried me away. I struggled, but somehow she held me in arms of iron, and I remember thinking: *Who did I get my strength from?*

I watched from within my mom's arms, my dog and Mr. Templeton going at it, and there were a few more blows to Bandit's head, each one a blow to my heart. Then Dad was there again, and he hauled Bandit off by the collar, dragged him a few feet away, told him to "*Stay!*" and he did, muzzle pink-smeared with blood, man's or his own I didn't know. Probably both.

Dad walked back towards Mr. Templeton. Shirt soaked in blood, the big man tried to stand. He was still smiling, and I thought: *He must be the devil.* Strings of spit and blood hanging from his mouth; clothes ripped, arms ripped; and he was still smiling.

He made it to one knee before Dad's kick to the ribs sent him sprawling again.

Dad knelt over him and threw a few punches to the side of the head and between the eyes, and then Mr. Templeton was still. Dad checked the man's pulse. Leaned in close to his mouth to hear the breathing.

He turned and nodded to Mom.

"Call the police," he said through his puffy and swollen face, and then Mom let go of me and went back in the house. "And an ambulance," Dad added after giving the prostrate bigger man another once over.

Free of her, I charged across the yard to my dog, kneeling and hugging him, squeezing him close, and in pain he looked wobbly and slightly delirious, and I knew my embrace must only be adding to his discomfort. But he endured it, my dog, my friend, my brother, smiling his wide smile and his long tongue hanging out, guardian of his family, proud and smiling.

### 4.

Can you guess who the responding officer was? Yup, God was taking a nice big shit on me that day, and the arrival of Sheriff Glover in his black-and-white made me want to roll myself up in a big wad of toilet tissue and flush myself away.

The fat man got out of his car as haughty as can be, this kind of wry smile on his face and the blue and red of the siren flashing casting a glow on it that made the smile seem demented. Which it probably would have seemed anyway without the dramatic lighting. An ambulance had arrived first and the drivers had taken it upon themselves to restrain and wheel Mr. Templeton away, and so it was just us and the round and smiling sheriff.

All of us were on the porch, making this sort of semicircle around Dad and Bandit, each with cold compresses to their respective faces; Dad applying his own, me pressing the cold bundle to Bandit. We watched the sheriff waddle towards us and climb the porch, the wooden stairs creaking under his weight.

He gave me a not so subtle glance before he spoke, and I know it was so I could get a nice long look at the fading cuts and bruises on his face. It was his way of saying: *I haven't forgotten.*

"Well," he said, looking squarely at Dad now, "it looks like you folks are just all kinds of trouble. And not even here a month." He made a *tsk-tsk* sound by clicking his tongue. "Not the best way to meet neighbors."

The sheriff grinned like this was a triumph.

I felt proud then for pelting another human being with rocks, and wondered if that was a sin and if I was going to burn for it.

"I told your dispatcher what happened," Mom said, a hand on Dad's shoulder.

"Yes, yes," Sheriff Glover said, nearly cutting her off. "Mr. Templeton has been a bad boy. That doesn't answer the reason why he was here, though," he said, and now looked at me again. "Have you seen his son around?"

I looked to Mom and Dad first, but they said nothing, and I knew this time around I wasn't going to receive any pardons. I was expected to answer the sheriff. Feeling trapped, with no time to think of a good lie, I told the truth. I felt like I was betraying Bobby. Knew beyond any doubt what was in store for him when he and his dad were reunited.

"Last time I saw him he was heading to the Connolly yard."

I wondered if Fat Bobby would look as bad as Dad next time I saw him. Inwardly, I shrunk and cringed, knowing I'd turned my friend over to a beating that could have been, if not avoided, at least delayed.

The sheriff nodded, and I knew what was playing in his mind, or at least an approximation, and it involved a lot of "niggers" and "coons" and "junglebunnies" with maybe a "spearchucker" or two thrown in for good measure.

"That man beats his son," Mom said. Her tone revealed she knew she was talking to a wall for all the good it would do, but it was something that had to be said and so she said it.

"That's a serious accusation," Sheriff Glover said. Then added: "And none of my concern anyway."

"This isn't fifty years ago," Dad said. "A man shouldn't get away with hitting his kid."

"Neither is this *California*," the sheriff retorted, drawing the word out like it was distasteful and made his mouth bitter. "Where any kid can sue his parents for getting a spanking."

"I have a feeling Mr. Templeton isn't the only one that hits his kid," I said, knowing I shouldn't have but unable to stop myself.

The stare the sheriff turned my way said he'd heard that and marked it, and the tally against me was growing. Payment would come, it promised. I believed him, and said nothing else.

"Inside," Mom said sharply, and, tail tucked between my legs, Bandit following me, I turned and went inside. I didn't go far, though, and turned back to creep to the side of the door to listen.

"Be assured Mr. Templeton won't be coming back on your property," Sheriff Glover said. "But I'd suggest that you folks don't stray too far from it yourselves, except for business and essentials that is, for awhile."

"You threatening us?" Mom asked.

"No, ma'am," he replied, and I was certain he had given one of his mocking tips of the hat with the "ma'am" there. "I'm just saying you folks aren't none too popular right now, and in a town this small even turds like Templeton have got friends, and those friends are your enemies now, I reckon."

With that I heard the porch creak and moan in torment as the sheriff turned and headed back down. I wondered if the Earth's plates were realigning under his weight, or if he was affecting the planet's axis of rotation and we'd be thrown into another ice age or something.

Then I thought of that look he'd given me, and things weren't so funny anymore. I wondered if they ever would be again, or if this was what awaited me all the rest of my days.

# CHAPTER EIGHT

## 1.

The day after the incident in our front yard, and the resultant confrontation with the sheriff afterwards, wasn't much better than the day itself. Dad stayed home from work, nursing his injuries and taking it easy. I wanted to go to the Connolly's to see if Bobby was okay, but Dad wanted me to stay home and I stewed in anxiety and fear for my friend. I tried to read, but couldn't concentrate on the words on the pages. Running about the yard with Bandit, who wasn't as badly hurt as he'd initially seemed, was distracting only for a while.

The ambulance had rolled away with Mr. Templeton strapped in the back, only half conscious at best, but I was pretty sure he wasn't the type of man to stay bedridden in a hospital, pitying himself, for very long. At some point, Fat Bobby and Tara had left the Connolly yard yesterday, and that meant they had gone home. And if Bobby was home when his dad got out of the hospital, things weren't going to be pretty.

"Dad," I said for the umpteenth time, plopping myself on the recliner next to the sofa, where he was lying with his head on a pillow and a compress on his head. "We've got to check on Bobby. You know what his dad's going to do."

"It's none of our business," Dad said.

His face wasn't as puffy as yesterday, but still purple and blue in places. If he'd been a lot smaller and wore white underoos, he could have passed for a Smurf.

"But it's our fault. His dad's angry with me for keeping Bobby from home all the time, and now he's angry with you for kicking his ass. He's going to take it out on Bobby."

"I said it's none of our business," he repeated. His eyes closed against the pain throbbing throughout his body, and his mouth was set thinly, teeth grinding. I knew not to press him any further. He recognized my distress even through his own, however, no doubt sympathized with it, and so added a belated: "Don't worry, son. As big an ass as Sheriff Glover is, he's now on notice about Bobby's family situation. To keep the peace between us and Mr. Templeton, he's going to want to keep tabs on him and his son."

Not fully satisfied with that answer, but knowing I wouldn't get anymore out of him, I went upstairs, where I found my sister standing in the restroom at the end of the hall. Sarah stood in the open doorway, watching me, and I knew she'd been listening. She wore a tan dress with the skirt down to her knees. Her hair was done up again like I'd seen it awhile back when she'd been getting ready for her date and I'd made fun of her, the sandal missiles launched at my head in retaliation.

For some reason she was still allowed to go out and that bothered me. Mom said it was because she was older, but just over two years didn't seem so much older to me, not enough to warrant her being treated special and me like a baby.

"Don't worry about your friend," Sarah said with genuine concern.

I was reminded of the night of the fair. How after coming home she'd come into my room and given me a hug. Standing there framed in the light and white of the restroom, I had to admit that my sister wasn't all that bad looking, and I thought of the days when maybe Tara would be spending time in the bathroom, putting on nice dresses and trying to look great for me.

156

"I'm sure he'll be okay," Sarah added.

I nodded but I couldn't fool myself. I knew Bobby was in for it, and it was my fault. Every punch or slap or kick or belt swing delivered to him when next he saw his father may as well have been delivered by my hands. It was that cut and dry to me.

But then I got to what was really on my mind, what Bobby needed to be okay for, and what I needed to get out of the house for.

"How am I going to get out tonight?" I asked.

Leaning out of the bathroom doorway, peering down the hall and towards the stairs as if to make sure no one was creeping up behind us, Sarah motioned me closer with a wave of her hand. Grabbing me by the arm, she pulled me into the restroom and swung the door so that it was only open a crack, enough to give us some privacy but also so that we could see and hear if either of our parents came trudging up the stairs.

"I'll get you out," she whispered.

"*How?*" I asked, keeping my voice low too.

"I'll have Barry pull up around ten o'clock."

Barry was the name of the guy that she'd ditched my parents for at the fair, as I'd learned in the days following. His name was seemingly one of the more frequent and important words in her vocabulary now. At breakfast and at dinner and all times between, it was Barry this and Barry that, so that you'd think Barry must have been an ayatollah or king or something, and not just some guy with a hard-on for my sister.

"You be in bed by then so Mom and Dad don't think to look in on you, but then go out the window and wait for us. I'll come walking in, then pretend like I've forgotten something at the theater or restaurant, and you get in the car while I have Mom and Dad busy. I'll have Barry drive us out to meet the others."

"Will that buy us enough time? Mom and Dad will wonder where you are if we're not back soon!"

She gave me a scowl and a sigh that spoke volumes, like she

was a frustrated special education instructor explaining things to an especially mentally handicapped student. That was me, the Dunce of Retards.

"Then I'll say we decided to stop by his house first so I could meet his parents! Don't worry! Dad will swallow anything I say, hook, line and sinker!"

I mulled this over, peeking out the crack in the door now and then to make sure the hallway was still clear. I thought her plan just might work, but then I was suspicious why she was going out of her way to help me. I told her this, making my tone accusatorial like Perry Mason, pointing at her and wagging my finger in her face. She slapped my hand away and gave me a scowl, but I repeated my question again anyways.

"Why do you want to help so bad?"

"Why do you think?" she said, and answered before I could get out even a syllable. "That creepo Collector guy said he was coming for both of us. We won't be safe until he's out of the picture."

Those words held a finality to them and I thought about our initial meeting on Lookout Mountain. I thought of Tara saying we'd need more than rocks, and I thought again about what me and my friends were planning on doing. My stomach briefly fluttered with nausea.

I thought also of what Jim and Tara and Bobby had been up to at the car yard yesterday, and the preparations they had presumably made. The things we were planning on doing were not things kids should be thinking about. They were things that maybe no one *at all* should be contemplating.

But I remembered the Collector, his long knife, and the finger flung through the air like a coin tossed. I thought of him telling us that he collected things that were owed, and sometimes he collected things for himself.

I had no doubt what category my sister and I fell into.

Of course there was the money to consider as well. I'm ashamed to say it now, but there's no reason in lying. The money occupied a sizable space in my mind. The imaginations of youth are fertile ground, and what the money could do, the things of this world that it could accomplish, weren't lost on me.

I have no doubt my sister and friends felt the same things, thought the same thoughts. I do not attempt to diminish my responsibility with that statement. Saying my friends felt the way I did about the money isn't some attempt at what psychologists call diffusion of responsibility. The stain on my soul will never diminish, never diffuse.

Not in this lifetime.

That money had been at the expense of some unknown's life, dead and rotted and now but a tangle of bones. Tied and bound and shut in a trunk, now gone as if scrubbed from existence. We wanted that money for our childish dreams, and how innocent can children be if we wanted what the dead had paid for?

## 2.

My bedside clock seemed to blink the minutes away at a torturously slow pace, like it was mocking me. I tried reading, with little success, then tried to nap, with even less success, and so finally settled on just turning out the lights and staring at the dark ceiling. The plaster contours above were fuzzy and vague in shadow.

I waited and hoped for my parents to climb the stairs and go to bed, but of course they didn't. Instead, they waited for their daughter to come home so they could quiz her on her evening out.

Did he open doors for you? Did he compliment you? What did you do? What movie did you see? I'd heard and seen the routine before in California with Mr. Greaseball, and knew my parents wouldn't settle down for the night until Sarah came home safe and sound.

The faint grinding of rubber on dirt and gravel announced her arrival. The crunches and grinding grew louder, the hum of an engine accompanying it. My chest pounded with anticipation, and I clutched my blankets in my fists.

Headlights through the window cast moving shadows like creeping things across the walls and floor of my room. The shadows passed over me in a brief eclipse, and the car pulled to a stop outside the house.

I sat up in bed, swung my legs over the edge of the mattress, and slipped on my shoes. Bandit awoke in the process, his eyes glowing in the dark like twin stars, and I shushed him softly. Creaks and stirs sounded from below as Mom and Dad got up to meet Sarah at the door.

I crept to my window and worked at it slowly so it pushed up silently. The curtains stirred in a soft and gentle evening breeze. Outside my window the apple tree swayed its branches in a leisurely dance.

Below my window and to the right, the enclosed porch was alight and the yellow cast by the bulbs seeped through the mesh screen like the ghost lights Fat Bobby had been so intent on seeing what seemed like ages ago. Sarah climbed the steps and hugged Mom and Dad both. Turning briefly to wave back at the car, she then walked inside and closed the door.

The porch lights winked off.

I swung one leg out the window and then the other, toeing the branches below me until I found a thick and sturdy one. My hands still on the windowsill for leverage and balance, the rattle of Bandit's chain collar made me look up, back into the dim interior of my room. The dog trotted to the window and peered out at me quizzically. I gave him another *shhhh* for good measure, then with one hand worked the window back down.

I knew if Sarah were to make it seem natural, I'd have only seconds before she reappeared on the porch, Mom and Dad most likely looking out the windows after her. Barry's car idling too long in the driveway, when he should have pulled away, would attract our parents' attention.

My hands left the windowsill and I turned and found the trunk of the tree. I lowered myself to awkward rungs on the scattered growth of branches. When these footholds terminated about halfway down the length of the trunk, I turned and leapt the last few feet to the lawn. I rolled with the fall to keep it as quiet as possible.

I moved fast in a crouch towards Barry's car.

I saw the lock buttons pop up as I scuttled towards the rear passenger door.

Gently, I opened it, climbed in, and shut it behind me as softly as possible. There was hardly more than a click, but in the otherwise quiet of the evening I felt as if I'd slammed the door. Waiting for Mom and Dad to come bursting out of the house, find me, and drag me back inside, I curled into a ball on the passenger seat, held my breath.

"Hey, kid," said the almost too handsome blond guy from the front seat. His pompadour bounced with the motions of his face and skull muscles.

"Hey, Fairy," I said.

"What'd you say?" he asked, turning in his seat to look back at me.

"Hey, Barry."

He looked at me like he was about to say something else, but then the light from the porch came on again and the slaps of sandaled feet flopping down the steps, coming our way across the lawn, silenced us both. Barry reached across the seat to pull the handle and swing the door open for my sister. Sarah climbed in the seat and when she turned to look at Barry I saw her eyes roll to look at me in her peripheral.

"Let's go, Barry," she said.

"*Let's go, Fairy*," I mocked in a high voice.

"Hey, kid," Barry said and started to turn around, until Sarah stopped him with a nudge of an elbow. I took that as Mom and

Dad still being at the door or the windows and watching. So Barry, instead, looked at me through the rearview mirror. "I'm doing you a favor, kid. I don't know if you're worried about me taking your sister away or something ..."

"Please, take her away," I said.

"Shut up, Joey," Sarah said. Then to Barry: "Just go."

I felt the car start to back out and then turn and shift into gear. We started down the road and when I thought we were a safe distance away I sat up and put on my seatbelt. Barry was looking at me in the rearview again and I gave him a winning smile, showing my pearly whites.

"Look kid, there's no reason for us to be rude to each other."

I stuck one hand beneath my shirt, under my arm. Cupping it there, I pumped my arm up and down a few times so that the mock farts squeaked loud and good.

"Was that rude enough?" I said. When he opened his mouth to respond, I gave him a few more.

"What the hell's wrong with your brother?" he said to Sarah, and I timed my armpit farts so that they coincided with his words. *What* FART! *the* FART! *hell's* FART! *wrong* FART! *with* FART! *your* FART! *brother?*

"Mom dropped him on his head," she said, crossing her arms and looking out the window. I knew I'd embarrassed her and was rightly proud.

"At least I have a head and not two asses," I said.

"I think this is going to be a long night," Barry said, and I made sure to accompany his words with another armpit fart orchestra.

* * *

We reached the end of the dirt road that led to the woods, the same road I had used to come to the stream where I'd first met

162

Fat Bobby. The same road from which Sheriff Glover had given chase, swinging his nightstick like a kid after a piñata. Barry put the car in park and turned to my sister.

"You sure you don't want me to come with you guys?"

"No," Sarah said, shaking her head. "Joey's just meeting some friends of his for something."

"Out here?" Barry prodded. "In the woods? At this hour?"

"Best time and place for Satanic worship," I said. Both of them turned and gave me exasperated and angry looks, and I realized I wasn't helping any, but it was fun and I couldn't help myself. "We cover ourselves in goat's blood and masturbate."

They did their best to ignore me.

"How're you going to get back?" Barry asked.

"We'll walk," Sarah said. "It isn't far."

Barry's expression said he didn't like that idea at all, and he took a moment to look around, peering at the wall of trees and the night sky outside the car. I knew what he was thinking. The silence save the breeze and the bobbing and swaying of the trees, the dark and shadows: anything could be out there. Though your mind on the verge of adulthood or something close to it insisted there was nothing more dangerous out here at night than there was in the day, another part of your mind, perhaps some primitive genetic remainders of distant and long dead ancestors, told you otherwise. This voice warned you to remain near the fire, stay in the light.

"I don't know about this," Barry said. "I think maybe I should wait for you. I can give you guys a ride back after ... you do whatever it is you're doing out here."

I looked at the time on the digital clock set into the dashboard, saw it was almost ten thirty. We had to find Jim and the others and get set up before midnight. I opened the door and stepped out, started walking towards the woods.

"Joey!" my sister called after me. "Wait!"

"We don't have much time," I said, turning to look back at her.

She got out, then leaned back in the open door and said: "Fine, wait, but I can't say how long this will be."

Sarah closed the door and jogged awkwardly in her skirt and sandals to catch up, her purse slapping against her side like a riding crop. The headlights of Barry's car spotlighted us as we stepped through the trees and into the forest. This gave us some light to see by for the first several yards before dwindling out and leaving us in near pitch-dark.

The zip of Sarah opening her purse sounded serpentine in the night. When the beam of the flashlight she'd stowed in there blinked on, I was relieved.

"Let's go," she said, and we followed the small light into the greater darkness.

\* \* \*

We met Jim and Tara at the bend in the stream where not so long ago a fat kid had been pelted by rocks and sticks by three older guys who'd later held us at knife point in a mockup haunted house. Jim was wearing a heavy dark sweater that billowed out and made him look heavier than he was, with a backpack slung across one shoulder. Tara was wearing jeans and a sweater too, though her top didn't make her look fat at all, but clung to her in places that I would've liked to investigate closer if we'd been alone.

"Where's Bobby?" I asked, fearing the worst, knowing that the worst in my head was probably fairly accurate.

"He didn't show up," Jim said, his eyes set in his dark face like little bright stars dangling in the night.

I recapped for them what had happened at our place the day before, the fight between my dad and Mr. Templeton. We looked about ourselves and at each other for a few anxious moments, wondering how this affected things, thinking about our friend. I knew we were all wondering if he was curled in a ball right now, somewhere in that little trailer of his, being whipped or pummeled and whimpering for his dad to stop. Or worse, maybe not whimpering or begging at all, because maybe his dad had gone too far this time, seeing *my* dad, seeing Bandit, seeing me as he brought the belt or fists down on his son.

I resolved then and there that I had to find out about my friend, even if I had to go to the trailer by myself. But first was this business tonight.

"Okay," I said, "so we make do without him."

The words out of my mouth made me feel like the most callous asshole ever, but there was nothing to be done about it. Not tonight anyway. Though I'd met him only once, I knew the Collector wasn't going away until he got what he wanted. You got that message loud and clear when he was holding a big bowie knife to your throat and tossing severed fingers around like jacks or marbles.

"You guys got everything?" I asked Jim and Tara, and Jim stepped closer to me, shrugging the backpack off his shoulder and kneeling to unzip it. Sarah, Tara, and I knelt too, looking into the depths of the pack as he opened it, seeing what was there, staring at it, then staring at each other.

The look that passed among us spoke of things beyond our years, things we weren't ready for. Things that once done could never be undone and would stay with us for the rest of our days.

"Good," I said, giving the contents of the backpack one last lingering look, then standing. Tara and Sarah stood as well, and Jim zipped up the pack again and hefted it back over his shoulder. I looked at my sister and my friends again. I was suddenly afraid. I wished Bandit were with me. "We all know what to do?"

They nodded.

"Then let's get started," I said.

I wondered with a stark realization if this would be the night that I saw some or all of them for the last time. That realization—that things could go wrong, that we were ill-equipped players in a game far greater than us—made me want to run and hide.

And I almost did. Then and there, I almost turned and ran.

The moving waters of the stream whispered secrets in the night; tantalizing, urgent, frightening. But also alluring, seductive, and mysterious. I didn't run.

Instead, we, the members of the Outsiders' Club, looked at each other one last time. Some of us nodded slightly. Some of us offered weak, half smiles.

Then we parted, my sister and I going west, Tara and Jim east, and Bobby out there somewhere, directionless, lost to us for the time, lost to us perhaps forever. Or maybe all of us were lost, and we just didn't know it yet.

### 3.

The rutted and pitted access road, overgrown with weeds and detritus, looked like the abandoned road of some old pagan city long gone to ruin. With every pop and snap of a twig, there was the expectation that something would dart from the shadows; something with a wide-brimmed fedora and long flowing trench coat. Something wielding a large, gleaming knife. It would grab and snatch at us, pull one or perhaps both of us into the shadows and feast upon us with its lone long, sharp tooth.

I knew he was out there, the Collector. I could feel him, waiting, watching. Watching from within the shadows of his upturned collar and fedora.

In front of us, the car came into view, catching the moonlight in its windows and headlights and patches of body yet untouched by the skin of rust spreading upon it like a cancer. The doors were open as before, like wings. The old bent grill and bumper grinned at us.

And from the shadows, as if stepping out from another dimension, a portal from darkness to darkness, the Collector arrived. He stopped in front of the old dead car, his collar upturned and the hat pulled low. Like last time, nothing of his face could be seen but a pale blur and the whites of eyes looking at us.

It was time.

I remembered his words, his dark poetry.

*This is the night. These are the times.*

No words had ever seemed truer to me for some reason. They rang in my head like the grim tolling of a despondent church tower bell.

"The money," he said, his voice like the voice of a poet too. Casual, fluidic, underscored with restrained passions. Passions of pain and violence. Blood passions.

I couldn't speak. I knew I had to, but it seemed as if my voice had left me for greener, and safer, pastures. Somehow Sarah found hers, though, and again I was filled with an appreciation and love for my sister that I'd rarely consciously felt.

"We have it," she said, and turned to point behind us. "It's up on a small hill down the road, past the stream."

The Collector's hands moved to his pockets. They shuffled in there, and I remembered with stark clarity what had been in those recesses last time. What I had no doubt was in there this time as well. Just a casual motion, as if he were turning about a set of keys or a pile of change.

His shadowed visage moved the slightest of degrees, looking at Sarah, looking at the road beyond her.

"No tricks," he said, not a question, not a request.

Sarah shook her head, the beam of the flashlight playing on the ground between us and him. Still he didn't move. I think he could see through us, see our thoughts and our deceits. In the shadows of his upturned collar and wide-brimmed hat, that small cave of lightlessness, was something altogether inhuman. Something that could see things we couldn't, that processed ideas and thoughts and feelings we'd never understand. A way of perceiving that was *impossible* for us.

He doubted us.

He sensed our intentions.

The knife came out: a flick of the wrist, a dance of fingers. The twirl of the blade like a pirouette. A flash of metal.

He didn't believe us, and now came the cutting. Unless we could regain his trust in our fear. I remembered what had made him believe me two nights ago when he held the knife to my throat. The thing that had probably saved my life.

I did what I had to.

For the second time that summer, I pissed my pants.

The warmth of it spreading across the front of my jeans was startling in the cool night. Trickles of it ran down my legs. The smell of it; tart, astringent.

The Collector saw it. The vaguest sense of motion in that cave of shadows: a smile. He knew the fear. We all did. Its bitter smell filled the distance between us.

"Be afraid, little boy," he said, and the knife spun again in his long and dexterous fingers. "But not of death, not this night. Not if I get what I came to collect."

I nodded, swallowing a lump in my throat the size of a basketball.

"There will be a death," he said. "We all owe one. But show me what I want and yours will be for another day. That I promise."

I nodded again. Tears threatened at the corners of my eyes. A knot in my stomach twisted, squirmed. My heart bucked and thumped a primal, tribal beat.

The Collector motioned with his knife, and I knew the command: *Walk.*

I turned, and with Sarah at my side we started back the way we came.

For awhile, save for the sound of our footfalls, the crunching of leaves and twigs underfoot sounding like the snapping of small and brittle bones, we walked in silence. Silence and darkness don't go well together, not for me. The darkness, the inability to see things more than a few feet around you, is unsettling by itself. But with silence, and no idea what is out there and no sounds to identify it, the feeling of helplessness and vulnerability is intensified a thousandfold.

Then the Collector began to speak, and I wished for the silence to return.

"I once collected from a woman and her family," he began. "She owed to my employer at the time and refused to pay. She said the contract was null and void. She hadn't the authority to make that determination. And so I was sent to collect."

He paused briefly as if to let it sink in, to make sure we were paying attention.

"I collected from the woman and from her husband, and from their two daughters," he said. He said this all as if recounting a particularly fond familial memory. Maybe a barbecue with Uncle Ned, or the graduation of a favorite nephew. "There is collecting, and then there is collecting. Sometimes it's only business, and sometimes there's the opportunity for gratification. That night I was intensely gratified."

That last hung in the air, undefined, unexplained, and for that I was grateful.

"That was long ago," the Collector said. "It was winter, it was cold, not at all like these warm summer months we're in now. But that night I was warm and the winter didn't touch me. Do you understand?"

I understood nothing of what the fucking nutjob was saying. I only knew this whole thing had been a bad idea, the fucking king of all bad ideas, and I wished that I could hop into a time machine, reverse myself a couple of days, and tell my dad about this freak. Dad would take care of it, or he'd call the police and they would. Then I thought of Sheriff Glover, and didn't know if that last was true or not.

I understood nothing of what the Collector said, but I nodded.

Or maybe I understood only too well, and was afraid of that knowledge.

"Once, in Mexico," the Collector said as we continued walking, the swell of the mountain seen rising above the tree line ahead of us, "there was this rich *hombre* who lived in this beautiful private *villa*. He had something of importance to a man in Brazil. This something of importance wasn't rightfully the Mexican's. He had stolen it. I was sent to collect this item and return it to the Brazilian."

I wanted nothing of his collection stories. I snuck a glance at my sister from the corner of my eye. Saw her looking back at me with the same look of disgust and fear. I wanted to reach out and hold her hand. Smelling of piss, scared, I wanted to hold my sister's hand.

Yet I feared the consequences of the slightest movement. The Collector had told me to walk, nothing else, and I didn't want to give him any reason to collect from me.

"The Mexican's estate was large and had many guards," the Collector said. "To move with shadows, though, is a talent I learned long ago, out of necessity. I moved through the Mexican's estate with ease, unseen. I came upon the Mexican in a lush and silken bedroom making use of a little *niña*. The kind of youth only money can buy. He didn't notice me until I was at his bedside, and when I asked for the item owed he reached for the nightstand and the gun inside. He was fat and slow. The girl screamed, and I silenced her, and then I made the Mexican tell me where the item was. In time, he told me. I collected the item, and then I collected more, from him, for myself. Do you under-stand?"

Standing beneath the rise of Lookout Mountain, its shade over us like a blanket, I nodded. Up there, somewhere, were Tara and Jim, and I wanted to scream for them to run, to forget the whole thing. To run and get the police, to run and get my dad, but I knew I'd die from the teeth of the knife before the first word was even out.

Sensing my hesitancy, the Collector felt compelled to extol upon us one last treatise on collecting.

"I have collected for many individuals, for many years. My employers are numerous, but the outcome is always the same. They get what they want, as do I. I have never failed, and I never will. My present employer will get what is his, as well. That is my reputation, as collector, and reputation is everything. Do you understand?"

I did indeed understand more of the Collector now. He had been doing this for a long time, probably longer than I'd been alive. He was a man, but during the course of his life, the pursuits of his profession, he had become something more. Something of this world, and beyond it. Something malignant; something poisonous. I felt sullied and tainted just by his presence.

I nodded my understanding.

"It's ... up there," I said, somehow finding my voice. "All of it."

"Let's go," he said, and my sister and I started up the rocky incline.

I had to fight the urge to race up the hill. Each foothold and handhold I placed with a determined and consciously feigned care, as if I were unfamiliar with the climb. Eagerness to get to the top might betray mere fear and alert the Collector to something else.

I took an opportunity with one difficult foothold to look down, and I saw the Collector still there, yards away, at the bottom. The bowie knife flashed in his hands like lightning, and yet it was an idle motion almost without thought. He was standing there, looking up, but not looking at me or even at the top of the mountain. Maybe he was looking at the sky and the moon, and maybe the strange gears of his mind were in the middle of some dark and alien purpose I'd never comprehend. That I'd never *want* to comprehend.

This is the night. These are the times.

I realized he was made for the night, and the night for him.

Then he looked at me looking at him. The pale blur of his face in the dimness. A smear of off-white and the faintest hint of eyes and mouth.

He started up after us, and I turned and continued climbing. We made it to the top before him, and Sarah and I stood at the peak and looked about. At first I didn't see my friends, and then my eyes roamed up the wall of stone and there they were lying flat atop it, staring down at us, vague in the moonlight like wispy spirits.

Except for the gun in Jim's hands, the metal gleaming in the night. On his belly atop the upright stone, he held the pistol in both hands, aimed in our general direction.

I heard the approach of the Collector from behind us. The tumble of dislodged stones and pebbles, tiny avalanches, as he scaled Lookout Mountain. Turning, I thought of kicking him as he rose to join us, sending him sprawling back down the rocky hill. But he was *right there*, hands clasping the edge and pulling himself up, and the knife, the knife in the moonlight, silver streaks across the blade like wicked smiles.

I turned back towards the peak of the small mountain, and the upright stone like a large tombstone. Jim, atop it, motioned us with a nod to move aside. Sarah did, but I was too slow, and then the Collector was standing behind me, one arm wrapping around me like the first time, the knife at my throat.

The Collector saw them immediately.

The blade pressed dangerously against my flesh.

"No tricks," he said, his voice still calm and stoic even with a gun pointed at him. "That was the deal."

"You're a liar," I said, my voice little more than a wheeze with a knife at my throat, and the smell of piss permeating the air like a strong and stringent perfume. "You ... would have killed us ... anyway."

172

"Perhaps," he said in his silken poet's tone. "Perhaps not. Now you'll never know."

"We ... we don't want to hurt you!" Jim said from his perch, his voice tremulous and high. Not at all like the confident kid I'd met not so long ago. "Just leave my friend alone! Go away and leave us alone!"

"I'm afraid that, my dear boy," the Collector replied, his minty breath puffing against my cheek, "is not an option."

I knew it was coming then, the end, the end of me, the end of it all. There was going to be a lot of collecting, a harvest of collecting. I doubted Jim could shoot a man, even in self-defense. Shooting cans off a stump in your backyard, and shooting a human being, were worlds apart. Even if Jim *did* take a shot, I doubted he could kill this man, this *thing*, the Collector, in one shot once he slit my throat and went for the others. I doubted if bullets, if anything, could kill this creature that held me. It was over, all of it, and I'd only just met these friends, who in such a few short weeks were the best friends I'd ever had. Worst of all, one kiss, and one kiss only, from the most beautiful girl I'd ever known.

A slight sense of motion as the Collector's fingers tightened their grip on the knife. The tensing of movement to come. The cutting.

A sound below us.

The stomping of feet. Heavy, thunderous as they grew closer. Shouts. Panting. The crackle and snap of branches.

The Collector relaxed his hold on me so that he could turn and look down. Acting before thinking, I slipped down against him, under his loose arms and the guillotine blade, fell to the ground and rolled away, towards my sister and the upright stone and my friends with the gun above me. The Collector looked at us, then looked back down the slope of the mountain to whatever was coming.

Something heavy hit the incline and scrabbled up, kicking

loose cascades of pebbles and dirt. Heavy breathing could be heard even from this distance. Shouts pursued the climber, the voice violent and familiar, and more footfalls close behind.

The Collector turned again towards us and then looked down once more, uncertain.

"*Don't move*," Jim said to him in little more than a whisper, and the Collector faced us and the gun pointed at him. His motions were lithe and casual and unbothered. He seemed a lazy and complacent audience member watching a boring play on a lackluster stage.

The second set of footfalls below and out of sight at the bottom of the mountain slowed, then started up the incline also, kicking and stomping footholds into the face of it. Shouting still, wordless grunts and noises of intended violence carried up to us. Almost at the top now and I knew who was coming, both of them, pursued and pursuer, by the shouts of the second and the promise of pain he brought with him.

"Bobby!" I yelled. "Don't come up!"

But there he was, clawing up over the edge now, meaty hands grasping and pulling and him rolling over the top. He didn't see the Collector until the man was grabbing at him and pulling him up and wrapping an arm around his throat and bringing the knife up, sliding it between two rolls of chin.

Bobby's face was frantic and confused. He looked at us across the peak of the mountain, saw Sarah and I standing and Tara and Jim on top of the rock with the gun. His eyes tried to roll down and to the side at the sound of his dad's ascent, kicking and slapping stone and dirt for purchase. The size of the man, the mountain of him, came over the edge and arose, like a leviathan from the ocean of night and shadow.

The Collector stepped aside as Mr. Templeton rose to full height.

Bobby's father, streaked with sweat and glimmering in the night, looked about. He saw the Collector holding his son, and the knife in the shadowy man's hands. He saw us and the gun, and his gaze narrowed on me and Sarah, and he smiled. His face was bandaged and purple with bruises, and his smile was gapped in places by missing teeth.

In the arms of the Collector, Fat Bobby was likewise streaked with sweat and reminded me of a large and wet Thanksgiving turkey. His face was bruised as well, his mouth bloody, and a knot the size of a golf ball perched atop his forehead. I wondered how many other bruises, or worse, were hidden underneath Bobby's clothing.

Images of him huddled in his bedroom, or what served as a room in their trailer, the belt and fists and kicks raining down, came to me. The pain, the resigned horror at what had always been endured, the hopelessness. The blows still coming and nothing you could do about it.

Such an existence made no sense to me.

I hated the bull man before me all the more.

"That's my son," Mr. Templeton said, facing the Collector now and pointing as if for emphasis in case the other man didn't know what he was talking about. "Give me my son."

"I'm afraid that can't be done," the Collector said, his voice like soft music from the darkness about his face. "These children have something of mine."

"Let Bobby go or I'll fucking blow your head off!"

Jim's voice from above was sudden and loud and made me jump.

The Collector ignored him and focused on Bobby's father.

"There is money here," he said in his lilting tone. "Lots of it. Help me collect it from these children, and perhaps you can walk away with a bit of it."

"Money, huh?" Mr. Templeton said and his ruined face showed interest. Fat Bobby jiggled and quivered in stark terror in the iron grasp of the Collector. He watched his dad as if seeing an alien creature. "And where is this money?"

175

"I was just about to acquire that information," the Collector said. "But there was the little problem of a gun ..." he said and then his arm shot out like he was casting dice. The arc of the blade flashed through the space between us.

I thought it was coming for me. Rooted as I was by fear, I waited for the blade to find me, pierce my heart and bleed my life away.

But the air parted above me as it passed, and a yelp of pain from Jim followed its passing. The pistol discharged and a thunder close to my ear drowned out the rest of the world.

I slumped back against the stone in pain, cupping the side of my head. The world around me spun in kaleidoscopic swirls and rollercoaster tilts and loops.

Bobby was cast aside like a fat and doughy rag doll by the Collector. His face collided with rock and he remained on the ground, unmoving.

Mr. Templeton charged across the small space and met the Collector with a thud. The momentum carried them both down and over the side of the mountain. The tumbling and smacks and thumps of their descent were like drumbeats.

A brief rustle of motion as I felt more than saw Jim's form roll off the stone above and thump down beside me. He moved and groaned in pain, and though I was glad to see him alive my eyes fixed on what dropped along with him.

The gun clattered against the stone floor beneath me with a metallic clacking. I saw in blurs and whorls and tried to grab it. The world tilted again as I moved and I vomited hot and steaming chunks that splattered the ground like a gruesome rain.

Tara jumped down from above, knelt before me, found the gun, snatched it up. She strode the few yards to the edge and peered over. Sarah crab-walk shuffled on her knees between me, Jim, and Fat Bobby, her hands coming away from each of us bloody. The scarlet wetness alight by the moon was very red.

I'd never seen so much blood before. I wondered how much

of it was mine, how much that of my friends.

The thunder of gunshots clapped atop our little mountain, startlingly loud even through the ringing in my head. I jumped with each explosion, my hands to my ears, and looked to their source.

Tara stood at the precipice of the hill, her arm outstretched over the brink and pointing down. The pistol in her grip issued a curl of smoke from the muzzle, like a ghost snake rising.

The drumming in my ears faded and I brought my hands away and there was blood there, but I could hear, and I heard rocks and dirt sliding down the hillside. Thumps and grunts. I crawled over to Tara with the smoking gun, and at the edge I looked down and there was Mr. Templeton looking back up at us far below.

But his head was backwards, the rest of his body belly down against the forest floor. His arms and legs were bent at weird and impossible angles, like an action figure in broken poses.

A few feet from Mr. Templeton, the Collector lay sprawled in the bushes, his fedora still on his head even after falling so far so that I thought maybe it was part of him, attached to him like a strange organ. His coat spread out from beneath him, wide and open like the wings of an insect.

Near his right shoulder two holes like eyes stared back at me, though these eyes bled. The cloth of his black shirt was torn about the holes.

Holes in cloth, holes in flesh.

Seeing these, I wished for a hole of another sort, to bury myself in and hide from all that had transpired.

The Collector, motionless, collecting nothing, yet still I feared him and looked away. Only to see the other bodies strewn about, those of my friends, and I buried my face in my hands so I saw nothing.

**4.**

Barry, having heard the gunshots, came minutes later, rushing through the trees like a would-be hero, too late in the last reel of a movie. Meeting him at the bottom of the hill, we looked at him, saw him take in the bodies of Mr. Templeton and the Collector, and the horror on his face was what we all felt inside.

Jim, a hand pressed tightly to the nasty gash on his shoulder, wanted to check on the Collector. He took a step in that direction before Barry stopped him. Told him that we shouldn't disturb anything. This was a crime scene and the police would take care of everything. None of us put up much of a fight against this proclamation.

I least of all. I just wanted out of there.

Barry told us to follow him back to the car and he'd take us all over to the hospital and call the police. Once, as we started away, I looked over my shoulder back at where Mr. Templeton and the Collector lay sprawled. Whether it was a trick of the moonlight, shadow, or wind I thought I saw the merest twitch from beneath that fedora and high collar.

Trick of the light or not, I quickened my pace.

At Barry's car we loaded ourselves in, and on the dark roads in the heavy night, only the headlights shining through the bleakness about us, it seemed the world had vanished, abandoning us.

We drove into town and arrived at the hospital and its comforting world of white.

\* \* \*

A trip to the police station was unnecessary, as they came to us at the hospital. As did our parents. With a little protesting, Jim, Bobby and I got to stay in the same room. Jim was stitched up at the shoulder where the Collector's knife had stuck him; Bobby's face was cleaned and patched up; and various things were stuck in my ear as the doctor snapped his fingers a couple times to make sure I could hear.

Like a small band or tribe, our parents stood outside the room and came in after the doctor was done. They were all in robes and flannels and slippers like maybe that was the traditional garb of their culture. Mr. Connolly tall and thin and dark; Tara's dad, wiry and gawky and with the hawkish face, her mom moving around Tara like a guard setting a perimeter; Mom and Dad, staring at me and Sarah, sending us those private telepathies that said there was a lot to answer for, and we would, oh, by God, those looks told us, we would.

I couldn't help but notice that Bobby, save for us his friends, had no family and was alone, and I wondered what that felt like. Even if you hated your dad, as I was pretty sure he did, there must be something inside that was different when he was no longer around. Something gone and maybe a hole where it had been.

Sheriff Glover showed up but Mom and Dad refused to allow him to be the one to interview us, and so things were on hold until other officers arrived. The police questioned us with our parents present and it was Fat Bobby who spoke first and we listened and got the gist of what he was saying and so formulated our story around that. He told the police how we had a club and we met at this abandoned car on one of the forest access roads and just talked about stuff and played games and such. We had agreed to get together at night sometime, thinking it would be cool and spooky, and so we had set it up. But then his dad found out and wouldn't let him go and started to beat him. Sarah and I picked it up from there and we were as honest as could be and told how Sarah had asked her boyfriend to sneak me and her out at night to take us out to the woods where we'd meet the others. Jim and Tara told how they'd arrived together and met us and how the four of us had waited a couple minutes for Bobby, but when he didn't show up we went on by ourselves.

At the old Buick we found someone else there. Someone in a wide-brimmed hat and a long coat, and it was here that our story necessarily spiraled into lies again. This strange man asked us to take off our clothes, I told the deputies. We said no and he took out a large knife. We ran, and he ran after us.

We ran to the mountain and climbed up it, the strange man in the coat and hat still chasing us. Here Bobby picked up the story again, saying how he tried sneaking out of the trailer so that he could still meet us, and how his dad caught him and started to hit him again. So Bobby had started to run and his dad, drunk and slow, followed him. Bobby went to the old Buick on the access road first, and when he didn't find us there he headed on to the mountain. There he saw us and climbed up to us and his dad followed.

Barry started to speak for the first time and that was when his parents arrived at the hospital. Seeing them in their silk pajamas I realized again that he wasn't anything like Sarah's greaseball in California, but Barry and his family weren't like us either. And I think maybe that's why Sarah liked him so much. He was from a different world than ours, and had money and was polite and well mannered, and maybe those things were appealing to a girl.

Then I wondered why Tara liked me because I didn't have any of that. I wasn't too well mannered; I'd almost gotten us killed a few times; and what money I may have had was blood money. But Barry's story interrupted this train of thought, and I listened as he told the police how he'd heard some gunshots and left the car to come find us. His disheveled yet still dignified parents coddled him and engulfed him in hugs at this revelation.

*Gunshots?* one of the deputies said, and so looking down, avoiding his father's gaze, Jim told how he'd snuck out one of his father's guns and brought it with him. He thought maybe it'd be cool to show us all and maybe shoot a few cans or bottles off some stumps or something. Mr. Connolly's face filled with a fire then, and I knew Jim's lies for our sake was costing him dearly, that the downcast of his eyes and shame in his face was genuine and he wasn't at that moment lying about anything. His father had had a deep trust in him and Jim had broken it. Intentionally and for good purpose to protect us against the Collector, but that neither the police nor our parents could know about.

There'd been a struggle between Mr. Templeton and the strange man in the coat and hat. During this melee the man in the coat had thrown his knife. Hitting Jim, the gun had discharged and Jim had dropped it. In the course of their brawl, Mr. Templeton and the other man went over the side of the mountain. Tara had picked up the gun and walked to the edge. Both men were right there, she said, just a few feet down on a small ledge of rock, fighting, and then they'd both seen her and reached for her and she'd pulled the trigger.

She wasn't sure if she'd hit either or both of them, Tara said through the sobs that shook her as she took up the narrative. But both men stumbled backwards, fell again, and tumbled all the way down.

The story told, or at least a version of it, we stood or sat there in the hospital room and waited for what would befall us. By the faces of the police and our parents, a great shit storm was a-blowing.

## 5.

The story was in the local paper for weeks.

Jim's father was fined heavily for his gun finding its way into the hands of minors and all his firearms were confiscated from his home. Bobby was put into a group home for a few days until my mom and dad did some heavy and persistent legwork, after which he was placed in our home until his case could be further reviewed by Child Protective Services and the state. For having shot a man, Tara's parents were required to provide her with counseling, and I didn't see her for over a week. Sarah and I were restricted to the house, and so I really didn't see much of anything.

Then another week passed and finally I saw the light of day again.

I met my friends at Lookout Mountain after calling them all, and we stood there not looking at each other but looking at the upright stone and the top of it. Finally Jim walked over and boosted himself up. He peered down inside and then looked back at us.

"It's still there," he said, and we exchanged glances.

My sister was with us, indelibly part of the club now, having seen what she'd seen, been through what she had, what we all had. I looked at her, she looked at me, and though the day was warm and bright it somehow seemed as dark as the night it had all happened. Jim reached inside the fissure between the stones and started pulling the sacks out one by one and tossing them down among us. When he was done he jumped back down and we made a circle around the sacks of money.

"Are we sure we want to do this?" he said. "After all we've been through?"

Tara held up the box of matches and we all leaned forward and took a couple out.

"I guess that answers that," Jim said, rolling his own matches between his fingers.

With scratches and hisses we all struck the heads of our matches in turn and knelt and applied the small flames to the bundles of money. We watched the flames grow and lick the air, and we wondered how long before someone noticed the smoke. The smoke wasn't thick, but it was gray and black and conspicuous against the blue sky. With my feet I kicked stray bundles closer to the center of the blaze. Seeing what I was doing everyone else followed suit. Soon, the whole mound was ablaze, and the heat wafting off of it was palpable and uncomfortable.

"Millions of dollars," Jim said, "up in smoke."

But his heart wasn't in the words, and I knew he wasn't terribly disappointed. Neither was I, and I don't think any of us were. Mr. Templeton looking up at me from the bottom of Lookout Mountain, crooked and broken like a toy was what I was thinking about, and other thoughts like it. The bound and rotted skeleton in the trunk of the Buick with the hole in its skull; the Collector's knife at my throat, then at Bobby's; Tara at the precipice, gun in hand, the flashes of it firing.

The Collector …

When the police had gone to search the access road and then the mountain, they'd found everything as we'd said, except for one thing. There were spent bullet casings, and a knife, and at the bottom of the hill, crumpled and broken, Mr. Templeton.

But no man in a coat and hat, though they'd found a crushed bush where he'd landed, and footprints leading off into the woods. Blood presumably from bullet wounds made another trail along with the prints. Lots of blood. The police assured us he couldn't have gotten far after losing so much blood.

But we knew differently.

He'd obviously made it far enough. They didn't find him.

I tried to pretend it was over, as I and the rest of the Outsiders' Club stood atop Lookout Mountain and watched the money burn and the ashes carried away, some in the breeze, some down the slopes and mixed into the grass and trees. I told myself that maybe wild animals, like coyotes or bobcats, had collected the Collector when he'd finally collapsed from exhaustion and blood loss.

I tried to tell myself many things, but none of them brought the slightest comfort.

Because I think I understood him now. I remembered his poetry and it echoed in my mind whenever the silence allowed the memories to stir.

*This is the night. These are the times.*

Life itself is on loan, a price that must ultimately be collected.

PART THREE

# This is the Night

# CHAPTER NINE

## 1.

Try as I might, I couldn't be family to Fat Bobby. He had been alone at his father's funeral—my parents, Sarah and I having driven him to the cemetery, but at his insistence not accompanying him to the coffin—and he'd been alone ever since. I tried to understand his sadness, depression, or whatever it was, for a wicked and evil man, but I couldn't. He'd been freed from his prison, the monster had been slain, and yet he moped around as if still bound by what was gone, and that irritated me.

This irritation on my end worried me. I remembered what I'd felt like initially befriending this kid, and how it had made me feel good being there for him. Whether showing him the wonders of comics or listening to him on a hilltop talk about wanting to get away from it all; being there for another human being had stirred something in me that I now had trouble retrieving.

I think I understood on some level what was happening. It wasn't just Fat Bobby and his despair over a dead father who didn't deserve a single tear shed for him. So much had changed about the people, and the world, around me. It was as if I were seeing the world through a prism and the image of things was broken up. I was seeing behind it all, catching a glimpse of the true nature of things.

Since the night on Lookout Mountain and the death of Bobby's father and the disappearance of the Collector, Tara and I hadn't spent a single moment alone. We didn't touch or hold hands, and a second kiss like the first at the fair seemed impossible and distant, like an astronomical body.

*This is the night. These are the times.*

The Collector's words lived on in my mind, haunting me even though the man himself was gone. The fedora and the coat and the shadows they cast were thrown far and wide and seemed to eclipse the rest of my life. In the aftermath of death, something I'd never truly seen until the broken neck and crooked face of Mr. Templeton at the bottom of the hill, nothing seemed the same. They *couldn't* be the same.

Fat Bobby was tainted by his father's death, in a way, as strongly as he'd been tainted by the man in life. The rest of us were tainted also, by the desire for money that was blood bought and never ours, and our momentary claim over it was paid in death. Maybe that's why Tara and I couldn't touch each other. Stained by the pain and suffering our actions had inadvertently caused, such a warmth and comfort as human contact maybe wasn't ours to have.

We didn't deserve it.

Not merely an eight-hour stretch when the earth had turned and the sun had left our hemisphere, *this* was the night: pain and death and the memory of it playing endlessly in a loop in your mind. The darkness that pervaded the mind, heart, and spirit, born of the grim things in life that were always there. Catch a glimpse of the devil and maybe he never went away but camped out in the corners of consciousness, ready to hold up the pictures of sins and remind us all of how far we'd fallen.

These are the times.

I couldn't read the things I'd so enjoyed reading since as far back as I could remember. I'd open a book, lying on my bed or sitting on the porch, and five minutes later I'd close it again. The words wouldn't come together, they didn't make sense. The story they built page after page fell absently through my mind like sand through a sieve.

I walked the house aimlessly, and Bobby did the same. We passed each other like lost drivers on a directionless highway, feeding off the invisible hurt and silent suffering of each other.

I think he disgusted me a little.

And I disgusted myself.

My sister and I didn't so much avoid each other, as we did wordlessly agree with tentative nods and furtive glances that maybe a little distance was necessary. Although we were brother and sister and annoyed each other, I think we both knew that the kind of barrier that was between me and Bobby couldn't be allowed to divide family.

But we could give each other a respectful buffer. A measure of time to permit the healing that only time could effect.

There seemed no cure to it, no end. Just day after day of the muck and mire, the heavy shadow over us and nightmares that overflowed from sleep to wakefulness. My parents felt it as well. After Dad reluctantly went back to work it was just Mom in the house, and she'd try to talk to me at times, ask how I was doing, if I was sleeping well, if there was anything I wanted to talk about. She said that Bobby and I should go out and play; she offered me money to go walk the shops in town; and yet none of it seemed right or proper.

To return to life as if nothing had happened would be a lie, one more atop the mountain of lies we'd already told. I couldn't do it.

Then came the Fourth of July. The flyers posted about town and inserted in the morning paper promised fireworks and hotdogs and drinks in Town Square. Dad wanted us to go, thought it would be good for the family, and we went, along with most of the rest of the town. Under the evening sky with the expectation for the coming light blooming like flowers above, a work was done. For a time it seemed like things might return to a semblance of the way they were, and I felt a thing in my young heart like hope.

189

My parents picked out a spot for our family, Fat Bobby and Bandit included, atop a small rise not quite a hill but a mild roll like a small wave passing through the earth. Mom unfolded a blanket and set out the basket of food and the cooler with frosted drinks like cold ambrosia on that hot summer evening. People were everywhere along the green expanse of Town Square, like ants milling about, and the courthouse provided a backdrop that brought to mind again that Wild West image of hanging criminals and dust-trailed wagons and saloons.

Set apart from the gathering families and lovers holding hands was a roped-off area with several devices like miniature space shuttle launch pads pointing up at the sky. Here people with bright yellow shirts with "VOLUNTEER" stenciled in black pulled fireworks like little rockets from boxes and wrappers and organized them on folding tables and on the grass. It seemed like an arsenal being laid out and I grimly wondered about the mayhem that could ensue if all those little rockets exploded accidentally here on the ground, instead of high up in the sky.

I leaned over to my sister and told her about this, and how maybe if one landed on her head it would improve her face. She pushed me as I tried to take a bite of a sandwich, and my food landed on the ground. I picked it up, saw the dirt and grass stuck to the bread, and wiped it on her arm.

"You retard!" she said and wiped her stained arm on my shirt. I saw Fat Bobby sitting across from me flash the slightest hint of a grin, and that small miracle made me smile too.

"Leave your sister alone," Mom said.

But it was a forceless command, and I looked at her, saw the hint of a smile on her face also. I thought that maybe she wasn't so mad that things were getting back to a semblance of normalcy, even if that normalcy meant us driving each other, and her, insane.

At eight o'clock the fireworks began and the explosions of

them in the black night sky was like watching the universe becoming. Stars and planets colliding in bursts of color and fire and light. Flashing and then dimming in the dark to be replaced anew by further cascades of brilliant light. Reds and blues and yellows opening like hands and fingers of sparks darting out in every direction. Blooms of light and us below in the illumination of it all.

I looked about for Jim and Tara among the throngs in the dark. Trying to find a familiar face in a sea of strangers staring up at the lightshow in the sky was nearly impossible. Not wanting to miss the fireworks myself, I gave up, likewise turning my gaze skyward.

Cheers, clapping, and oohs and ahhs made a discordant yet cheerful chorus for the better part of an hour, until, finally, the lightshow slowed, then ended.

With the spectacle over, people started to trickle away. Slowly at first, so that it was like a small stream breaking away from the larger body. I turned and asked my parents if I could look around a bit, and they said for a couple minutes.

Despite the smile that had temporarily returned to his face under the lights of the fireworks, Fat Bobby didn't accompany me. Healing is a slow thing, I guess, and we all do it in our own time.

With only Bandit at my side, I walked amidst the stirring yet still sizable crowd. It wasn't unlike moving through the woods, stepping around and ducking, dodging people instead of trees.

I came to the steps of the courthouse, and a large sycamore to the side of them stretched high and the branches of it reached wide and far. I thought again of the town as a throwback in time and imagined the outlaws on their steeds and the sheriff's posse in pursuit on desert landscapes, dirt clouds kicked up high by plodding hooves.

Climbing the courthouse steps I looked back over the crowd from my better vantage point. None of those I saw were those I was looking for and I started down the stairs again, slightly disappointed. This night of flowered lights and blooming universes was something that should have been shared with Jim and Tara, and that neither of them could be found, even after the show, was disheartening. I aimed myself in the general direction of my family and started back.

"That was quite a display," a voice called from behind me. I stopped and turned in the direction of the speaker.

Two figures left the shadows under the sycamore and stepped into the light cast by the bulbs of the courthouse. In gray suits and ties, with shoes polished to such a shine that I thought if I bent over and peered at the leather surfaces I'd see myself staring back, the pair looked like distinguished businessmen.

Bandit growled beside me, and I pulled him close by the collar.

The speaker was the shorter of the two, an older man somewhere in his fifties, with silver-gray hair streaked back tight against his skull. Lines like borders and rivers on roadmaps spread across his face. Despite these signs of age, his black eyes were alert and aware and intelligent.

His companion was large and blockish, and a buzz cut like a marine made his head even more sharp-edged and angular. I remember thinking that block of a head could be used maybe as a carpentering tool to measure right angles if the need ever arose. The blockish man's nose was crooked, pointing off to the right like it didn't care for the smells of the world and turned away in disgust.

I knew without having to ask that these men weren't locals, and the events of the past month had given me a good radar upgrade when it came to reading trouble. Wondering if I gave off some sort of pheromone that attracted trouble, I made a silent promise to start showering better.

"Yeah," I said, stepping backwards and continuing back towards the crowd and my family somewhere among them. "It was cool."

I turned and kept walking, and they fell in to either side of me, the older man on my left, Mr. Blockhead to my right. I felt like the innards of a sandwich, and the big guy especially looked hungry.

Bandit beside me looked to either side, that low growl still rumbling in his throat, and I shushed him sternly. I was thinking of the punches he'd taken from Bobby's dad, and for some reason I thought these two men would do more than punch my dog, and that made me sick inside.

"I bet people from all over come to this small town," the man with the silver hair and black eyes said. He leaned a bit towards me like we were buddies palavering. "Just to see the country, take in all this open space. Breathe the air."

He stretched out his arms as if to embrace it all. Closed his eyes and took a deep breath.

"Sure," I said. We reached the outskirts of the remaining crowd still milling about. Though the fireworks were over, people idly talked and shook hands with friends, and little bouts of laughter danced about the park. "I guess so."

"I bet people even come here for business," the older man said. His voice was slightly accented, and that along with his suit and fine hair made me think of maître d's at fine Italian restaurants. "In fact, now that I mention it, I think this is just the sort of place I'd come to if I had business matters to attend to or associates to meet."

I felt one hand touch me at the small of the back in a familiar way like we were friends, and I looked up at him and he looked down at me and smiled. His teeth were straight and white and reminded me of tombstones.

"An out of the way place like this might be just the sort of place big city folk might come for business affairs that require a bit of—how should I say this—*discretion*," he said and tapped his chin with a finger like he was thinking carefully. "Wouldn't you say so, Brock? That this is just the sort of place for a quiet, professional retreat?"

I turned to look at Mr. Blockhead (Brock) but he didn't look at me. He was looking straight ahead, and as he walked people parted for him like the waters of the Red Sea for Moses.

"Yes, Mr. Perrelli," he said with a voice like a buzz saw. "A fine place for business affairs."

I could see my family now, through the moving bodies of the crowd. I thought about running, and the two men seemed to sense my intention and moved in closer, squeezing me more tightly between them. Bandit had to dart out from between the closing vise of the men and, trotting a few steps before us, he turned and showed his teeth.

"Now this isn't the place for a scene," the older man, Mr. Perrelli, said. "Not on a nice evening like this, the Fourth of July, celebrating the independence of our great nation. Is it, Joey?"

He knew my name and my heart skipped a beat when he said it. My name out of his mouth was like a poison and I wondered if I was infected. He knew me, and I was sure that wasn't something I wanted.

"No, sir," I said, giving up on running, seeing we were still moving towards my family anyway. Realizing that neither he nor the behemoth on the other side of me would do anything rash with so many witnesses about. At least I hoped not.

"Good boy," Mr. Perrelli said and he clapped me on the back and gave my shoulder a little squeeze. "I'm in town for awhile on business, Joey. And I think you know what that business entails."

With that his arm left my shoulders and the two men fell behind me and it was just me and Bandit now, walking towards my family. I didn't look back until I was there, standing close to my dad, and him looking down and smiling at me.

I tried to smile back.

When I finally turned and looked behind me the two men were gone. In their suits, so out of place on a summer evening, they should have been easy to pick out of the crowd. I scanned the throng but didn't see them.

I'd see them soon enough, though. That I knew.

They had business to attend to and that business was me.


## 3.


Even the incident with Mr. Perrelli and his man Brock couldn't fully dispel the magic of the Fourth of July fireworks display. Those lights in the sky and the people gathered below watching them reminded me of the way things had been. The simple joy that could be had with others. Life in its fundamentals.

The day following, I called Jim and I learned that he and Tara had indeed been there, he with his dad and she with her parents. We simply hadn't come across each other in the multitudes present.

But we'd all seen it, and in our minds maybe we'd been together. Transmitting the wonder of it, the majesty of the lights and the power of the spectacle, to each other.

After talking to Jim, I called Tara, and hearing her on the other end was like hearing an old song on the radio. A favorite you hadn't heard for awhile and your heart kind of fluttered at hearing it again.

We agreed to meet at the sandwich place in town where we'd eaten last time. Having recently passed her driver's exam, Sarah borrowed Mom's car and drove us all into town, Bandit in the backseat with Fat Bobby.

After the incident on Lookout Mountain, Sarah and Barry hadn't seen much of each other. Through overheard secondhand snippets of conversation between my parents and sister, I got the gist of the situation. Barry's parents didn't want him around my sister anymore and Barry, though going on eighteen, didn't offer up any sort of resistance. It seemed his parents were paying his tuition after his senior year of high school for some expensive East Coast university, and he really wanted out of the dead end of Arizona.

So he did what his parents wanted him to, which included politely, but succinctly, dropping my sister like a bad habit.

This ended up with Sarah locking herself in her room for three days straight, the wracking of her sobs shaking the wall between our rooms. The sound of it was like the moans from torture chambers in hell. She came out only to eat and use the bathroom, and though several remarks came to mind on the spare moments during those days when I passed her, red-faced and bleary-eyed, her hair in tangles, I for some reason checked myself and kept my mouth shut.

All of this, along with what she'd gone through with the rest of us atop the hill, led to a strange outcome the likes of which I'd never imagined: I didn't mind my sister's company, almost preferred it.

Sarah pulled over at the curb in front of the restaurant's patio.

The look Jim gave me when we approached the patio table he and Tara had already claimed, said he wasn't too thrilled with this turn of events.

I gave him a not so subtle middle finger scratching my chin and he smiled. Tara rose to give Fat Bobby a hug, and I think I heard her whisper an "I'm sorry." I didn't need to ask what she was sorry about. Though she hadn't shot Mr. Templeton, it was the chaos of the gunfire that had sent he and the Collector tumbling down. No doubt, she would feel at least indirectly responsible for Bobby's dad's passing. Bobby, to his credit, didn't show any animosity, and he hugged her back.

Then we all sat down, no one else made an issue of Sarah's inclusion, and we ordered and ate.

Tara was to my right and her presence sent periodic tingles through me like an electric charge. There was a feeling like sparks jumping between us, and I remembered my old thoughts in the first days following the events on the mountain. How I thought things would never be the same and how we deserved it.

But there she was, and here I was, and I still felt things, and even if I didn't deserve it I wanted it. I wanted her, and not merely in the pop a boner way either. I wanted what she represented: happiness and friendship and good things.

The five of us talked about stuff as we ate, Bandit under the table waiting for the stray crumb or scrap. The things we talked of were incidental and unimportant, and that's why we spoke of them. We talked about movies and music and books. We recounted the fireworks and how they lit up the sky. Jim told dirty jokes and we laughed and food sprayed out of our mouths and soda out of our noses.

What had happened on Lookout Mountain was still there, hanging over us like a cloud, but it didn't seem to me as oppressive. Like maybe it was breaking apart and in time the light would shine through.

In the back of my mind lurked also Mr. Perrelli and Brock, and I wondered if I should mention them to my friends. I knew the answer to that, yet the laughter and smiles around the table made me push those darker thoughts away.

Then as if to slap me in the face and show me the error of my ways, some more people came onto the patio, taking a table nearby, and I saw them and they saw me, and that storm cloud seemed to settle overhead again. Dillon Glover gave me a little wave as he sat, that familiar smirk spread upon his face. Stu and Max settled into chairs on either side of him, their gazes aimed our way as well.

Jim was telling another joke and everyone else was laughing around me but it was like hearing noise through a thick wall. I saw only the three older kids looking at us across the patio.

"What's wrong?" Tara said from beside me, poking me on the shoulder. She followed my gaze and then said: "Oh shit."

Jim heard this, and Fat Bobby too, and they turned and looked at the table behind them. Dillon smiled at us like he was privy to a joke the punch line of which he wasn't sharing. Only it wasn't a funny, ha-ha joke, but a mean one. Sarah realized no one else was laughing anymore, and her laughter trailed off as well as she turned to see what we were looking at, then turned back to me.

"Who are they?" she asked.

I told her.

"Those are the guys from the fair? He's the one that pulled the knife on you?"

She motioned at Dillon with a slight nod, and I nodded too.

She looked to Dillon again, seemed to measure him. I knew what she was seeing. His face, his sneer, the eyes that screamed *Hey, I like pulling knives on people.* He had that face of casual, suppressed violence, the kind of face you passed in a crowd and felt a chill down your spine like you'd just come too close to something soiled. Something not right and maybe filaments of it had reached out to touch you.

"Maybe we should call the police," Fat Bobby said, and I turned to look at him, saw his face pale like maybe he was going to get sick.

I shook my head.

"They're not going to do anything in public," Jim said, apparently sharing my assessment of the situation. "They're just fucking with us."

"And doing a good job," Tara said.

Dillon gave us another wave.

Tara flipped him off.

Instead of exploding in anger and running over to stab us all to death with the knife he no doubt had secreted in his jacket somewhere, as I half expected him to, Dillon just leaned back in his seat and his smile broadened. Pudgy Stu and acne-scarred Max did the same, and I knew something wasn't right. These weren't guys who had patience or tolerance to spare. These were guys who flew by the seat of their pants, reacted, gave in to impulses rather than thinking things through.

"I think we should go," I said, knowing that they wouldn't do anything in broad daylight with other strollers and diners about. But that wasn't the fear: that they'd do something. The fear was that maybe they didn't have to, and I wasn't sure what made me think that until I scooted my chair back and stood.

A hand on my shoulder like a clamp pushed me back down.

The sound of a chair scraped along the patio concrete behind me, drawing up to our table, and Mr. Perrelli in his black-gray suit and with his hair like spun silver scooted in between me and Tara. He folded his hands on the table and looked at everyone— Jim, Bobby, Tara, and my sister—and then turned sideways slightly so that he was looking at me. He seemed like an executive at a board meeting, us all around the conference table, and I remembered his words from the night before, that he was here on business. We were about to learn what that business was.

"What a fine day for a bite to eat," he said, sitting head and shoulders above the rest of us. That hand was still on my shoulder, and I knew if I turned I'd see the man-mountain Brock. The head like a granite slab looking down on me. "A fine day for a friendly chat."

My friends and my sister looked at him and at the figure behind me, unseen by yours truly but the hand on me firm, and the confusion on their faces was clear.

Bandit growled from beneath the table. I felt him rise under there, brushing against my legs.

I wondered why the other patrons on the patio or those in the restaurant didn't come out to ask us how we were doing. Didn't they know something was wrong? Wasn't it obvious? There was a young couple at the far end of the patio, in their twenties maybe, and they spared us not a single glance. People walked past on the sidewalk, and not one stopped to ask why this old man and his square-headed companion were bothering five kids eating lunch.

In suits and for all appearances professional and affable, they nonetheless nearly reeked of danger and malice. It was like it lived beneath their skin, oozed from their pores, and could be smelled on the air that came along and carried it from them.

These two men weren't like Dillon and his two buddies. They weren't thugs or punks. These two weren't even like Mr. Templeton, Bobby's late father, bored and complacent with the suppressed violence within him. They weren't like the Collector either, who collected what was owed, yeah, but also sometimes collected for himself and was gratified by it.

These two men were of a different breed.

I knew their potential for violence, but it wouldn't be violence out of vengeance or vendetta. They would hurt people—they would hurt us—because it was what they did. It was their business, their livelihood, and when Mr. Perrelli pulled the trigger and blew your face off, or brought the garrote over your throat and choked the life out of you, there would be no personal malice in it at all.

He was just doing a job.

"I hear you kids came across something pretty interesting some weeks back," Mr. Perrelli said, again favoring everyone around the table with a glance. The CEO and his board members all around. "These fellas," and he pointed at Dillon and company with a thumb, "were kind enough to fill us in on the details. When we told them what we were looking for, they were only too eager to help us find you."

I looked again at Dillon Glover. His smile was still there and again he waved, just a twiddling of his fingers like a patron flagging a waiter.

"I've spoken to lots of people," Mr. Perrelli said, "and I've read the newspaper stories about what happened out in the woods a couple weeks back. But I think maybe there were some parts left out."

He looked at me and his eyes twinkled with a light that spoke of profound intelligence. He favored me with a chummy grin again like we were old friends, and then he passed that grin around the table to my friends and sister.

"It's those parts that were left out that interest me," he said. "There was a car mentioned in the papers. An old car. A Buick.

But the paper treated it like just a small detail. Some place you kids liked to hang out."

All of us exchanged glances at this, and I remembered a fire on the hilltop, and millions burning to ash and carried away on the wind like dust.

"I think there was something in the car," Mr. Perrelli said. "Maybe a couple somethings depending on where you looked. And those somethings belonged to me."

He said this again not with malice or accusation or anger, but as simple fact.

"I'd like to have these possessions of mine returned to me."

The hand on my shoulder clenched and unclenched not gently but not painfully either. Like maybe I was getting a firm massage. I spared the large knuckles and thick fingers there a nervous glance. Looked back at Mr. Perrelli.

I said nothing, unsure of what the best course of action would be here. Honesty? Lie to buy us time? Apparently reading my hesitancy as if I were leaning towards option two, Mr. Perrelli spoke again.

"There's nothing to be gained from lying, young man," he said, and patted my leg chummily. "I believe you met an associate of mine out there in the woods. He kept me apprised of all that transpired."

"The Collector …" Jim muttered from across the table, his ability to speak when I couldn't a reminder again of his strength.

"Bingo," Mr. Perrelli said, winking at my friend and giving a finger and thumb gunshot his way. It was all too easy to superimpose a real gun upon that familiar gesture, and it didn't seem at all friendly. Rather like a warning, a hint of things to come, instead of a jovial, casual motion.

That more than anything, the implied threat towards my friend, spurred me to honesty instead of option number two. It was lies that had got us to where we were in the first place. More lies could only bring about more consequences.

"We burned the money," I said more calmly than I felt. Inside, my stomach was churning and quaking like geologic plates. "The Collector took the body."

Mr. Perrelli smiled. Closed his eyes like he was enjoying the feel of the sun on his face, the heat of it and the warmth.

"You burned the money?" he asked. It wasn't like he wanted the question answered, but merely like he was repeating it to himself for clarity. "A bunch of teenagers burnt ten million dollars?"

That number echoed in my head. Stated so casually, so unceremoniously, that figure giving a concreteness to what we had seen. It brought a reality to what we had so briefly dreamt of doing with the money in the sacks.

Ten million dollars.

Ashes in the wind. Lost and gone.

"That's what you want me to believe?" Mr. Perrelli asked and he again circled the table with his gaze. His black eyes were like pools of darkness. "You burnt the money?"

Having nothing else to do, I nodded.

I thought about pissing my pants again, but having to inconspicuously throw out ruined jockey shorts without my mom noticing was getting old.

"Well," Mr. Perrelli said and pushed with his hands on the table to stand. "This really is quite an unfortunate situation."

Once on his feet, he pulled on the lapels of his suit jacket, straightening it. He brushed off unseen dust particles and lint from his pants. Then he offered me a smile and it seemed to me like a shark grinning before he chomped you in half at the torso.

"I guess we'll have to come to some sort of arrangement then," he said.

I had no idea what that meant, didn't like the sound of it, and didn't want to ask for clarification. And I didn't have a chance to, anyways, because then he was walking away and the hand left my shoulder. Turning in my seat so that I was peering over the backrest, I watched the two men in suits walk a distance, climb into a long black car, and then the car pull away from the curb and roll away down the street. It rounded a corner and was soon out of sight.

Turning to face front again, I started to get up and stopped when I saw Dillon Glover there, standing over our table, his friends to either side of him. His fists were on the tabletop, and like Mr. Perrelli he looked around at each of us.

"You little fucks are in all kinds of trouble," he said, and he smiled and the pure joy on his face was of a perversion I'll never forget. He too had an idea of what kind of people Mr. Perrelli and Brock were and he found it amusing, a game, and he was glad to have been a part of it.

Then they too were gone, and it was just me and my friends, and we looked at each other across the table, all of us waiting for someone else to say something first.

"Well," I said, "it looks like there's more people that want to kill us."

"Yeah," Jim said, picking up his sandwich, taking a bite, washing it down with a long swallow of soda. "I was starting to feel normal again."

"You're not normal," I said. "You're colored."

He grinned, gave me the finger, called me a "honkey."

"So what do we do?" Fat Bobby asked. Surprisingly, he seemed to have recovered from his bout of sickness rather quickly.

"Same as always," Tara said. She used the last of her French fries to mop up the last dabs of ketchup on her plate, stuffed them in her mouth, chewed.

"What's that?" Sarah asked. "Coming up with stupid nick-names? Collecting decoder rings and playing *Dungeons and Dragons*?"

"At least we don't play with ourselves," I said.

"Yeah, right," my sister said. "I bet your shorts are stiff as crackers with all the crank-yanking you do."

I wanted to punch her but blushed instead and avoided looking at Tara.

"We deal with it," Tara said, ignoring our exchange.

None of us said anything in response to that, and to me it seemed maybe there was no need to say anything else. Because maybe there wasn't much else that could be said or done. What happened, would, and that was that.

*Deal with it* seemed to me like the summation of all things.

## 4.

One evening Tara called and asked if I could go out. She'd just gotten her driver's learner permit and was borrowing her dad's car. It was my birthday, and this fact must have slipped out earlier in the week, because she wanted to give me a present. I asked my dad, and he gave me a wry smile like he knew a secret and he wasn't going to tell me what it was. He nodded and told me to have a good time. I relayed his answer over the phone to Tara and she said she'd be over soon. It took fifteen or twenty minutes to drive from town to the outskirts where we lived, and those minutes ticked away so slowly the anxiety of it made me pleasantly sick.

I remembered the kiss under the moon at the fair.

The feel of her hand in mine at the top of the Ferris wheel.

But then the other things had happened: Sheriff Glover in the woods; the events on Lookout Mountain; the strain in our friendship and the dread that things could never be put right again; the arrival of Mr. Perrelli and the business he was about.

I thought of my sister in the bathroom not so long ago, getting herself all prettied up for Barry, and wondering if someday Tara would be doing that for me. Now here I was in the restroom in front of the mirror, looking from this angle and that like the slightly different view would reveal some hideous deformation that I'd somehow missed my entire life. Making sure each strand of hair was just so seemed a task of monumental importance. When I heard the sound of a car approaching, headlights skewing shadows through the windows of the house, I wasn't ready, thought maybe I'd never be ready.

The knock on the door announced Tara, and I bounded down the stairs. Dad was there, looking over the back of the sofa at me, again with that wry smile like he had a secret.

"I'll be back in a couple hours?" I said, my hopes turning into a question, my hand on the knob at the ready.

"Sure thing," Dad said and I turned to go but stopped again when he called my name. "And son?" he began, the door still unopened, Tara still on the other side waiting. I turned back to him.

"Yes, sir?"

"I was wrong," he said, and I wondered more about why he was bothering me at such a time more so than whatever he was wrong about.

"Sir?" I asked out of necessity because he was addressing me, not because I gave a shit.

"About her," he said with a little nod towards the door. My heart lurched. Something in my stomach did a few somersaults. "She's not too old for you. I think she's just about right."

He was saying more with those words than I could understand. Maybe it was what me and my friends had been through, and he saw something in her and the others that he approved of. Maybe it was just something between a father and a son, and the secrets of growing up, the secrets of girls, that he was imparting to me or trying to. Both, maybe, and something more or less, and it didn't matter. All that mattered was that girl on the other side of the door. She had a car waiting and we'd drive through the evening and go places in the last hours of this, my birthday, and I had one more gift coming and I wanted whatever it was more than anything.

"Thanks, Dad," I said.

He nodded again, I opened the door, and there she was. The night was curtained behind her like a stage backdrop just to outline her for me. She waved over my shoulder to my dad, and then she had me by the arm and I was hers and the world was mine.

* * *

The truck wound through the dark roads and we descended into the sparse lights of town. A faint glow like a halo encircled the desert town, and I didn't know if it was the sodium vapor street lamps and business neon and lights from houses, or something else, something in me, and something in her, and the expectation of things lighting up the world. I watched her hands maneuver the wheel and handle the gearshift. I knew she saw me watching her, but her eyes were on the road. Yet there was a slight tick at the corner of her mouth as if she were struggling against a smile.

"Where we going?" I asked.

"You'll see," she said and I saw that tick again at the corner of her mouth.

Through town we rolled and then it was dwindling behind us as we continued north. Eventually the lights of it blinked away as the bumps and rises of the road blocked them out. Tara took a turn and steered onto a dirt road. There was a sign but it was dark and we passed it before I could read it. She let her foot off the gas as the unpaved path jostled the truck and soon she slowed the pickup even more and stopped.

Tara cut the engine and got out.

I followed, coming around the truck to see her duck quickly back in to pull something out from behind the driver's seat. A large bundle wrapped in birthday cake print gift wrap appeared in the cradle of her arms, the paper crinkling as Tara handed it over to me.

"Your present. But don't open it yet."

I nodded and tucked it under my arm. It was malleable and soft, squishing under my arm a bit like a pillow.

"Come on," she said and hooked my arm with hers to pull me along towards the trees.

"Do you think it's safe?" I said, thinking of Mr. Perrelli and his man Brock. "Maybe we shouldn't be out by ourselves."

Mentally, I cursed myself for making the suggestion.

"I watched to make sure we weren't followed."

So had I, in between bouts of staring at her and her hands and the dark desert rolling past outside the truck. Indeed, there hadn't been a car on the road other than us since we had left Payne behind. But it wasn't like we were experts at spotting tails either.

I nodded.

"Besides," she said, "with the headlights off no one would know where we'd pulled off the road anyways."

This made sense and I nodded again.

We strolled into the trees but it wasn't like entering the forest from near my home or the Connolly yard. These were proper trails and along the trails were cleared spaces and wooden picnic tables. In one clearing was the squat brick structure of a public restroom, looking like a small military bunker in the night. Green signs made a darker hue in the night dotted the trails, telling passersby how far to where. We continued walking, Tara leading the way, and the area around the trees became more spacious so that off in the distance I could see a rippling and moving surface— almost black—and the light of the moon and stars glinting off of it like a million diamonds.

We walked to the shore of the lake and there Tara stopped, and I stopped with her. On the lakeshore was a large rock shaped like a state I couldn't name and in front of it a length of drift-wood, washed up like the last plank of a lost and sunken ship. Tara sat on the rock and patted the space beside her, and I lowered myself next to her.

There wasn't much space and our shoulders brushed when we moved.

She folded her hands in her lap and turned to me. Now she was smiling and it reached her eyes, along with the reflected sparkle of the heavens, and it seemed like there was a whole universe in her eyes.

"You can open your present now," she said, and I blinked, confused, then remembered the package under my arm and pulled it free.

I tore at the wrapping like I imagined tearing at her clothes someday, the way ruggedly handsome actors did it in the movies. When the paper was tossed away and I saw what I held in my hands, I felt both extremely unmanly, as far from Mel Gibson or Tom Cruise as a guy could get, and very, very happy at the same time. To be completely honest, the happiness outweighed the embarrassment.

The stuffed plush Batman, previously gutted in the Haunted House, stared back up at me, stitched inexpertly but charmingly across his midsection so that it looked like train tracks crossed the width of him. Batman as the Frankenstein monster maybe.

I knew the grin on my face was wide and foolish, and I didn't care.

I held Batman tightly in my lap, my fists squishing him.

"I went back that night to get him," Tara said and I looked at her and she looked away, off across the dark waters of the lake. "It seemed wrong to leave him there. You know, after all he's done for Gotham."

"Wow," I said. "You just might be the biggest nerd I've ever met."

She laughed and nudged me with her shoulder.

"Don't make fun. He may have saved our lives."

I thought of that night in the Haunted House, and Dillon pulling the knife away from me to go to work on the stuffed Batman. Tara acting quicker than any of us, turning and kicking the guy a good one on the shin.

I don't think it was the Caped Crusader who saved me that night.

I stared at Tara by the lake with the trees rustling and whispering in the evening breeze, and she finally looked back at me. I think she may have seen a hint of my thoughts. She nudged me with her shoulder again and then leaned over and I leaned over to meet her.

Our lips met and time seemed to stop. Again there was that feeling that the world was moving just for us: this night was ours, and this lake, and the wind in our hair. And this girl, this most beautiful of creatures, was mine, here and now and mine alone.

I had the notion to use my hands this time and wanted to do it oh so badly. To touch her, let my fingers roam her. To feel the curve of her back with the skin of my fingertips. Maybe to put one on her leg and let it spider-crawl there, seeking, feeling. If I was real daring, to encircle her with my arms and pull her close so that our bodies were touching too, shoulder to shoulder, hip to hip, a dozen little places, a dozen little meetings of us and the tingle of it like electric pulses.

But she pulled away before I could command my hands to act.

Just that kiss and the contact was broken.

Again she stared out over the lake and embarrassed, disappointed maybe too, I did the same, trying to find whatever it was she was looking for. Knowing she wasn't really looking for anything in particular, or perhaps one very important thing. The most important thing ever: understanding.

"What do you think will happen to us?" she asked in little more than a whisper, a sigh.

I didn't know if she meant me and her; or Jim and Bobby too and the whole Outsiders' Club; maybe Mr. Perrelli and Brock, and the things that had come before; Dillon, Max and Stu at the Haunted House; Sheriff Glover at the access road near the Buick; the Collector and Mr. Templeton on the mountain. Perhaps she meant all of it and that feeling I'd had for awhile after it all, that feeling that things were closing in on us, that we'd been too lucky for a bunch of kids who'd wanted what wasn't rightly theirs. That maybe all there was for us was pain after pain, trial after trial, and a special place in hell for kids who plotted to steal money that didn't belong to them and killed people who wanted it back.

I shook my head, not knowing what to say.

"What if it doesn't end with this Perrelli guy?" she said. "What if we do … something … again, and someone else comes after him?"

Silence was all I had to give.

The trees continued their murmurs, better conversationalists than I.

"When I had to do that counseling," Tara continued and I knew without having to ask she was talking about what the court had ordered after her having shot the Collector up on Lookout Mountain, "the doctor kept asking me about my feelings and what I thought about shooting that guy. Shooting the Collector."

She stood and stepped over the driftwood so that the toes of her shoes were almost touching the water. I stood up and walked over to stand beside her.

"All I wanted was to be out of there," she said. "His office was so drab and dull. Just all these leather doctor's books. And on the walls were just a bunch of degrees in fancy frames. It was a dead place, and it reminded me of being up there on the mountain and pulling the trigger and watching that man fall all the way down."

I was looking for something again out on the lake. Looking anywhere to find it, anywhere but in Tara's eyes.

"He wanted to know if I had nightmares," she said. "But I just wanted to go home. So I kept it all in. I didn't tell him about my feelings, and I said nothing about nightmares."

She grabbed me and turned me towards her, turned me away from that something I sought over the black waters, and towards her and the pain in her eyes. The pain in her eyes maybe reflecting what was in me, and me not wanting to see it.

"But I do have feelings. And I have nightmares."

I had nightmares too, remembered the one about us high in the Ferris wheel, the ride falling apart around us, and us crashing down among the ruins of its mechanisms. I didn't share this though and said nothing.

I was becoming real good at saying nothing.

I thought maybe I could major in it in college. Probably get full tuition paid by the United Mutes of America Foundation.

"I think about you all the time, Joey," she said, and those words filled me with a sense of contentment so profound I felt airy and light. I wondered if I should strap myself to something lest I float away like a balloon in the wind. "And I have nightmares about one of us not making it."

That deflated me right quick.

Dread replaced my momentary elation, pushing its way like a bully cutting in line.

"This Mr. Perrelli doesn't seem like a nice guy," she said. "And I get the feeling his blockheaded friend likes to hurt things. Ten million dollars is a lot of money to lose. When he finally believes that we don't have it, he's going to be pissed."

I agreed with all of this and so continued my record-breaking silence.

"I got the distinct impression," Tara continued, "that when Mr. Perrelli gets pissed, people get hurt. I think those people are going to be us."

She sought my hand again and squeezed it. My fingers inter-twined with hers, each touch like dynamite going off inside me.

"Jim or Bobby. Your sister maybe. You or me. I don't think this thing will pass without us suffering for it."

Finally, I found words and said them, knowing they were inadequate even before I spoke them, but saying them anyway.

"We seem to have done alright so far."

211

"Is that so?" Tara said. "We beat up some punks; threw rocks at a fat sheriff; and killed a man." In my mind I corrected her, saying: *No, you killed a man; you're the one that shot him.* Horrified at my own selfishness, I wisely kept my mouth shut. "And for what? A bunch of money we ended up burning anyway?"

She looked away from me again. Dropped my hand.

"I wonder if it isn't all our fault," she said in a near whisper. "I wonder if maybe we wouldn't have been better off never meeting."

"Don't say that," I said, wondering how the conversation had turned in this manner, my heart sinking. *She* had called *me*. *She* had picked me up and driven us out here. *She* had walked me out to the lake and given me my present and then kissed me. This time I grabbed her hands and held them tightly. "Don't ever say that," I repeated and then I was moving forward and kissing her. At first she tried to pull away but I pulled her back, and then she was yielding, accepting it.

This time I did use my hands, desperately, almost without even thinking about it. First they were on her hips, moving up and down the denim of her jeans, finding the seam there between her blouse and waistband, touching that small strip of skin. Then they were under her blouse and touching the flat of her stomach, smooth and taut like leather. I felt her gasp into my mouth, tasted her breath in puffs. I pulled her close like I'd wanted to minutes ago, making those dozen small contacts: legs brushing legs, stomach to stomach, chest to chest and the swell of her breasts mashed against me, and her heartbeat behind them. Our faces were close, and when the kiss was done, but my hands still moving, roaming like they had minds of their own along the hidden skin beneath her shirt, we leaned against each other so that our foreheads rested one against the other.

"*Don't ever say that again,*" I repeated once more, whispering it fiercely to her, breathing it on her, wanting the words to go into her and take root there. "This will be over soon." I realized that like a hero in a movie I was making my first promise to a girl, and I wondered if I'd be able to keep it. "It'll be over and we'll still be here."

That was the last thing either of us said there in the night by the black water, the trees whispering their devious secrets, their own promises maybe, of shadowy things and hidden things. And suddenly, despite the kisses and the touches, the girl in my arms and the taste of her on my lips, I didn't want to be out there anymore.

Tara felt this, I think, as well and we walked back to the truck and she drove me home, where I had many feelings in the long night in my bed, and many nightmares. Oh, God, were there nightmares, and morning seemed so far away.

### 5.

Dad was off to work and Mom went into town for shopping when Sarah came into my room and tried to rouse me from bed. I was awake but not wanting to be, trying to make up for the sleep lost the night before. My breath had that morning stench like sour things and I hoped it hadn't smelled that way yesterday when I'd kissed Tara.

I purposely blew it into my sister's face.

"You stupid troll!" she said, backing away and holding her nose. "You smell like ass! Go brush your teeth or something!"

"*Don't ... bother me then*," I croaked. I added a fart too, just for good measure, hoping it would scare her away. But Sarah held her ground. "*What do you want?*"

"If you weren't so stupid and gross I would have told you by now."

She went to my bedroom window and looked out. Then she turned back to me.

"Hurry and get up. I have something to show you."

"A ... new face?" I said through a yawn. "No need for me to see it. I'm sure it's an improvement."

Sarah moved quickly to the bed, grabbed my leg and the covers, and pulled hard. I slid along the mattress and then there was no mattress and I fell in a tangle of sheets to the floor. Bandit leapt down from the bed at the disturbance. My head hit the wall.

"You tampon!" I said, rubbing my head. "What's your problem?"

"Remember those journalism skills you asked me about?" she said, and she smiled in triumph. "I went on Dad's computer and found out some stuff about your friend Mr. Perrelli."

The triumph quickly left her face and was replaced by something else. Worry, maybe, or fear.

"I think you should come take a look."

I was already struggling to my feet at the mention of Mr. Perrelli. We moved quickly out the door and down the hall towards Dad's office. Bandit brought up the rear, his nails clacking madly as he rushed to follow the excitement.

In Dad's office I moved around his large oak desk and took the swivel chair, rolling it close so I could reach the keyboard, mouse, and lean in close to the monitor. Sarah at first stood close behind me, looming, and so I puffed another burst of dragon breath in her face and she backed up a few steps, looking like she was deciding whether to retch or punch me in the face. In the end she did neither, but just stood back as I read what she had pulled up on the computer screen.

As my eyes roamed down the screen, taking in the words and pictures there, stark validity was brought to the fears that Tara had voiced last night. I added my own blooming fears to those, and it seemed I'd stepped into another world.

"This is insane," I said.

Using the mouse to move the onscreen pages up and down, I re-read some of what I already had. I looked back over my shoulder at Sarah. She stood there, leaning against the wall in her pajamas, chewing on a fingernail.

"He's a mob boss," she said, speaking the words around the finger in her mouth. "Ties in Philadelphia and Chicago."

She glanced from me to the screen.

"He's the real thing," she said.

I turned slowly back to the computer screen.

On the screen was one silver-haired, black-eyed Vincent Perrelli, a black-and-white photograph of him standing in front of a brownstone building. Around him were several uniformed police officers, one of them standing behind him, only partially seen. Mr. Perrelli's arms behind his back let the viewer of the photograph know what was happening, as if all the cops weren't enough of a hint. He was being arrested, though from the smile on his face and his casual, leisurely posture, he could have been surrounded by a personal escort, readying for a night on the town.

"Indicted on five counts of murder," I said, reading aloud the words on the screen before me. "Three counts of racketeering and two of extortion. He did seven years of a fifteen year sentence. Paroled after an appeal brought into question the chain-of-custody of certain forensic evidence, and one of the witnesses changed his story."

"I get the feeling this witness didn't just wake up one morning, realizing he'd given bad testimony," my sister said, and I agreed with her.

"And now Perrelli's after us."

"What do we do?" Sarah asked.

That was the ten-million-dollar question, which I had no answer for, because the ten million dollars that had briefly been in my possession had gone up in smoke.

I wondered if we were next for the flames.

* * *

Fat Bobby was out on the porch and I called him upstairs. The heavy thumps of his footfalls on the steps and then coming down the hall announced his approach. Poking his head into the room like he wasn't sure if he should be there, he looked at us in front of the computer, and I waved him over.

We showed him the stories about Vincent Perrelli. I even narrated some of it for him, like maybe he was dyslexic or retarded and wouldn't understand the gravity of what he was reading.

But he did grasp it, and there was that pasty pale hue to his face again like he might get sick. He rolled his eyes, leaned against a wall, and held his head in a way like he was thinking about it and coming to a determination. In the end he fortunately didn't spew all over my dad's computer, but there was this large lump that went down his throat like he'd swallowed what had been about to come up. This made me a little sick in turn.

"What do we do?" Fat Bobby asked. "That was obviously his money in the car, and we burned it all. What's he going to do when he doesn't get his money?"

I had no answer for him as I'd had no answer for my sister and myself. For a time in that room there was only silence, and I felt uncomfortably like someone had me in their crosshairs with their finger on the trigger. So strong was this feeling that I stepped away from the window, which brought me closer again to the computer monitor. Not wanting to, my gaze found the black-and-white of Vincent Perrelli again, smiling like a kindly grandfather or a man on a stroll.

I wondered if this was how our end would be: just another story in the morning paper. The totality of us summed up in a few paragraphs and maybe a poor photo and a caption.

# CHAPTER TEN

## 1.

The night with Tara at the lake, and my sister's findings on the Internet concerning Mr. Perrelli, made for a conflicting mess of hope and dread in my mind. One moment I would be thinking again of holding Tara's hands in mine, leaning in close, anticipation for the warmth of her lips on mine setting my heart aflutter; and the next those images were invaded and sent scurrying by that of Vincent Perrelli and the squat, brick-house figure of Brock, sandwiching me between them at the Fourth of July show in front of the courthouse.

Such a bundle of nerves had I become, that my mom noticed when I paced too often about the house, or peeked out the windows, and she asked what was wrong. I made some weak excuse about being restless and bored, and at the first opportunity when she left to run some errands, I picked up the phone and called Jim.

I told him what Sarah had found on the Internet about Mr. Perrelli, and Jim came over not twenty minutes later. The four of us—Jim and I, Bobby, and Sarah—tried to come up with some ideas on what to do. Should we tell our parents? Should we call the police?

After the events on Lookout Mountain, both these options held particular appeal. Yet I remembered what the Collector had said about collecting, how sometimes he collected for others, sometimes for himself, and the gratification such work brought him. This led naturally to Mr. Perrelli's businesslike impersonality, and the image I had of him back at the sandwich shop, like a CEO at the head of a conference table.

Mr. Perrelli, for all his professional demeanor, was no doubt a collector of a sort himself. Tallying his allotted dues on a ledger in his mind, the debtors filed just so in some mental Rolodex.

If we didn't give him what he wanted, I knew it wasn't just us kids that would pay. He would collect from our families as well.

I wouldn't allow that to happen, and, I was glad to see, my friends seemed to be of the same mindset. Gathered about the kitchen table, snacks, drinks, and printed copies of the articles on Mr. Perrelli spread before us like the articles of the world's lamest staff meeting, the four of us decided against telling our parents or the police. For the time being, at least.

Pushing up from our chairs, the four of us parted, Bobby to the guestroom he was using upstairs, complaining of feeling sick, which I understood only all too well; Sarah to her room, promising me she'd call Tara and fill her in; and Jim and I out to the porch, idly deciding what to do with the rest of the day. Jim suggested we go to his place, kill some time roaming about the car yard or playing video games.

I said fine, and we headed off.

* * *

Jim and I were walking down the highway towards the turnoff that led to his father's shop, Bandit gliding between us, when I heard the sound of an engine coming up the road from behind. Remembering the night Dillon Glover and his friends had pulled up beside me—Dillon in the shadows with his head and hands seeming to float in the darkness, and the click of his knife flicking open—I turned to watch the vehicle approach.

The long black Cadillac in which Vincent Perrelli and Brock had driven away from the restaurant patio just a couple days before, now cruised towards us. I turned back around and quickened my pace. Jim spun about to see what had captured my attention, saw the Cadillac approaching, and hurried to keep up with me.

"Shit," he muttered, jogging beside me. "What do we do?"

I shook my head.

There wasn't much we could do. The Connolly yard was still maybe a quarter mile away. We could make a dash for it, but even in that short distance the car would overtake us. Which it did just then, rolling past us and turning in a right angle across the shoulder of the highway, blocking our path.

I reminded myself that, like the incident at the diner, it was daylight, and nothing would happen to us. We were safe in the day.

The passenger and driver's doors opened.

Brock came out from behind the wheel. Vincent Perrelli stepped out onto the dirt shoulder from the passenger seat. His eyes hidden behind the sunglasses he wore was somehow worse than the black eyes themselves. Behind those tinted lenses I knew I was being watched, weighed, measured. He wore a gray-and-black pinstriped suit, the coat seeming heavy to me in this heat, yet the older man didn't produce a single bead of sweat.

He seemed in control of everything, even the biological function of perspiration.

I couldn't even reliably control when and where I pissed.

"Hello, Joey," he said. "I came to see about our little dilemma."

He looked from me to Jim, but neither of us spoke.

Bandit was growling and took a couple steps towards the man before I called his name and he stopped. He stood his ground, though, poised, legs and back tensed like he was ready to spring.

"You don't still expect me to believe that story about you kids burning the money, do you?" Mr. Perrelli said. "With all the stuff you could buy with that kind of money, you really think I believe even for a second that you burned it?"

"It's the truth," Jim said.

"Books and toys and maybe a new bike," Mr. Perrelli continued, speaking over Jim as if my friend hadn't spoken at all. "Maybe some girly magazines to peek through at night when the folks are asleep." He said this last with a sly and confidential grin that said: *Ahhh, I know what you kids do.* "The possibilities are endless. That's a lot of money." A sober and earnest expression replaced the warm smile, like he was a doctor with bad news.

"But it's not your money," he said. "And I would really like it back."

"You're gangsters," I said without thinking.

Mr. Perrelli gave a short bark of a laugh like he'd heard a good joke. But it must not have been all that funny because then he was all business again.

"I told you. I'm a businessman. And I think it's past time we ironed out the terms of the deal I have for you."

Brock came around the Cadillac to stand next to Mr. Perrelli. He stood casually with his substantial arms crossed over his chest. Bandit's growl rumbled again at the thick, squat man's approach, but he stayed where he was, back arched, ears pinned against his skull.

"Brock is what I like to call my contract negotiator," Mr. Perrelli said. "I tell him what I want and he sees to it that I get it. He can be very persuasive."

Brock's eyes were a steely gray, like chips of flint stone. I don't know if I'd say they were persuasive eyes, but they were cool and reflected nothing of emotion or anything resembling human sentiment. They seemed like the glass optics of some sort of machine.

"And I think that's what you children need right now. A little persuasion to bring you around to reason."

"We don't have the money," Jim repeated, and the tremor in his voice made me feel not so bad about the terror jumping around inside of me.

"Brock," Vincent Perrelli said and gave a slight gesture with one hand, "if you would."

Brock came forward, and Bandit charged to meet him.

I called out to my dog to stop.

One huge slab of a foot shod in a steel-toed leather boot came up and met Bandit's head with a *thunk* like something heavy hitting the floor. Bandit dropped to the ground and stayed there.

I charged the man-mountain and he backhanded me like he was swatting an insect. My head rang and my teeth clacked hard together and the ringing seemed to echo through my skull. I fell to the dirt, tried to stop my fall, skinned my arms and elbows in my awkward landing.

From my low perspective I saw the boot that had kicked my dog step past me and towards Jim. I lifted my head to watch, trying to push up. Dirt stuck to the blood at my lips where Brock's knuckles had cut me. Grains of it in my mouth ground between my teeth.

Jim turned to run, and, surprisingly, I wasn't angry. That was the right thing to do; the only thing to do. One of us had to get away. But my friend had waited too long to make a move. The man like a tank was there, intercepting him. One arm went around Jim's middle, pinning his arms to his sides. Brock's other arm brought Jim's left up and out at the elbow. Brock held Jim's hand out so that we could all see.

I didn't want to see. But I couldn't turn away.

The big man extended Jim's index finger. Yanked it backwards with one quick tug. There was a quick and brittle sound like a dry stick snapping.

Jim's scream climbed the sky in octaves I would have thought impossible outside an opera house.

Brock let go, and Jim fell to his knees, crying, holding his damaged left hand in his right. Cradling it to his chest like a baby at the teat, he cried, and I realized I was crying as well, and my finger hadn't even been the one pulled back.

"I want my money," Mr. Perrelli said. His tone was quiet and soft and in a way serene, yet it carried over Jim's cries of agony effortlessly. I looked up at him from the dirt, then away and at my dog still lying in a heap. I thought I saw the slight rise and fall of breathing, but wasn't sure. "I have all the time in the world. But the longer I have to wait, the more I have to use Brock to negotiate."

I didn't ask for elaboration.

He gave me a bit anyways.

"Escalation, Joey," he said. "Escalation is the key word here. I need my money or the negotiating gets tougher. And I expect our business to stay just that: *our* business. No parents, no police, no anyone but us."

I looked up at Mr. Perrelli again. Then I glanced side to side, up and down the highway. It was long and deserted both ways, like a road to nowhere. I wondered how far Jim's cries had carried. Wondered if anyone cared even if they'd heard them.

"Do we understand each other?" Vincent Perrelli asked, removing his sunglasses, fixing his gaze on me. His eyes sparkled like dark jewels.

I nodded.

He nodded also, turned, and climbed back into the Cadillac. Brock walked around the car and got in on the driver's side. They drove away, leaving us in a plume of dust. When the dust cleared there was only pain: the cries of my friend cradling his broken finger; my dog coming to with a whimper; me with my throbbing head in my hands, the world seemingly trembling with each thrum and pulse of my skull. As if it were on the verge of falling apart around us.

## 2.

We walked the rest of the way to the Connolly yard, Jim crying the whole time. I had my arm around his shoulders and wasn't the least bit embarrassed to be doing so with another guy. Bandit strode on wobbly legs beside us, like he'd just drunk an entire bowl of Purina Dog Beer.

Trying not to look at the horror of my friend's backwards pointing finger, I gave weak words of encouragement and consolation, like "It's not that bad" and "I've seen worse", which were both lies.

What should have been a walk of a few minutes turned out to take us, the sorry battered lot that we were, fifteen minutes or so, pausing now and again as Jim stumbled, cradling his finger, or Bandit stumbled, knotted head giving him faulty dog radar. Only when we were at the turnoff to Jim's home did another car finally pass, and seeing us stagger about drunkenly with our injuries, the driver slowed, rolled down his window, and asked if there was anything wrong. Why he couldn't have driven by twenty minutes earlier when two mobsters had been busy beating us, I didn't know. But it pissed me off and I flipped off the driver, a bald man in his fifties, and his eyes widened in shock. He cussed at me and drove on.

Mr. Connolly saw us coming up the road to the gate of the yard. He was leaning on the bumper of a car he'd been working on, still in a T-shirt and jeans like I'd always seen him, so that I wondered if that was all he owned. If maybe his whole closet was wall-to-wall grimy oil-stained white shirts and dirty, faded jeans. He saw me supporting his son, his son cradling his injured hand, and Mr. Connolly came running down the path, throwing the gate open. Ushering us in quickly, he led us to the garage.

"What happened?" he asked with a tone like a hammer blow.

Jim was still crying, his finger poking up like a crooked periscope, and though his face was stern and smooth, Mr. Connolly's eyes shone with an urgency. My friend unable to speak, it was left to me to think of a quick lie.

Vincent Perrelli had said no parents or police were to be involved.

223

He had spoken of escalation, and I knew he meant it.

So I said what first came to mind, and the simplicity and stupidity of it is what I think made Jim's father believe me.

"He fell," I said, and then thinking perhaps a little elaboration was needed: "We were running, horsing around, and he fell."

"I have to get him to the hospital," Mr. Connolly said.

Grabbing a set of keys from a pegboard on the wall, he herded his son out of the garage and into a jeep. The vehicle started smoothly and rolled out of the still open gate, leaving me alone in the car yard. Standing there with my woozy dog, I realized I'd have to make the short walk home back down the highway—alone.

\* \* \*

I made it home without any black cars full of mobsters pulling over to whack me. As I strode up the driveway I saw the garage door was rolled up. Inside, Dad was home for lunch and throwing some punches with Fat Bobby, who, I realized from a distance, wasn't as fat as he'd always been. I took this in with something like mild amazement, seeing that the rolls of fat were still there, but maybe not as many. Whereas previously he'd been monstrously fat, now he only seemed fat. Like there was freak show fat lady fat, and then baby fat, and Fat Bobby seemed to be leaning more towards the baby fat kind of fat, which was still fat, but not obscenely so.

It was all very complicated, these gradations of fatness.

I walked past and Dad saw me and waved, and Bobby turned and waved. I gave them one back and continued up the porch and went inside. Mom was there and noticed the redness where Brock had backhanded me across the face. She looked worried and asked what had happened, and I told her Jim and I had been wrestling. Her worry went from the type I'd seen after the episode at the Haunted House, or when Dad had tussled with Mr. Templeton—the urgent, wringing-her-hands worry—to the

224

motherly scorn of someone who had to deal with the trouble of boys on a daily basis. She took in the dirt smears on my clothes and shook her head and told me to go wash up. I gladly went upstairs, away from those probing eyes.

I made a beeline for Sarah's room.

Taking a cue from her, I went inside without knocking, found her sitting in front of her nightstand mirror, an array of pink and red goop in front of her. Applying some of it to her lips and face, she was making all sorts of weird expressions in the mirror. When the door opened, her hand jerked in surprise and the stick of red lipstick she'd been applying made a smear on her cheek, so that she looked like a brave putting on war paint. Or a clown putting on his funny paint.

I went with the clown and told her so.

She threw a makeup compact at me and it hit me on the chest.

"Get out of my room," she said, her face blushed red so now she looked more like an Indian, but a retarded one that couldn't put on their war paint correctly. Maybe her warrior name was Dumb Deer Clown Face.

I told her this, and she got up and came at me like she intended to hit me, which she did, hard, but instead of retreating I stayed in her room and closed the door. Though it was obvious I wasn't going anywhere, she hit me a few more times.

"*Would you stop hitting me?*" I said, bringing up my arms to fend her off.

"Get out of my room then!"

She moved past me to the door, as if ready to open it and throw me out if I didn't leave of my own accord.

I moved between her and the door.

"Mr. Perrelli got to me and Jim while we were walking down the highway," I said, blurting everything out in one big stream of words. "He broke Jim's finger, and told me not to tell Mom or Dad or the police. He said he still wants his money and he'd be back for it. That we better have it ready or—"

I didn't finish because Mr. Perrelli hadn't really detailed what would happen if we didn't have the money. But he had left the distinct impression that it wouldn't be pleasant. I walked over to my sister's bed and sat heavily on it. Burying my face in my hands, I started crying.

Sarah, wiping the streak of lipstick off her face, came over and sat beside me. She put a hand on my back and patted me there, and I again remembered that night after the Haunted House. When, later that night, having learned what had happened to me and my friends, Sarah had come to my room and hugged me.

No, she really wasn't that bad of a sister at all.

"What'll we do?" I said when my sobs died down enough for me to speak semi-coherently.

Like an epiphany, I realized I was asking the wrong question, and with that realization came the answer. It wasn't what "we" were going to do. This whole thing had started because of me seeing some light in the woods and wanting to know what it was. It was me that had brought everyone else into the whole mess. First my friends, and now, if I was unable to get Vincent Perrelli what he wanted, and since I didn't have his money I couldn't think of any way that I could, his threat of escalation might include my family also.

The responsibility was mine, and mine alone.

Knowing what I had to do, unable to tell my sister, I sat with her for a few minutes longer, then got up and walked out. Knowing what I had to do and knowing it might be the last thing I ever did was emotionally taxing, and I suddenly wanted to be alone with my burden.

## 3.

Hindsight being what it is, I can see that deciding to meet with Mr. Perrelli alone was the dumbest decision I'd ever made.

If you took all the dumb asses on the planet—the kind of

people who struck matches near aerosol sprays; set electronics on the edges of their bathtubs while bathing; stuck their hands in kitchen appliances to try to fix them while the machines were still plugged in—increased their stupidity by making them all mental retards, and gave them all lobotomies to top it off, you still wouldn't have reached the level of God-awful stupidity that I was possessed of when I made this decision.

Of course I didn't see it as foolish then. I thought I'd come to some sort of revelation. I would find Mr. Perrelli and confront him with the truth, alone, and by me being alone and having the courage to tell him face to face that the money was gone, he'd have no other option but to believe me.

Now, he might hurt me, hell, he might kill me. But I thought that even if he did hurt me or kill me, he would still see the truth of it, that his money was gone, and having taken his frustrations out on me, he'd leave everyone else alone. Didn't even gangsters have a code of honor? In the movies they did. And so, in a strange way, my death would be a heroic one.

Well, I never did claim to be the smartest kid around.

It was the day following the brutal assault on Jim that I walked into town by myself. I left Bandit at home, fluffing a pillow on my bed for him so that he could settle down and rest his battered skull.

The walk down the highway and into town was a long and nerve-wracking one. I expected to see the black Cadillac at any moment, swerving in a rubber-squealing arc to cut me off on the shoulder of the road. Brock would step out and grab me and throw me in the backseat and lock the doors. Then would come the finger breaking, this time not Jim's but mine. When all my little fingers were snapped back like those jointed straws they give kids at restaurants, I'd be driven out into the desert, like mobsters did on TV, and thrown out into a ditch. As I tried to crawl out of the ditch with my crippled hands, a hammer or a shovel or a baseball bat would come slamming down on the back of my head, and that would be it for me.

Broken, lifeless, left in a ditch.

With my luck, my body would probably be found in an embarrassing position. Maybe with my pants down around my ankles. Or I'd loosened my bowels upon dying. Or birds would shit all over me.

But I made it into town okay. Strolling past housing tracts and into the business district, I passed the bookstore and saw my dad's car there. I walked slowly by the storefront, looked through the glass, tried to spy Dad or Tara and, seeing neither, continued on my way.

People were milling about on the sidewalks, window shopping at the various mom and pop stores that lined the streets, or sitting on the outdoor patios of the diners and restaurants interspersed among them. I watched these people, trying to find a pair of particular faces, and I looked at the cars parked along the streets and in the small parking lots, keeping an eye out for the distinctive black Cadillac.

I knew they were out there somewhere, watching me. How else had they found me the first time at the courthouse and then, at lunch with my friends and, finally, walking down the highway with Jim? Yes, they were out there, watching, and I hoped if I lingered long enough they'd approach me. Then whatever happened after that would happen.

I found myself walking the Town Square park, strolling the low grassy hills where a few days earlier the fireworks had exploded above in kaleidoscopic patterns. The smell of sulfur and smoke still lingered in the air, and I had the sense of walking the outskirts of hell itself.

Crossing the courthouse lawn, I cut a path to the sycamore near the broad concrete porch steps, where Mr. Perrelli and Brock had stepped out of the shadows that first night. I figured this was as good a message as any, if they saw me. I was saying, as clearly as I could think of: *Hey, here I am, I want to talk, come over here.*

Even at that age, the irony wasn't lost on me.

Here I was at the steps of a courthouse, waiting for mobsters.

And they came, the silver-haired one and the blockheaded one, both in their black suits on that hot and arid summer day, walking across the park in my direction. Watching them approach, I thought briefly about calling my plan off, about running home and telling my parents everything, all of it, the truth about the money and the body in the trunk of the Buick. About the Collector and what he wanted, and the arrival of Mr. Perrelli and Brock, and how they wanted the same thing. But then I thought again of what Mr. Perrelli had promised—escalation—and what that could mean for the people close to me, those I cared about. My family, my dog, my friends; all of them. So I remained where I was and watched the two men approach. They stopped in front of me and I felt trapped, which I guess I was.

"You look like a kid with a lot on his mind," Mr. Perrelli said.

His hands were in his pinstriped jacket pockets like he was out for a casual stroll, not a murderer and monster walking the world in the guise of a man.

"I want to talk about the money," I said, my voice calmer than I felt inside. Inside I felt sick and fragile and tremulous, like I might fall apart at any moment.

"That's a wise decision," Mr. Perrelli said. He smiled what he probably thought was a friendly smile. "But not here. Take a ride with us."

He made a nodding motion with his head, the intention clear: *Follow.*

I didn't move.

Now that it was happening, my idea didn't seem so inspired and heroic anymore. I imagined being in a car alone with these two, maybe in the backseat with Brock or Perrelli, as one drove and the other guarded me. Or maybe in the front seat with both of them, trapped in between them and nowhere to go.

"As long as you tell us what we want to hear," Mr. Perrelli said, coming forward and putting a hand on my shoulder like a reassuring friend, "you have nothing to worry about."

With that arm he drew me towards them, and I had no choice but to follow or run. I didn't run, and we crossed through the precision-mowed, Irish-green grass, under the high and bright sun like a fiery eye. At the curb there it was, the black Cadillac, only it didn't seem like a Cadillac to me anymore, but a hearse, and there was going to be a funeral procession and I had the leaden feeling that it just might be in my honor.

* * *

We drove for several minutes, ending up in a nondescript rural neighborhood of spaced out manufactured houses dotting the land so that nature and construction appeared at a peaceable truce. The houses, about a half dozen, were hues of warm tans and whites, and the acreage of each plot leant the area an air of both seclusion and neighborliness. Here one could wave to a neighbor in the distance, and yet go about one's business in relative privacy.

The road curved in a wide cul-de-sac and Brock steered the Cadillac into the driveway of the house at the heel of the U. Beyond, the buzz of traffic along the highway we'd just departed could be heard, a background noise that lulled in this pocket neighborhood slightly removed from the rest of civilization. Mr. Perrelli got out and held the door open for me like a doorman. I got out, wondering how many doormen in the world had killed people and did time in prison. Scary thing to think of next time you're walking into a fancy hotel or restaurant and that bellhop is holding the door open for you.

My advice: tip big.

We walked up to the front door of the house together, me between the two men like the President escorted by Secret Service.

I don't think any president had to worry about finger-breaking Secret Service agents, though. Brock fished out a key and unlocked the door, and we stepped into the house together.

First thing I noticed was the dried rust-brown stains dotting the carpet and wall of the foyer. To the left of me more dots of that brown stain, and a couple smears leading to a door I guessed led to the garage. I wondered who had lived here before Mr. Perrelli and Brock had arrived in town, and where those people were now.

A faint astringent, unpleasant odor came from beyond that door to the garage, and I thought maybe I had an answer to where the owners of the house had gone off to. People stuffed in boxes or in the walls and dry-walled over came to mind, and I told my mind to shut up. I didn't want to think about it, turned away from the garage door, and followed Mr. Perrelli across the living room.

There was a lamp knocked over, little pieces of the bulb that had shattered shining in the shag of the carpet like diamonds. More smears of that ugly brown color on the dividing wall of the living and dining rooms could have merely been the careless prints of finger-painting children, I told myself. A couple pictures hanging askew gave away the lie. The pictures showed an elderly couple, gray-haired and wrinkled but lively and smiling like their company returned to each other the life that time sought to steal away.

The stains; the pictures; the smell from the garage.

I knew what had happened to the old couple, in broad strokes if not in the details. Escalation had happened. Escalation and business.

In the dining room was a sofa facing an entertainment center taking up one half of the room. The other half hosted a long dining table with frilly place settings and a glass vase with flowers at the center of it. The furniture was seen and registered almost by rote, though, like when you walk into your own home and you see the furnishings there but you don't really pay them any

231

mind because they're always there. It's just something you see, but don't *really* see.

Because although I saw the room itself, what I really saw were the people in it, and I probably would have turned and tried to run then if Brock and Perrelli weren't right next to me like a wall.

On the sofa facing the entertainment center was Dillon Glover and his friends: overweight Stu, and pimple-specked Max. Each had a can of beer in their hands, frosted and beaded with condensation, arms splayed on the armrests or back of the sofa, legs on the table before them. The three older boys looked at me when I walked in and smiled wicked smiles that would make a snake cringe. Dillon's smile was particularly eerie, that crooked smirk punctuated by a still fading yet noticeable blue bruising around his nose and eyes where my forehead had pounded his face some weeks ago. The bluish tint to his countenance made me think of zombies in movies, and his grin looked hungry.

On the other side of the room, the half dominated by the long dining table, sat Sheriff Glover, Dillon's father, facing me at the head of the table. It struck me that this was the first time I'd seen them together. Son muscled, father fat, the resemblance was still unmistakable in the vicious glint of their eyes, and the malice that radiated out from behind them like a hidden spectator peeking through curtains. Sheriff Glover was in his tan and brown uniform, which I thought was bold of him when in the presence of killers. Bold or stupid, or maybe he didn't care.

He too smiled at me, and I didn't care for that smile anymore than the winks he gave, or the tip of the hat. His every feigned display of propriety was a nuanced mockery and as much as the Collector or Mr. Perrelli and Brock, I knew Sheriff Glover wasn't really human anymore. Not in the ways that mattered. Whatever had been in him as a kid, whatever intangible is in each of us when we're born into this world, that made him human had long since rotted away.

The implications of his presence, along with that of his son and his son's friends, raced through my head. I wasn't sure about the how or why of it, but this whole thing was far bigger than a car full of money in the woods.

Or a car full of money was a far bigger deal than we kids had ever imagined.

"Have a seat," Mr. Perrelli said to me, and whether he meant the sofa with Misters Smirk, Pudge, and Pimple Head, or at the dining table with Sheriff Fatty, I didn't know. It was left up to me, I guess, and that was one of those lesser of two evils choices.

I chose the table, taking the seat at the far end across from the sheriff.

Don't ask me why I chose one over the other. I held no pretenses about one part of the room being safer than the other. I knew that not only had the shit hit the fan for me, it had short circuited the fan, caused a big fucking fire, and now I was smack in the middle of a shitfire that would probably burn me alive, and I'd die with the smell of shit in my nostrils.

Life is pretty shitty that way sometimes.

"Now," Mr. Perrelli said when I was seated, he and Brock remaining at the threshold of the room, still standing, like guards on high overlooking a prison yard, "let's hear about the money."

I took a deep breath, knowing what I was about to say wasn't what he wanted to hear. The Glovers and Glover Junior's friends weren't going to be very happy, either. They obviously had some sort of arrangement with Perrelli. I was about to stir up a hornet's nest, and this hornet's nest included a big bull of a hornet named Brock who broke fingers for fun, and I thought I was pretty much fucked.

"We burned the money," I said.

Looking up at Mr. Perrelli, I hoped against all odds that he'd see the truth in my face, that maybe Jesus would appear to him with this revelation, and he'd be moved by the Spirit to let me go. The look on his face told me he was definitely seeing something, but it wasn't the Lord Almighty.

"I see," Vincent Perrelli said, and his hands in his coat pockets withdrew and went behind his back, like a man idly thinking and measuring things in his head. "That is unfortunate."

I dared look away from Mr. Perrelli to Dillon Glover and his pals, then swung my gaze from them to the sheriff. No one was smiling anymore. I don't know if that was a good thing or not. I didn't miss their crocodile smiles much, but the flat looks on their faces weren't exactly winning any beauty pageants either.

"You promised me payment," Sheriff Glover said from the other end of the table. "You said I'd get a cut. I've been keeping an eye out for that car of yours a long time, Vinnie. I was to let you know if it was ever found, keep people away from it, and you'd send someone to collect. That was the deal."

"Yeah," said Glover Junior. "You said we'd get a cut if we took you to the kid."

The sheriff shot his son a hard look that wordlessly told the older boy to shut up, and shut up he did. I didn't feel vindicated by the confirmation of my long held suspicion of the less than loving nature of the Glover father-son relationship. This wasn't the time for me to gloat in anything.

This was a time for me to watch, carefully, and wait.

"It's not my fault your collector fucked things up," Sheriff Glover added. "Payment's still due, Vinnie."

Dillon, Stu, and Max vigorously nodded their agreement.

Mr. Perrelli didn't so much as look at any of them. I was the center of his universe and, right then, I wished for one of those *Star Trek* wormholes that could take me to an alternate universe.

"Now, what I think we need here," Mr. Perrelli began, "is another example of just how serious I take my business affairs, Joey." He pursed his lips as he looked at me, like he was considering something. Then he gave a quick little nod like he'd come to a determination. "Yes, I think I need to show you just how much ten million dollars is worth."

His hands came out from behind his back.

234

In his right hand he held a black pistol with a long and slim cylinder of metal attached at the muzzle. He held the gun out at me, and I stared down the muzzle of a gun for the second time in my life. That dark eye at the center was like a glimpse into eternity. He would pull the trigger, and with the silencer there'd hardly be a sound. He'd blow off a hand or a foot, or maybe he'd just kill me and go after my friends. Seek the answers from them that I didn't have, that none of us had.

Either way, great pain or the final darkness, it was going to suck big time.

Then the pistol swung away from me in an arc sweeping from the dining room to the living room. Towards the sofa and the three guys sitting there, holding their cool beers like the masters of everything.

Stu dropped his beer just as the pistol let out a *hiss* and *pop* and a brief jet of fire coughed out of it. His chubby head spit out a cloud of red behind it. He fell and rolled off the sofa to the ground. The can of beer followed beside him, liquor and blood pooling on the carpet.

The pistol spit fire twice more.

A bullet went through the beer can Max had in his hands, spraying the foamy amber liquid all over his pockmarked face. Then the second bullet went *through* his face, spraying everything behind it in red.

Dillon Glover watched his friends fall and, even as the surprise of it broke the comfortably drunk serenity on his face, he rolled off the sofa and the third bullet meant for him struck and chipped the fireplace behind him.

"*Whatthefuck?*" Sheriff Glover muttered, streaming the words together so that it came out like the muddled syllables of a primitive language. His eyes were wide and he watched the scene before him with disbelief.

He fumbled at his belt holster even as Mr. Perrelli swung the silencer equipped pistol his way. The sheriff looked like a kid caught jacking off, trying to reach down and pull his zipper up even as his mom or dad came into the room.

Gun at his belt, or gun in his pants, it didn't matter what Sheriff Glover had been reaching for, because the pistol sent out its lick of flame once more, the *hiss* and *pop* of it like a campfire crackling at the last twigs, and a bloom of red spread across his shirt like a blossom. The sheriff toppled sideways, sliding off the chair and hitting the floor with a thump.

Silence followed. Wisps of smoke curled from the pistol like spirits rising.

Sitting at the table, I watched all of this frozen in my seat, afraid beyond words, but at least I hadn't pissed my pants like with the Collector, and so I figured I was making progress.

Vincent Perrelli's eyes fell on me for a moment, and the pistol began an arc back in my direction. His eyes sparkled with a sinister satisfaction.

"This is escalation," he said.

Movement from near the sofa. Dillon Glover rising, turning, running.

Mr. Perrelli swung the gun back that way. Brock also reached behind his back and his slab-like hand returned with his own silencer-tipped pistol.

Dillon dove past the dividing wall into the living room. Bullet holes appeared like magic in the plaster where he'd just been, trailing him.

Both men turned in pursuit.

Across the table from me, behind the now empty chair where the sheriff had been, a sliding glass door led to the backyard. I leapt up from my seat, dashed to the door, gripped it and slid it open.

Motion and a rustle of movement from behind me.

Darting into the backyard, I commanded my legs to move fast, faster. The sliding glass door shattered behind me, raining down on the paved patio in a million tinkling sounds like fairy music.

A set of heavy footfalls coming my way stomped a fast beat. I darted to the left, away from the remains of the glass door, towards the far side of the house and the alley there.

The pursuing footfalls slapped heavily onto the concrete patio behind me.

More *hisses* and *pops* from the whispering gun.

A pull of air and heat near my right ear made me yelp as I turned the corner into the alley between the house and the brick wall bordering the property. A jump of a spark flicked off the wall inches away. Far down the alley were a fence and gate and I ran for them.

Somewhere out of sight behind me, around the corner but close and getting closer, the heavier footfalls stomped after me.

My hands reached for the clasp holding the gate shut. I pulled at the contraption and the metal slipped through my fingers, wouldn't unlatch.

The plodding feet turned the corner, entering the mouth of the alley behind me.

I could almost feel the gun rising, taking aim.

The clasp lifted and the gate swung open. Ducking, I ran through.

More snags of air passed close by my head. I stumbled, bringing my hands to my head, feeling there like a boy on a first date checking his hair.

I ran, saw the black Cadillac, saw Mr. Perrelli some yards down the road, and Dillon even further, turning the far corner and disappearing out of sight. Standing at the center of the cul-de-sac, I shifted from foot to foot, took a step this way, then the other.

Brock's heavy footfalls were coming again, heavy and fast and determined.

Pivoting, I turned and darted around the end of the wall, leaving the property of the poor dead old couple lying lifeless somewhere in the garage behind me. A cement and dirt easement ran between the wall and the adjacent property, and I dashed down the narrow path. At the far end, a length of chain-link fence separated the neighborhood from the highway beyond. I ran for it, anxiously aware that the brick wall provided cover only until Brock turned the corner. Then, my back would provide an all too easy target in the narrow path of the easement.

I heard them calling out to each other, Perrelli saying that the Glover kid was gone. Here was the Hayworth kid, Brock shouted back, followed by two pairs of footfalls coming my way.

To my left, the old dead couple's nearest neighbor had an immense lawn, and several fruited trees. Recently watered, run-off from the sprinklers of the lawn had spilled across the concrete easement. Running at full speed, I hadn't the presence of mind to watch my footfalls, and I caromed from one side to the other as my rubber soles sought purchase on the wet concrete.

I fell hard, rolled, scrambled to my feet.

Grasped the wire of the chain-link, hoisted myself up and over. Dropped, landed awkwardly, almost fell again, then ran straight into the highway.

Traffic intermittent yet regular, I chose my path purposefully. With more than enough time to plot their courses around me or to slow down, drivers nonetheless greeted me with rude honks of their horns and ruder gestures out their windows.

I didn't stop until I was on the other side. Even then it was only a moment, a second or two, turning and looking back across the highway, over the hoods and roofs of the cars, past the honking, gesticulating motorists.

Peering through the links of the fence I'd leapt, staring across the highway at me, stood Mr. Perrelli and Brock. The older man waved. The big man only stared.

Perrelli mouthed one word at me, and even from the distance between us, I could read his lips and hear the word.

"Escalation."

# CHAPTER ELEVEN

## 1.

In comics the heroes are always in the right place at the right time to save the people that need to be saved. Oh, sure, you have the exception of the origin stories, in which almost every hero becomes a hero because of someone he or she lost. Spiderman is Spiderman because he failed to save Uncle Ben. Batman is Batman because he watched helplessly as his parents were murdered. Even Superman, before he decided to put on the cape and tights, watched his earth dad die of a heart attack. But after those early failures, the heroes always rise to the occasion. They take down the bad guys and save the world, no matter how diabolical the plot or seemingly insurmountable the odds against them.

But I wasn't a hero, and I was about as far away from the right place as could be. I was on foot while Mr. Perrelli and Brock had the Cadillac. To further complicate this, my family and friends lay in several different directions, and who to go to first, how to prioritize the value of their lives—not knowing who Mr. Perrelli would go after first, how he'd prioritize his killing, his *escalation*—made for a predicament that tore at my heart and mind.

* * *

239

I ran the two miles home as fast as I could. My chest was heaving, my heart pumping and thudding so hard there were echoes of it in my ears. Sweat drenched my shirt like it was a wash rag by the time I turned off the shoulder of the highway and into my neighborhood.

Dad's truck was in the driveway, and I realized he must be home for lunch with Mom, and the fact that they were together and Dad would never let anything happen to her lifted at least one responsibility off my shoulders. As I pushed through the front door and saw my parents at the dining table, I briefly thought about telling Dad everything, letting him carry the burden of figuring out how to deal with Mr. Perrelli and Brock.

Then I thought of Dad being pummeled by Mr. Templeton. That had been my fault also, and Dad had paid the price for it. I knew I might yet have to pass the burden of my troubles on to him but, before I did that, I had to get everyone together in one place.

That much at least was my responsibility.

"Joey, you alright?" Mom asked as I walked briskly past them and headed for the stairs.

"Son, you're sweating like you've run a marathon," Dad said.

"I'm … fine," I croaked.

Taking the stairs two at a time, I glanced back, eyeing the clock hanging on the wall in the foyer. Dad must have just arrived before I had. It was only a few minutes past noon, which gave him another forty-five minutes or so for his lunch hour before he had to leave again. That would be cutting it close for what I had planned.

Very close.

I headed straight for Sarah's room and pushed the door open. Like last time, she was planted in front of her dresser mirror, compacts like a painter's palette in front of her, and a tube of lipstick in one hand. Again, the sudden opening of her door made her jerk, and the lipstick nearly went up her nose, leaving a red streak over her upper lip and a smear across her nostrils.

"Can't you knock?" she barked at me.

I struggled to catch my breath. Taking my silence as defiance, she got up, fists clenched. Then reading something in my demeanor other than brotherly annoyance, she stopped short.

"What's wrong, Joey?"

I didn't immediately answer.

Thoughts of the dead froze me in place. The older couple that were probably putrefying in the sweltering summer heat in the closed garage. Mr. Pudge and Mr. Pimple, shot in the head and face. Sheriff Glover and his chest blooming red, like the fireworks exploding in color on the Fourth of July.

Then I thought of Mr. Templeton at the bottom of Lookout Mountain, twisted and broken. That took me even further back to the Collector and his knife at my throat. Which in turn led to the Haunted House and Dillon's switchblade prodding me in similar fashion.

The money.

The bound body in the trunk of the Buick, and the hole in its skull.

Everything that had occurred that summer came rushing back in one great tidal wave of terror. No longer did I feel like a teenager on the brink of something greater, those mysterious years past school, summer breaks, and days spent with friends. No longer did I feel like being brave and strong as my dad had taught me to be, not taking shit as I'd told Fat Bobby that first day by the stream in the woods. The boy who'd shattered an older boy's nose in the mirrored dark halls of a haunted house seemed far and distant.

Then and there in my sister's room, I just felt like a kid. A kid deep over his head in things he couldn't handle.

I realized I was trembling, tried to consciously will myself still.

"What happened?" Sarah asked, moving closer.

I told her everything. About deciding to speak with Mr. Perrelli by myself; he and Brock escorting me back to their car; the tract house in the nondescript neighborhood; the owners who were probably dead and the smell from the garage; and the shooting that left Dillon's pals and dad dead.

"We've got to tell Dad!" Sarah said. "He'll call the police!"

"And what do we tell them? How we wanted to steal ten million dollars? How we knew about a dead body and kept it a secret? How I just watched two kids and an officer murdered?" I shook my head. "We'd be stuck at the police station for who knows how long, all the while Mr. Perrelli would be out there tracking my friends down and—"

I didn't finish that thought, but our imaginations did just fine.

"Then what do we do?" she asked, her tone taking on an edge of panic.

"We get to everyone before Perrelli does."

"How?"

"We'll take Mom's car. You drive."

"And then what? If we get to everyone before they do?"

"We bring everyone back here," I said. I took a deep breath. Let it out slowly as if it might be the last breath I ever took and I wanted to relish it. "*Then* we tell Dad everything."

"And what if Mr. Perrelli follows us back home? What're we going to do? Have a big shoot-out?"

I said nothing after that, and Sarah looked at me as if I'd gone mad. I couldn't argue so much with that, but wondered if it was just me or the entire world.

## 2.

We decided on Jim's first since it was the closest. Not wanting him to get hurt, but not wanting to go completely unprotected, I decided to take Bandit with us and for once Sarah didn't complain about him. She even knelt briefly in the hallway and scratched him behind the ears. Downstairs, we headed for the door and Sarah snatched the extra pair of keys hanging from the pegboard on the wall nearby.

"I'm borrowing the car, Mom!" she called out behind us.

Mom and Dad were still at the dining table, finishing lunch, and one or both of them said something back, but we were already out the door. I threw it shut against any protestations, and we raced down the porch and across the walkway to the driveway. I loaded Bandit into the backseat of the car, then climbed in myself, Sarah getting in behind the wheel and starting the car. Pulling out with a squeal of tires and kicking up gravel, we backed out of the driveway and onto the road.

"Where's Bobby?" I asked, just now realizing I hadn't seen him at home.

Sarah looked at me as she turned the steering wheel.

"I think he went for a walk or something," she said.

"You *think*?"

My voice rose in near hysteria at the end there.

"I don't know!" Sarah said, almost yelling. "I think he just said he was going out! Maybe he went to Jim's."

Moments later we were on the highway, heading for the Connolly yard and racing against time—a force that waited for no one.

\* \* \*

I saw the rooms that Jim and his dad called home for the first time that day. Sarah pulled up to the gate of the Connolly car yard, and I got out to open it for her. We parked in front of the garage where the working bay doors were rolled up. The lights inside were on so that it looked like a trio of huge eyes looking out on the grounds.

Walking inside I saw one of the side doors open that Fat Bobby had pointed out to me before, and my sister and I walked

243

over to it. Our footfalls echoed like ghost footsteps on the concrete floor of the garage. We peeked through the door hesitantly like maybe we were looking in on a secret chamber. Sounds of crashes and explosions and gunfire came from inside, and the flashes cast by the television screen on the walls lent an eerie cast to things.

Inside it was startling to see, like some sort of optical illusion. It was far more spacious than I would have thought possible judging from the exterior of the garage. There was a small dining nook, complete with stove, cluttered island counter, refrigerator, and cupboards. A booth and table lined one wall, and adjacent to this was the living area, where a sofa and reclining chair sat in front of a television set atop a small wheeled stand. A VCR and a pile of movies were stacked atop the television like an electronic totem pole for some pagan techno-religion, and at the far end past all of this was a door open to another room. In this room were double bunks, a dresser, and a small desk.

Jim and his dad were on the sofa in front of the television. Seeing us, Mr. Connolly reached for the remote and muted the blaring speakers, but not before Bruce Willis yelled a "*Yippie kai-yay motherfucker!*" so loud it shook the walls.

"Hey, how you guys doing?" Mr. Connolly said.

We gave them little waves, Jim waved back from beside his dad, and I saw the large splint on his hand. The metal and gauze made his finger large and fat, making me think of those big foam rubber fingers at baseball games. I felt a quick surge of sickness rise up in me as I remembered Brock holding him, extending Jim's hand, and snapping the finger back so casually like a twig he'd picked up from the ground. I was glad to see Jim and his dad okay, Mr. Perrelli and Brock nowhere about, but that left Tara and Bobby out there still unaccounted for, and that added to the sick feeling in my gut.

"Fine," Sarah said. "We were hoping Jim could come out for awhile."

I looked at Jim across the room, he looked back at me, and it was clear that he read something in our expressions and knew something was up. Apparently Mr. Connolly was on the same wavelength, or close to it, because his eyes swept from me to my sister, and then back again before he spoke.

"It seems you kids keep getting in trouble when you're all together," he said. A half grin on his face made this seem like a joke that wasn't particularly funny the second and third time around. "Stabbings, broken fingers. I don't know how many more lives poor Jim's got hanging around you kids."

Mr. Connolly's tone, though half joking was also half serious, and it was that serious part that made me look away from him. I couldn't meet his eyes knowing what had just happened to me that morning in the tract house in town, and what I was probably dragging Jim into. But I could think of no other way to protect my friends unless we were all together, with the exception of telling the whole truth, right now, and I wasn't ready to do that with an adult who wasn't much more than a stranger to me. A nice man, I had no doubt Jim's dad was, but a stranger still.

I'd save the truth for my dad once I had all my friends with me. He'd know what to do. He always did.

"We're just going to pick up Tara, sir," my sister said. "Then we're all going back to our place. Just to hang out."

"Uh huh," Mr. Connolly murmured, and by his tone I thought the scales were leaning towards the joking side of things. "But if my son comes back blinded, decapitated, burnt to a crisp, or otherwise crippled, dismembered, or dead, just know I'll be sorely pissed."

Sarah and I both nodded. Jim smiled and pushed up from the sofa, attentive of where he put his bandaged finger and the weight and pressure he put on it. He walked over to us and said goodbye to his dad. Sarah did too, but I kept walking and for some reason I felt something like daggers on my back and I knew that if I turned to look I'd see Mr. Connolly looking at me, and me alone.

His eyes would shine like lanterns and he'd see through me and know what was going on inside.

The dark and hidden things all of us hide.

\* \* \*

On the highway into town, I stared out the window and the desert to either side was like a sheet of ancient and brown parchment rolled out. Jim asked what was happening, leaning forward from the backseat so that his head was poking out like a jack-in-the-box between my sister driving and me.

I told him about meeting Perrelli at the park. Told him about being driven to the nondescript neighborhood and led into the house. The smell inside and the bloodstains. The others inside waiting: our old friends the Glovers along with Glover Junior's pals. The shooting that followed and how I made a run for it.

"He still doesn't believe we burned the money?" Jim asked.

I shook my head.

"What if we didn't?" Jim said, and Sarah and I both snapped our heads towards him. Sarah had to turn hers back to the road when the car started drifting, but my gaze remained fixed on my friend.

"What're you talking about?" I asked.

Jim eased back from between the front seats, settling into his like he was trying to get as much distance between us as possible. He even looked down and away, and he'd never looked away from me before, always looked me square in the eyes. I knew I wasn't going to like what I was about to hear.

He didn't answer immediately, but looked out the window at the desert landscape whizzing by. Like there was something out there he wanted to see but couldn't find it.

"Jim?" I said, with more than a hint of anger in my voice. "What the hell are you talking about?"

After a moment he looked at me again. There wasn't shame or embarrassment in his expression, but neither was there defensive anger aimed back at me. Instead, he wore a sort of dead expression, a resignation, and somehow that was worse.

"Bobby took some of the money before we burned it," Jim said, looking at me with that flaccid face.

"What?" Sarah exclaimed, shooting a look at Jim through the windshield rearview mirror.

"What the fuck are you talking about?" I repeated.

"Before moving the money to Lookout Mountain," Jim began flatly, like he was lecturing about the thrills of watching grass grow to an audience of rocks, "Bobby wanted to put some of the money somewhere else, in case things went wrong."

"In case things went wrong …" I said, shaking my head, thinking that was the understatement of the year.

"Which they did," Jim said, a tinge of emotion returning to his voice, and then it dawned on me why and I actually lowered my head into my hands.

"It wasn't just Bobby," I said. "You wanted the money too."

It wasn't a question.

Now he did meet my gaze, and a spark of that old Jim—the Jim who was raised like me and didn't take shit from anyone— returned. His brow was furrowed and his mouth did something like a sneer or growl, as if he might bite.

"We all wanted the money," he said. "That was the plan when we found it, and we didn't see why it should change just because some weirdo threatened you."

"He didn't just threaten me, Jim!" Stretching, I leaned towards the backseat like I was on the verge of climbing back there and fighting him, which maybe I was. "He threatened all of us! And it wasn't just threats! The Collector would've killed us all! Maybe keep parts of us for souvenirs and shit!"

"But he didn't kill us!" Jim shouted back, leaning forward again so that we were nearly face to face. Spittle leapt between us like

247

little liquid gymnasts. "We killed him and we still burnt the money! What kind of sense does that make? We were in the clear! The money was ours! And we burned it!"

"The money wasn't ours!" I threw the words back at him, our faces close enough to kiss if I suddenly chose to go gay and wanted some hot black action. "It was never ours!"

Bandit, on the seat beside Jim, looked back and forth between us, confused.

I knew I was talking to myself as much as I was to Jim. I think he realized that too because we both almost instantly calmed, moving away from each other and settling back into our respective seats.

"How much did you guys hide?" I asked.

"Two million," Jim said without hesitation.

Even then that number rolled around my head. It wasn't ten million, but it was sure still a hell of a lot more than I'd probably ever see at one time if I lived to be a hundred. Divided five ways and that was four hundred thousand each. That was still a lot of comics and books and all sorts of things.

Everything in me told me these thoughts were wrong.

I tried to push them away, but they wouldn't go.

Then something else dawned on me, and why it wasn't the first thing on my mind after hearing Jim's confession about the money, I didn't know. Dad would have been deeply ashamed, and that was the clincher that helped me refocus my thoughts.

"Bobby's the only other one that knows about the two million?" I asked.

"Yeah," Jim said.

"Any idea where he is?"

"No," Jim said, and his mental wheels and cogs began to move the same as mine. He again leaned forward so that he was between Sarah and me. "He's not at your house?"

I shook my head.

"So he's out there somewhere," Jim said, and the vagueness of

248

that, like Bobby was lost in a formless and directionless world, seemed somehow right and true, but that wasn't entirely accurate either. Because out there, separated from us, Fat Bobby wasn't truly alone. There were others out there, looking, searching, hunting. And if they found him before we did I think then he truly would be lost.

We all would.

### 3.

Though she'd given me her address a while ago, I realized with a mild surprise that this was the first time I'd been to Tara's house. That I'd kissed her and touched her, and she'd kissed and touched me, and yet I'd never seen where she'd lived seemed strange. I wondered if that meant something: two people in some ways so close, and yet keeping a certain distance.

I wondered not for the first time if the old Buick, the money and the body inside it, had tainted us in some way. Soiled us and left us stained at the deepest of levels, at the root and core, so deep maybe that you couldn't see it. Perhaps so far down it could only be felt. Yet its effect on things was nonetheless real and acted as a force and attracted certain things and kept certain things away.

Gravities and polarities, I thought, those words coming to me from somewhere, with the beginning of a meaning I'd never attached to them before.

When we pulled into the driveway, I stepped out and strode up the walkway to the front door. Pressing the doorbell, I waited in dread. As at the Connolly yard under Mr. Connolly's scrutinizing gaze, I felt that when the door opened my deceit would be laid bare.

I realized that I should be there on that doorstep asking Tara to a movie, or asking her out to eat somewhere.

But that's not why I was there.

I was there to gather her up and take her somewhere where bad things would happen. The understanding that maybe this was all I could ever give her, all that I would ever have to give, brought a heavy sadness upon me.

Yet it was necessary, I told myself, clinging to that fragile and clumsy belief. The alternative—all of us apart, separate, easy pickings for those in the black Cadillac searching for us—was no alternative at all.

Her dad opened the door. Tall and lean, his sharp face again reminded me of a bird of prey looking down. His smile, no doubt intended as a pleasantry, made him look hungry. I wanted nothing more than to be away from him as soon as possible.

"Hello, Joey," he said.

"Hi, sir. I was hoping I could see Tara."

He looked over my shoulder at the car in his driveway. He waved. I looked back, saw my sister and friend waving in return. Bandit looked out the window like a forlorn stowaway.

"Kids have a day planned?" he said. In his uniform, the gun at his belt, he seemed not merely a park ranger, but a Gestapo ready for an interrogation.

"Nothing special," I said. "Just board games maybe. My mom's going to bake something. Just thought, you know, school's getting closer and we're not going to have much time once it starts."

He nodded as if this all made sense. I hoped he didn't ask why I hadn't called beforehand. That seemed an obvious question to me, and I had no ready reply if it should become one for him too.

He didn't have a chance to ask it.

Tara came down the stairs then and to the front door. Her dad moved aside a bit to let her in the doorway. We looked at each other and something like what had passed between me and Jim back at his place seemed to pass between her and I.

"Mind if I go out for a bit, Daddy?" she asked, looking up at

250

her dad like Sarah had done with ours back at the fair, like Mom had done that same night to get him to let me go with my friends. The batting of eyelashes, a little tilt of the head like a puppy; kryptonite to any man, be him father or love-struck boy.

"Sure," he said. "I don't see why not."

Tara and I hurried back across the lawn together to the car. I wished again that someday I could make that walk to her front door and it would be for that movie or lunch. It seemed to me the denial of this was in some ways as much a crime as clubbing a man to death and sticking him in the trunk of a Buick.

* * *

On the highway heading back home, each of us scanned the shoulders of the road looking for Bobby. I'd filled Tara in on my morning with Mr. Perrelli and Brock, and the mention of the shootings made her go a shade of white so pale that the blue of her veins stood out beneath her skin like cords. I didn't have to hold any psychology degrees to know that my story had pulled her back to Lookout Mountain, when she'd shot the Collector. After that, no one said anything for awhile.

Until I noticed Sarah's eyes moving again and again to the rearview mirror, her face frantic. I turned around to look out through the rear window, craning my neck side to side to see past the heads of my friends and my dog.

A black Cadillac, long and sleek, sped towards us like a torpedo zeroing in on its target. Soon, bumper to bumper with us, it hung there, straying only the merest of inches. So close, the roar of its engine behind us was like a beast. The windows were tinted, shadowed, so that there seemed no driver. Just a black ghost car rumbling down the highway.

Jim and Tara both turned to see what I was looking at, what had Sarah so frenzied. Immediately, Jim turned back, pushed forward again so he was between the front seats, a hand gripping either one, me having to move back into mine so he didn't collide with me.

"Don't stop!" he shouted in Sarah's ear.

My sister hit the gas pedal and the car surged forward.

The Cadillac swerved and picked up speed also. It drew up alongside our car with ease, so close that if Sarah rolled down her window she could reach out and touch it.

It swerved towards us, striking the driver's side and sending sparks showering about like radioactive rain. Sarah screamed; we all screamed. The impact rocked us, sending me hard into the passenger window. For a moment the steering wheel spun out of my sister's hand and the car jerked to the right. The tires left the road and crunched gravel. Grains of it struck the undercarriage with a Morse Code-like *tap tap tap tap*.

Sarah caught the wheel. Pulled the car back onto the road.

Where the Cadillac again swerved and broadsided us.

More glowing sparks like hot rain; more screams; the crunch and crinkle of tortured metal. The tires left the road again. More gravel *tap tap tapping* underneath the car.

My sister tried to get us on the highway again, hit the gas pedal harder and tried to bring us forward, ahead, and around the Cadillac. But it was there blocking our path, black and malignant. Dark metal like a thing of shadows, a sliver of the night come alive.

The Cadillac swerved again, striking the side of our mother's car, and insanely I thought: *Well, I don't think either of us will ever be allowed to drive again.*

With this collision, the driver's side tires were forced off the road too, and the car dipped as we hit the shoulder. Dirt plumes rose about us like we were at the base of a tornado. Sarah hit the brakes, and the car squealed to a stop.

Bandit barked from the backseat.

Jim was chanting something that sounded druidic, but I don't think druids ever gathered around Easter Island chanting: "*shit-shitshitshitshit.*"

Tara or Sarah was crying. Maybe both of them. Or maybe it was me.

Through the dirt clouds I saw the vague form of the Cadillac speed ahead of us, and then the shape of it lost in dusty vapors. I realized I was gripping the armrest beside me as if to secure myself against another impact.

I let go.

Opening the door, I stepped out.

Breathing in deeply, I inhaled dirt as well as air, and coughed violently like a black-lunged smoker. I waved the billows of dirt away with little effect, waited for them to settle.

Other doors opened and everyone else got out.

"Was that them?" my sister asked. No one answered. No one had to. "They're trying to fucking kill us!"

Again, there was no need to answer.

Bandit trotted beside me, his tail hung low.

Then he was barking and, at first, I tried to shush him, until I heard what he heard and I turned to stare down the highway. Saw what he saw. I called out to everyone else, pointing.

There was a scrabble of footfalls as everyone lined up to look down the highway at what I needlessly pointed at.

I thought maybe we should have been getting back in the car, then wondered how much protection that would give us.

The shiny grill like a metal sneer preceding it, the Cadillac roared our way. It ate up the highway between us like a starving animal licking up a length of intestines. We stood where we were as if anchored to the ground, watching the car draw nearer, moving fast and yet seeming to approach us in slow motion at the same time.

The Cadillac slowed as it neared.

The rear door opened as it rolled past.

Mr. Perrelli was in the backseat. So was Bobby. Mr. Perrelli held Bobby around the throat with one arm. With the other he fished underneath his black suit jacket and pulled out a pistol.

He put it to the back of Fat Bobby's skull.

Feeling the chill and solidity of it, Bobby's eyes widened in shock. He reached out for us, fingers splayed.

Vincent Perrelli pulled the trigger.

Bobby's head exploded.

Mr. Perrelli kicked out with a foot to Bobby's back. Bobby slumped forward, did a half somersault, landed on the pavement in front of us. The top of his head was missing and some of him poured out like the contents of a capsized soup bowl.

The Cadillac continued to roll past.

I stared down at my friend. His fingers and one leg jittered and twitched as the remaining electricity in him misfired, trying to fuel life where there was none.

I realized someone was screaming again, but it was muted and distant as if I'd somehow turned off the world. I saw only my friend there, his insides on the outside, on the pavement, under the sun, dead.

Something in me loosened, fell, was lost.

I turned in the direction towards town, where the Cadillac was still rolling slowly away, taunting us with its leisurely pace. I took a step or two towards it. A wet squish as one shoe landed in something underfoot that I didn't want to think about.

"*We have the money!*" I shouted, and now the world returned to life, and I heard my words above all other sounds. It was loud, angry, seemed to shake all of creation like the voice of God.

The Cadillac braked. The rear door was still open.

"My house! Midnight!"

A black-sleeved arm reached out and pulled the Cadillac door shut. The black car picked up speed and I watched it for a distance until it crested a rise, went down it and was gone, creature of ebony in the bleached desert white.

254

# 4.

We loaded Bobby into the backseat. The others wanted to put him in the trunk, but I refused to let that happen and sat in the back with him, cradling his ruined head and looking into a face that was no longer all there, trying to remember that face. Bandit sniffed at the mess, and I let him. Maybe my dog had a way of seeing what I no longer could.

Jim was on the other end of the rear seat, pressed as far against the door as possible, not looking at what lay between us.

Tara had taken my place in the front passenger seat.

Sarah still drove.

I told her where to go, speaking softly, as if not to disturb the boy in my lap. As if he were just napping. I expected some resistance to my directions, was ready to scream it to submission, but nobody offered any.

Looking down on my dead friend, his clothes specked with his own blood, the juices of him staining my lap, I cried, I think, but it wasn't hysterical. They were tears of shame, tears of loss. I cried at what I had done; at what I had failed to do; at the things that I could never do again.

If I cried, I like to think that my tears fell and mingled with his blood. That way a part of me is with him always. My tears, his blood, the various waters of life.

Jim had once told me about other access roads into the woods. I tried to think of the nearest one and told Sarah how to get there. We found it and turned onto it, the trees sprouted up around us out of the desert, and again I was struck by this strange land. How there was nothingness and desert, and then the green and majesty of forestry just around the bend. Life and death; color and the void; those polarities that seemed so intent on finding me, revealing themselves in all their apathetic glory.

This access road eventually met with the familiar fork that was ours. I knew if I leaned over and looked out the window I'd see the old rusted sign, fallen in the grass in the rutted road. Here we turned and kept driving, and sometime later we came to the old Buick, sitting there unmoving, immovable perhaps, waiting for us as if it belonged to us, and us to it. That it hadn't been moved by the police, even after the incident on Lookout Mountain, didn't seem strange at all to me then, nor does it now. Some things are monolithic in their existence, transcending all the orders of the world.

That old Buick was just such a thing. A permanent fixture upon the earth, testament to life and death and all things between.

I told my friends what I wanted to do and looks were exchanged, but no one argued which I thought was a good idea. I wouldn't have argued with me at that moment either. Plus, I think they understood.

We were Bobby's family. He belonged to us, and we to him. It was for us to decide what to do with him.

The Outsiders' Club: we always watched out for each other, no matter what.

The four of us grabbed and lifted Fat Bobby, Jim and I at his arms, Tara and Sarah each at a leg, Bandit plodding along beside us like an honor guard. We carried him from our car to the Buick. The trunk was still open as it had been since that night we'd met the Collector and led him to Lookout Mountain. The old body, bound hand and foot and with a hole in its skull, gone, I thought: *Out with the old, in with the new*, and I had the brief and incredible urge to laugh. Then it was replaced with the urge to cry again, and we lifted Fat Bobby and hefted him into the trunk of the Buick.

For a time we all stood there and stared down at him.

His head was in shadow and you could barely make out the ruin of it and for a moment he looked almost normal. I could almost pretend as if he were just lying there, sleeping. Then reality crept in and I knew I was looking at a corpse. He was asleep alright. A sleep from which he would never awaken.

I reached up and closed the trunk lid.

"There's a pond not too much farther down the road," Jim said. "The stream feeds into it."

I nodded.

"Will the car move without a key?" Tara whispered, as if she were afraid to speak.

A thought came to me then as if out of the ether. Something, in all our time with the Buick, we'd never thought of doing. Leaning in across the driver's seat, I reached for the glove compartment, gripped the latch, and pulled it open with a brief, harsh tug.

Inside were some old yellowed papers like ancient documents, an owner's manual, and … a set of keys. Grabbing the keys by the fob, I settled in the driver's seat. The third key I tried fit into the ignition. Turning it, the steering wheel unlocked, and I looked out at my friends as if for affirmation.

"Put it in neutral," Jim said, "and we'll push it."

I got out, and Sarah settled behind the wheel of the Buick, put it in neutral, and released the emergency brake. Jim and I got behind the car. Tara stood at the passenger side behind the open door, using the doorframe for leverage. Sarah steering, we pushed the car, turning it around slowly, the ancient tires flaking away in black drifts. I groaned and huffed with the effort, heard Jim and Tara doing the same. Then we had it facing the other direction, and going straight, the going was a bit easier.

We rolled it along beneath the intermittent shade of the over-reaching forest trees—for how long I don't know. Occasionally, deeper ruts in the road gave us problems, so that we had to heave-ho and rock the Buick rhythmically until we built momentum and could roll it out of the rut and get it moving again. Soon, I was sweating as if I'd run a mile. I could smell myself, the sour sweat and pine of the forest and the heat of the day mixing into a noxious odor.

Finally we came to it, glimpsed through a break in the trees, glimmering with the green of fallen leaves and reflected leaves and the moss beneath its surface coating the rocks like fine earthen pelts: an emerald pond, almost magical in its strange color and still, fluid face. Only just larger than the Buick itself, I wondered if it had been waiting here for the car, as the car had been waiting on the road for us.

Through the break in the trees we steered off of the road, branches snapping under the nearly tireless rims. As it rolled nearer, Sarah climbed carefully out from behind the wheel and stood and walked alongside the car, positioning herself like Tara opposite her, pushing the car ever closer to the placid green water. Then the front of the Buick dipped down and we all pushed harder, groaning and gritting our teeth, and Sarah and Tara left their positions and came around to the rear to join Jim and I. There the four of us pushed together, digging our heels into the ground with the effort.

The car rolled into the pond.

It sunk to the door handles, seemed to bob there for a moment like a child's bathtub float toy. It rolled forward a bit more. Water cascaded into the open doors, filling the space inside, weighing it down, pulling it down.

The water of the pond bubbled as the car sank lower, and then there was just the roof of it, almost even with the surface of the pond, so that if you were to wade out and climb atop it you could probably do a good imitation of Jesus walking on water. In time that too was gone, and a gurgle of water like a faint burp seemed to announce this. Bubbles rose to the surface and popped.

A ripple followed and then that too faded, and we stood there gathered at the tiny shore of the watery grave. In our silence we felt the passing of the dead in the quiet of the woods. The light of the sun seemed muted in the tall imposing stillness of the woods and the cold, wider world beyond.

# CHAPTER TWELVE

## 1.

It was afternoon when our little funeral was done and we were back on the highway heading home. No one spoke and there was nothing to say.

We pulled in the driveway and filed out. I thought briefly of what Mom would say when she saw her car, then decided it didn't matter because she and Dad would soon know everything. Dad's car was still in the driveway, although his lunch hour had long passed, but this was just fine by me. Mr. Perrelli had obviously been busy with us, which meant my parents were safe and sound. Whatever the reason he was still home, we could now tell him everything without having to wait. The sooner everything was on the table, the sooner we could prepare for what was coming.

Trudging up the porch, I opened the screen door, left behind a rusty smear. A smear of Bobby.

Sarah opened the front door and we all stepped inside.

The curtains were all pulled shut, and the lamps and overhead bulbs were off, putting the house in an artificial and premature dimness. Mom and Dad were at the dining table as they had been earlier in the day. For a moment there was a sense of déjà vu, and I thought briefly of science fiction stories of temporal loops where people lived the same day over and over again. I wondered why my parents would sit or eat in darkness, and was about to ask them when I noticed something.

They weren't sitting across from each other as they had been during Dad's lunch earlier. Instead, they were side by side, facing us from across the table. Underneath the table, I could see their legs were tied to the legs of the chairs. The way their arms were hooked out of sight around the backs of the chairs, I assumed they were likewise bound.

Blood streaked their faces.

The deep purple-green of ripe bruises complemented the blood.

Taking a hesitant step or two forward, I saw Mom's makeup was running down her face and I knew she'd been crying. She made noises when she saw us enter, but the wadded cloth stuffed in her mouth made her gag on the sounds. Dad rolled his head and tried to open his swollen eyes when he heard her, and his squinty stare made him look vaguely Asian. He saw us and tried to talk as well, but the gag in his mouth allowed him only weak moans and incomprehensible utterances.

Sarah and I ran towards our parents, fell to our knees beside them, working frantically and ineffectually at the tight fishing line knots that bound them. The fishing wire bit deeply into their wrists, and seeing the rawness and redness of their flesh made me wince.

I heard Bandit growl, his claws clacking on the hardwood foyer floor, then the light clacking of him bounding upstairs.

Behind us I heard Tara's gasps as she took in our parents. I heard Jim utter something with "fuck" and "shit" in it.

From upstairs came a pained yelp and the sound of something heavy hitting the floor.

I stood when I heard Bandit's cry of pain, trapped in indecision. The knots around my mom's wrists and ankles may as well have been iron chains. Did I find something to cut her free or charge upstairs to find my dog?

"*We don't have the money yet!*" I screamed upstairs in frustration and anger. There were supposed to be rules, I thought. In school and at home, everywhere in life there were rules. I'd said midnight. That was the rule I'd established and they were supposed to follow it, and yet here they were. "*I said midnight!*"

But something didn't make sense. I hadn't seen the black Cadillac anywhere outside. Also, Perrelli and Brock had driven in the opposite direction after dumping Bobby, back towards town.

How had they gotten here ahead of us? Had they turned around while we were busy with Bobby? Headed back here? Even without knowing where the money was?

From above me a rustling issued at the top of the stairs.

Turning, I saw the figure flowing down like moving shadows, fluid darkness, billowing coat and wide fedora, face in darkness, face of shadows. Here he came, drifting down as if smoke given form, and the knife, the knife in his hands, sprung from nowhere, from the void, that long and sharp knife, that cruel tooth. The Collector descended, shot and supposedly dead, but not dead, definitely not; instead, here in my house, floating down like a living storm cloud. His coat flapped like large black wings as he descended on us, enveloping us, eclipsing all else.

Jim tried to turn and open the door. But the Collector was there, across the distance between them as if teleported, and grabbed my friend by the arm and twirled and threw him. Jim danced across the room and collided with the stairway banister, crashing to the floor in a heap.

Tara tried for the door next, and the Collector glided towards her, intercepting her, grabbing her and likewise tossing her as he had Jim. Tara met the door of the foyer closet face first with a thud, rebounded off of it, and crumpled to the floor also.

"*Get Dad loose!*" I yelled at my sister, and then I was running across the room at the dark form of the Collector. His face was pale and vague in the midst of the shadows, a blur, a ghost of color, watching me coming at him.

His knife rose as I ran at him.

Skidding to a stop feet from him, I twirled, did a little pirouette, and shot out one leg. I didn't really expect much against
this man, the thing of shadows, but my foot met his knife hand
and then the knife was arcing through the air and fell to the floor
with a clatter.

I sent another kick at his crotch, hoping for the satisfying
crunch and pop of his testicles against my foot. But my kick was
stopped in midair by one pale hand, and he lifted and threw and
I was flying backwards, doing an impression of a novice tumbler,
first looking up, then down, the house around me right side up,
then upside down, whirling and twirling like I was caught in a
whirlwind. My face met the floor and all motion stopped, the
world seemed to pause, and then blackness seeped in like a fluttering blanket settling atop me.

* * *

When next I opened my eyes I found myself in a chair at the
dining table next to my parents. My sister and Jim were also in
chairs across the table from us. We could have been sitting down
for dinner if not for the fact that we were all bound to the furniture we sat on.

The fishing line bit cruelly into my wrists and ankles, and
when I tried to wriggle them I felt a numbness and tingling like
the pins and needles when a limb has fallen asleep. Through the
slim partings in the curtains at the windows, it seemed all the
darkness wasn't just from the lack of lighting in here. Afternoon
had passed and evening had settled in.

The clock on the wall above the television read nine o'clock.
I'd been out for awhile.

Looking around the table, first at my parents then at my sister
and friend, I saw they were all conscious or close to it. Panicked
eyes looked back at me, and I guessed I probably looked much

the same to them. I wanted to say something to them, but jammed deep into my mouth was a cloth of some sort, tasting of old food and carrying with it the faint smells of long ago meals.

I didn't see Tara anywhere.

She wasn't at the table with us, and from my mostly unobstructed view of the kitchen and living room, she wasn't in those rooms either. Unless she was lying on the floor, unconscious or dead, out of sight behind the sofa.

I remembered where she'd hit the foyer closet door. Where she'd fallen to the ground. That spot was visible from where I sat, and she wasn't there.

I also thought of Bandit upstairs somewhere, injured, maybe worse, and I renewed my struggles against the fishing line. The numbness initially allowed my fingers and toes to only move in brief and spastic wiggles. Across from me, Jim shook his head and the message was clear: we've all tried, there's no use. But slowly feeling returned to my arms and legs and I was able to pull harder against the fishing line. My chair rocked with my struggles, tilting from side to side and nudged against my parents to either side of me.

Dad moaned, and I looked at him and the expression on his face matched that of Jim's. I wasn't trying anything the rest of them hadn't, and I was wasting my time and energy.

Disconsolate, I ceased my rocking.

Instead, I nodded at each of them, then nodded at an empty space beside Jim and Sarah. My meaning was clear as well: *Where's Tara?*

I looked at my mom first, then Dad.

The sorrow and fear on their faces was plain and raw.

I looked across the table at Jim and my sister. They both looked away, unwilling to meet my eyes.

I turned back to Dad, panic again rising to the forefront, and I tensed, ready to begin pulling anew at the fishing wire around my hands and feet.

*Where is she?* I tried to send wordlessly to him. I was breathing hard against the balled-up cloth in my mouth, so that I was making a frantic Darth Vader sort of breathing sound. Dad nodded and I followed the direction of his gesture to the stairs, and I looked back at him and he nodded again towards the stairs.

Upstairs.

Tara was up there somewhere with the Collector.

I remembered Lookout Mountain and Tara standing at the edge with the gun where the Collector and Mr. Templeton had fallen over. The gun in her hand, smoking at the muzzle.

She had shot the Collector at least twice, she told us later.

We had thought, or hoped, that he had died that night. I remembered the police telling me that he had probably stumbled a little ways, then fallen, unconscious, and probably dragged away by animals. That story had been so appealing after the horror preceding it, I think we all just accepted it with a tired, resigned hope.

But he wasn't dead.

And now he'd come back to collect. Sometimes he collected things that were owed. Sometimes he collected for himself. *This is the night*, I remembered him saying, his dark and insane poetry. *These are the times.*

He was upstairs with Tara, and he was collecting.

## 2.

He came down sometime later, seeming to float down the stairs as he had done the first time. In the dark he seemed like a part of the night, a piece of it separated from the rest, a disengaged probe of shadow and substance. He crossed the living room to the dining table, his hands in his pockets like a leisurely stroller through the park. I thought of the first time I'd seen him walking down our street from my bedroom window, and thinking that maybe if I threw the window up I'd hear him whistling some lackadaisical tune. Maybe something like the *Andy Griffith* theme.

There in our home, walking towards us, he *was* whistling, but it wasn't anything as upbeat as a 60s television theme. It had sharp and abrupt fits and starts, like a song he was making up as he went along.

Strolling and whistling, relaxed and calm.

Collecting must be meditative and stress relieving in some way, I remember thinking, and wondered what that meant for Tara.

I shook my head and groaned loudly against the gag in my mouth as the Collector came up alongside the table. He stopped whistling and looked at everyone in turn. Even from this close his face was only a smudge of whiteness beneath the low hanging brim of his black fedora. Then he was looking at me. How I knew this since I couldn't even make out his eyes, I don't know. But he was looking at me, and I think that perhaps he was smiling.

He pulled up a chair to the free space at the table beside Jim and Sarah, directly across from me. Sitting, the length of his coat draped the chair like a cover and rustled with leathery whispers as it settled.

"There is a price that must be paid for every action," the Collector said, leaning towards me ever so slightly over the table. "In this life there is a balance to all things."

I had no idea what the fuck he was talking about, but I didn't look away from him. I couldn't. I was pretty sure he wouldn't allow it anyway.

"Last time we met," the Collector continued, "you and your friends impeded me from my collection. As a matter of fact, in a lesson of irony, you collected from me instead of the other way around."

He removed his right hand from his coat pocket and raised it to his collar. In the dimness of the dining room I was still able to discern that the hand was wet and gleamed with its

265

wetness. A deep scarlet in the darkened room, I didn't want to think about what that redness on his hand meant. The bloodied hand went to the collar of his black coat and pulled it down and over his shoulder. Baring flesh whiter than my ass cheeks, so pale as to almost be translucent, I saw a puckered scar still partially scabbed over, just under his collarbone. He covered the white flesh again, pulling up the collar of the coat so it was only his face and hands that broke the pattern of blackness about him.

His wet hand went back into his coat pocket.

"You collected from me," he said, me only half listening at first, still thinking about that patch of pale flesh like marble, "and so I collected in turn."

This last brought my attention back from the shock of the glimpse of his pallid skin, and I was again enthralled by the words he spoke. He had collected in turn, and I was about to learn what that meant.

"I have a gift for you," he said and looked down to indicate his hands in his coat pockets. "I will allow you to choose."

I bit down on the cloth in my mouth. I was shaking, looking from either side of him, down below the table where his hands were out of sight, in his pockets, holding my possible "gifts." I didn't want to choose, didn't want to play his games.

But I knew I had no choice.

If I refused, who knew who he would collect from next: my mom or dad; Sarah or Jim; or even me. I'd felt the touch of his knife before; felt it draw my blood. I didn't want to ever feel that again.

I nodded towards his right hand. The one I'd already seen. The one with the blood coating it like paint.

The Collector nodded.

"Excellent choice." Withdrawing his hand again from the coat, he cupped something in his palm, looking down on it like a jeweler considering a gem. I couldn't see it yet from my perspective, but Jim, right next to the Collector, did, and his eyes widened even more, so wide I thought they might roll out of his head and onto the table like spilled marbles. The Collector looked up from his cupped hand to me, then stretched his arm out across the table, showing me what he held. "Here is some of what I have collected thus far."

Lying in his palm in a circle of blood was an ear.

Not a human ear, though.

The triangular, fur-covered ear of a German shepherd dog.

I screamed behind the gag. I bolted forward against the fishing wire that held me to the chair. My midsection collided with the edge of the table as I tried to get to the Collector across from me. The collision knocked me backwards. The chair rocked back on its legs. I didn't try to stand again, but I kept screaming, the breath of it pushing against the gag.

"You wish to speak?" the Collector asked calmly. As if he held nothing remarkable in his bloodied hand.

I nodded, still huffing behind the cloth stuffed in my mouth.

"I'd like to hear what you have to say."

He leaned forward, stretching his right arm across the length of the table. He reached for my face, my mouth, the blood-soaked hand beneath my nose so that I could smell it, the rawness of it, and two fingers darted between my lips and I could taste it, the coppery and salty taste of my dog's blood. These bloody probes sought the gag, snatched it, and yanked it out of my mouth. I tried to bite him at the last moment, missed, and my teeth clacked together painfully.

"You fucker! What'd you do to my dog? I'll kill you! What'd you do you fucker!"

I thought the force of my words must blow him back like a gale force wind, but he merely sat there across from me. Watching from the shadows of himself as I spewed my venom, trying to burn him with it, to engulf and destroy him with it.

I kept at it until he reached across the table and slapped me hard. The blow was staggering, sent my chair again rocking so that for a moment I thought I'd spill backwards.

"I am the Collector. I collect what is owed, and sometimes I collect for myself."

He may have been ready to say more, or he may have said all that he wanted to me. I'd never know. His left hand came out of the coat too, and it was holding the long bowie knife. The point of it pointed in my direction.

Then the front door flew inward with a crash, splinters of it rattling to the ground. The Collector turned away from me at the disturbance. I craned to look past him.

Brock was in the doorway, moving in, pistol in hand.

Silver-haired Vincent Perrelli was close behind, his gun at the ready as well.

The two men took in the scene quickly. They saw us at the table, the moonlight outside casting us in its glow. They saw the Collector, moving towards them across the room, knife in hand.

"You failed," Mr. Perrelli said to the dark figure gliding his way. "Our contract is nullified."

Who fired first, I don't know, but one moment there was a silence after Mr. Perrelli's pronouncement, like a dramatic pause onstage, and then both he and Brock were shooting, the pistols spitting fire like tiny rocket engines. The Collector danced a spastic dance like a broken marionette dangled by a drunken puppeteer. His knife was jerked out of his hands and flew past my head. It hit the wall and clattered somewhere behind me.

The Collector fell to the ground in a black mass.

The guns fell silent with empty magazines.

I looked at my dad. He looked at me, nodded.

We both rocked backwards and sent ourselves in our chairs falling. The collision of my back on the dining room floor was hard and painful. I tried to hold my breath and steel myself, and still most of the wind was knocked out of me. My hands tied to the back of the chair were smashed and throbbed under the weight of me.

But I gritted my teeth, looked to either side from my new horizontal perspective. I saw my dad, also dazed by the fall. He saw me. We both saw the knife between us.

We both scooted awkwardly towards it.

Footsteps coming across the floor marched in our direction.

I lifted my head, stared down the length of my body, between my legs and under the table. Saw two pairs of black slacks and shiny black loafers coming our way.

"Hurry, Dad!"

I felt my fingers brush the knife.

My dad's grasped it first and pulled it away.

The black panted legs planted themselves in front of me, above us, and the bodies they were attached to, Mr. Perrelli and Brock, towered high. Perrelli smiled down at me as he ejected the spent magazine, pulled out a spare from his jacket pocket.

"Well, well," Perrelli said. "Lucky we came early. Looks like the party was starting without us."

He fit the new magazine into the pistol. Aimed it at me.

Brock likewise reloaded and pointed his pistol at Dad.

Mom was crying behind her gag, still upright in her chair. Looking from Perrelli to me and Dad on the floor, her eyes flitted frantically, trying to see everything at the same time.

"I think you need to tell us where the money is," Mr. Perrelli said.

"*It's not midnight,*" I said stupidly, unable to think of anything else to say, thinking only of the unfairness of it all. I stared up into the muzzle of that gun and there was nothing else to say.

There was no money, this man would never believe that, and I was dead. That was the short and sweet of it, that was the ending to my short life, and there was nothing to be done about it.

"The money, Joey," he repeated.

And since I was dead anyway, I decided I might as well go out with style.

"Have Brock bend over," I said. "You'll find it with your dick up his ass."

Mr. Perrelli's smile faltered and that made me smile, and me smiling made his smile fade completely, and that made me laugh.

"We burnt the money, dickhead," I said. "A bunch of kids burnt ten million dollars, you stupid tool."

Vincent Perrelli shook his head like this was disappointing news, and he extended his arm and the pistol was there, mere inches away. His finger curled around the trigger.

"How unfortunate that our business had to end this way," he said.

An explosion; a small thunder. I waited for the feel of the bullet shattering my face. Then I realized that it should have happened before that thought was even complete.

More gunfire, and I was still alive.

Mr. Perrelli dropped to the ground beside me, rolled away, taking cover behind the table. I saw him holding his left arm. Saw the moonlight glitter and reflect off the blood there.

I looked in the other direction, towards Dad. Saw him fumbling for the knife again, grasping it, trying to turn the blade towards the fishing wire at his wrists.

Brock had darted into the kitchen, putting a wall between him and whoever had opened fire. I thought of Tara, upstairs, and maybe she'd found one of Dad's guns, had come down charging to the rescue.

I looked down the length of my body again, saw the table and my mom and sister and Jim still sitting there, prominently in the line of crossfire. Under the table and across the room towards the front door, I saw the lower half of someone in the doorway.

A guy, not a girl. Not Tara.

I saw the hem of a brown suede jacket.

On the floor near me, Mr. Perrelli stood and fired. The guy at the front door dropped to the ground, rolled behind the sofa. I saw his face as he rolled and scrambled for cover. The greasy hair, the crooked smile like everything was a game.

Mr. Smirk. Dillon Glover.

*"You killed my dad, shithead!"* he called from behind his cover.

Even in the midst of this chaos, I wondered why a kid like him would give a shit about his asshole of a dad dying. Then I remembered Fat Bobby, and how he'd moped about for days following the death of his dad atop Lookout Mountain. How he'd had us drive to the funeral so he could say his goodbyes.

Maybe, regardless of who brings us into this world, there's still something owed. A loyalty or devotion beyond sense and reason.

Dillon jumped up from behind the sofa, took sloppy aim at Mr. Perrelli, pulled the trigger. Vincent Perrelli dropped behind the table again. Splinters of wood spit into the air and rained down on me, and I turned my head.

Looking towards the kitchen I saw Brock leaning against the wall, tensing, and darting out. Dillon saw him, swung his gun towards the tombstone-headed man, fired. Brock fired also.

Both of them went down. Neither got up.

In the sudden silence I could hear the breathing of many people. A chorus of breathing. A choir of fear and expectation.

Mr. Perrelli stood, favoring his injured arm. He turned this way and that, almost as if hypnotized, surveying the scene around him.

"Well," he said, "that was unexpected."

Dad leapt to his feet beside me, hopped over me, charged Mr. Perrelli, buried the bowie knife into the older man's stomach. Wrenching his gun hand down and to the side so that the reflexive pulls of Perrelli's trigger finger fired the rounds harmlessly into the floor, Dad's momentum carried them into the far wall.

The impact shook the house and framed pictures swung on the wall as if by poltergeist hands. Dad twisted and thrust with the knife, skewering Perrelli and lifting the man almost off the ground, so that he slid *up* the wall a bit. Blood oozed from his

271

stomach, and Mr. Perrelli spit some of it up like scarlet vomit. It rolled down his lips and chin in trickles. His eyes widened. He scowled and looked down on my dad.

"*This … isn't supposed … to happen …*" he rasped, the words punctuated by liquid pops as blood bubbles burst from between his lips. "*This … isn't right …*"

Dad leaned close to Vincent Perrelli, still working the knife side to side and twisting it about, ripping and tearing the older man's innards.

"Welcome to life, asshole," Dad said, let go, and we all watched the silver-haired man slide to the floor, coming to rest in a sitting position, back against the wall like a petulant child. His breath slowed, his eyes glazed over, and the rise and fall of the chest ceased, then he was still.

## 3.

Having already freed me, Dad was kneeling to cut the fishing line from around Mom's wrists and ankles, me in the kitchen looking for a knife or scissors to do the same for Jim and Sarah, when I heard a sound like rustling leaves or the whisper of distant voices. I turned, and the Collector was standing, riddled with holes in his coat and redness seeping from those holes like piping sprung leaks, but standing.

I watched the rising shadow moving silently towards Dad, tried to shout a warning, but my voice caught in fear at this phantom that wouldn't die. This thing of shadows and night with the hat of darkness and the coat like wings, scooped up a mug from the kitchen counter that separated me from him and, still unseen by Dad, inched closer.

Finally I found my voice and called out "*Dad!*" but the Collector was already swinging and Dad was turning, turning *into* the swing. The mug struck his temple, shattered in ceramic chunks, and Dad fell to the ground.

The Collector turned to me. Shambled towards me, even shambling, legs carrying him weakly, still moving like smoke, a mist rolling over the earth.

The front door was past him. I couldn't go that way.

I turned around towards the rear of the kitchen, the door there leading to the backyard. I ran across the kitchen and out the back door.

Running, I realized I'd never been out here before, never had an occasion to. There were weeds and where the weeds didn't cover, barren dirt ground and rocks like the lifeless landscape of another planet. I remembered Dad saying something about a pool when we first moved here, and how he'd fix it up for the summer and have it filled and we could swim in our very first pool.

A hole loomed before me like a large quarry.

I skid to a stop. My foot slid on loose pebbles. A monster weed that I swore intentionally reached out and snagged me sent me sprawling. The hole in the earth yawned open as I tumbled towards it. A cavernous mouth waiting to swallow a tasty morsel. I rolled. My feet went over the edge. I grabbed at the ground rolling away from me. My chin hit the rim of the hole and I bit my tongue, tasted blood.

Dangling over the edge there, I looked down. Ten feet below, the sloped concrete siding of the dry, empty pool bottomed out in jagged chunks of rock and more concrete.

Facing forward again, I was afforded a ground-level view of the backyard, and the Collector coming down the porch, shambling, rocking, unsteady, but still flowing as if smoke, blowing like vapors. The phantom of the night drifting my way.

I tried to pull myself up. Tried for purchase with my feet on the sloped concrete wall. Thought about dropping down, taking my chance with a broken leg or ankle. Tried pulling myself up again and seeing the Collector so close now, too close, there was nowhere to go. He had me and he was going to collect.

Beyond him a demon spilled out of the house and into the night. Wild matted hair covered it and clumps of it were coated red. Eyes glowed green with the moonlight. Fangs long and pointed were bright in an open maw and tendrils of spittle stretched from gum to gum. A one-eared demon, bloodied, snarling, dashed across the barren backyard as if the fires of hell itself spurred it forward.

The Collector right there, right in front of me, towered over me, and I stared between his legs even as he reached down for me. Watching this beast, this white-furred beast, this bloody monstrosity, running, and the spittle flying from its clacking jaws.

The Collector's scarlet-stained fingers reached for me, then paused, hearing the approach from behind him. Turning, he saw the demon bearing down on him, and the hellhound leapt, flying through the air between them, colliding with the Collector, the man-shadow, the thing of the night. Opening his arms as if to embrace the demon dog, the force of the impact carried them both over me, down into the hole below, the rocks and jagged protrusions at the bottom of the pit.

The sound of bodies breaking was loud in the otherwise quiet night.

# CHAPTER THIRTEEN

## 1.

There was a gathering of parents and police and lots of vehicles with sirens that filled the night with flashes of blue and red. The neighbors stood outside up and down the street to watch and I was reminded of the masses gathered on the Fourth of July to watch the fireworks. We told Dad and the other parents and police gathered everything, just as we had planned on. Or damn near everything.

There were some things Jim, Tara, Sarah and I kept to ourselves even then.

Like a little mossy pond out in the woods.

But most everything else we went over. The old Buick and the Outsiders' Club; the things we'd done from finding the money to stoning Sheriff Glover when he pulled his gun on us; the incident in the Haunted House with his son and his son's friends; the events on Lookout Mountain and hiding the money up there; and concluding with the arrival of Mr. Perrelli and his claim to the money and his promise of escalation and the shoot-out at my house.

One other exception that wasn't talked about, or at least that I didn't hear anything about, was Tara. She was found in the upstairs master bedroom by my dad, alive and seemingly unhurt. She'd been tied to the bed, my dad told the police, and he had tried looking her over as best he could for any serious injuries, without crossing any lines of propriety.

She spent nearly three hours up there alone with the Collector, and she was the only one not to say a single word during our retelling of events to the police and our parents. She merely stared at the walls, or down at something in her hands or lap that none of the rest of us could see, and the vacancy in her eyes frightened me.

Her dad, tall and imposing in his ranger uniform, put an arm around her shoulders and led her away. I watched her climb into the jeep and her dad start the vehicle and they drove off and out of sight.

Of course, to corroborate our stories the police looked for the Buick, and they looked for the money, and there was a long search for Bobby Templeton that never brought about any leads. These details we didn't expand upon. We just shrugged our shoulders like everyone else, chalking it up to the mystery of things.

Obviously, the natural conclusion, the ending that found its way into the newspapers and the local television station's evening news, was that Vincent Perrelli or the man who'd called himself the Collector had found the money and relocated it. Or maybe found some of it but not all, and probably had done the same to Bobby Templeton, finding him and relocating him, catching the poor kid alone sometime during the day and maybe tried to extract information from the boy.

The newspapers speculated on the Buick, the money inside it, and the body in the trunk. Many a journalist pored over Vincent Perrelli's criminal past, looking for missing associates who'd perhaps wronged him, attempted to rip him off. There were many candidates in such a man's life, and no one could ever pin down a prime suspect. Tracking down the owner of the old Buick proved likewise fruitless, as the Buick itself was gone, and no one had previously written down its plate number.

All of this seemed to me very appropriate, very natural. Easy answers were for movies and comic books, not real life. Real life is far more unsettling, and only seldom provides us the answers we seek.

I remember watching the police and coroner dragging the body of the Collector out of the concrete pit of the dried and empty swimming pool. His head had been bust like a melon. Mom tried to shield me from the sight but I saw him pulled out and loaded into a black bag almost the color of his hat and coat.

The hat had fallen off when Bandit had jumped on the Collector and pushed him into the empty pool. As the zipper of the body bag was pulled up, I saw his pale and nondescript face for the first time. It was a face I thought I'd never forget, so plain and ordinary and not at all what I thought evil would look like. Yet today I find it very difficult to pull up from my memory the details of him. The lines and contours of his countenance seem lost, like maybe it could be any face at all, or none that I'd ever seen.

I do remember thinking, as the bag zippered the Collector out of sight, leaving only the shape of him there under the plastic, that there'd been the slightest of twitches on that drab and boring face. Then he was gone, loaded into an ambulance and, like Tara, rolling away into the night.

Bandit broke two legs and suffered the smallest of hairline fractures to the spine as a result of his headlong plunge into the empty pool. He was a one-eared gimp of a dog for the rest of his life, which ended at the ripe old age of his fifteenth year. I buried him under the apple tree in the year before I left home for college. I still go there sometimes, since I own the place, and sit there on the small brick wall under the trees. Under the bright light of the desert sun, I remember him in my bed at night, curled against me, his heartbeat and mine indistinguishable at times.

I watched Mom and Dad grow old and Sarah get married. I went to school in Phoenix so I was never far away. On visits on holidays and every other weekend or so, I still threw down with my dad in the garage, working the punching bag and sparring. He made a pretty good sparring partner all the way to his sixty-fifth year, when a heart attack took him in the night and Mom's phone call woke me up in the dorm.

Mom died a year after that.

They were both fighters, Dad of the physical sort when necessary, Mom's strength from the heart, but they were a team, and I think when Dad went the fight went out of Mom. Sarah and I buried them side by side in a small plot at the local cemetery. Everything was left to us and I don't think we'll ever sell that house.

The school year following that summer in Payne with the short-lived Outsiders' Club, I didn't see much of either Jim or Tara. We'd see each other over the heads of other students in the crowded halls once in a while. Occasionally we'd have classes together. We'd nod and sometimes wave. But we never hung out together again, and I think that was for the best.

With distance and time, I think things get easier. Pain is never forgotten, especially of the sort that was bestowed upon us that summer and that we bestowed upon ourselves. But with distance and time, all things become bearable.

Last I read, Jim did indeed follow his dad's advice. He ran for sheriff of Payne straight out of college. Won by a landslide. Every time I visit the old house, I pick up a copy of the local paper, and see his name somewhere in the Crime section, talking about statistics, doling out safety advice for residents, and maybe a photo of him in uniform posing with school children.

As far as I know he's the only person who knows where the remaining two million dollars is located. Sometimes, I wonder what's become of it. Then, knowing if my old friend has retrieved it over the years it's been put to good use, my curiosity quickly ebbs.

I met Tara once more, years later, after college, after Mom and

278

Dad had passed, and I was a man out on my own trying to find the ways of things. I was walking down the streets of a business district in Phoenix and I saw this beautiful woman with swirls and spirals of brown hair like galaxies, and she walked with this gait that made her skirt twirl in the cutest of ways.

She saw me coming and I saw her and we stopped there on the sidewalk and after the longest time we smiled and shook hands. I noticed the ring on her finger. She introduced me to her daughter standing shyly beside her, holding her mommy's leg for comfort and safety. I smiled at the little girl and gave her a little wave.

"Hi," I said, looking back at the mom.

"Hi," she said right back.

I like to think her hand lingered on mine before we let go and kept walking our separate ways. I didn't look back, and knowing her for that brief time in that short summer, I don't think she did either.

That time in my life was so short and yet, as I get older I find myself thinking back to it more and more often, almost to the exclusion of all other things. All the other decades of my life seem to fall by the wayside in the wake of that summer of the Outsiders' Club. I remember the words the Collector spoke, and I'm worried by the sense they make to me now.

*This is the night. These are the times.*

There seems a dark wisdom in there, his grim poetry, and I want to find it. Then knowing I will, eventually, I'm afraid of it, afraid of that knowledge.

I also think of what my dad said as he buried the knife into Mr. Perrelli's gut, in reply to Mr. Perrelli's protestations that this wasn't how it was supposed to be, his life draining out of him, it wasn't right.

*Welcome to life, asshole.*

There seems wisdom in that too.

About love and hope and good things, I'm not so sure I know

much about, or ever did. This saddens me, because I know that in the years of the flow of my life, there have been good things. I just can't seem to hold onto them. Then I remember there once was a boy saved by a dog.

And, for a moment, there is peace.